The Book of Bones

Sam Hawksmoor

Hammer & Tong

Hammer & Tong
www.samhawksmoor.com

Book Layout © 2022 BookDesignTemplates.com
Cover Design – Debs Cooper -
 https://debjcooper.wordpress.com
Cover Photo: Front: ben-parker-H3FBy3i9Q7E-unsplash

The Book of Ashes/ Sam Hawksmoor. -- 1st ed.
ISBN 979-8-837434-952

Reviews from the first Delaney and Asha mystery -
We Feel Your Pain *(So you don't have to)*

*'a captivating adventure that ... could be compared to a
Roald Dahl tale filmed by Wes Anderson'*
Lionel Darmendrail - France

*'A great human story that wears it's heart on its sleeve.'
Dr Allen Cook - Bridgeport University*

*'Mysterious, angsty, emotional and thrilling!' -
BookAddicted Girl*

*'brilliant and intriguing - unlike any book I've read be-
fore.'*
Inscribed Inkling - Goodreads

CHAPTER ONE

The Showing

"You know what an unhappy customer is, Mr Delaney? Do you?"

Delaney suppressed a temptation to swear. He put down his wood plane and stepped back from the bench to view his complainant who was now pointing a fat finger at him. Her face was red and her neck pulsating with anger, her eyes bulging a little. He began to comprehend exactly why her husband had fled. He debated whether to be polite or blunt. This Duchkov woman had been a pain right from the off.

"As I recall Ms Duchkov, you asked me to locate your errant husband and I fulfilled that obligation a month ago."

She sneered at him. "Look at you in your fancy new premises. I paid for that desk."

Delaney looked down at the just-smoothed work surface and wiped the sweat from his brow. "This workbench has been here since 1864, Ms Duchkov. I have merely restored it. You have no grounds for complaint. I found him. The fact that he chose not to return to you is his choice to make. Get a lawyer, I already recommended one if I recall."

"You think I can afford a lawyer after paying you?" She snarled.

Delaney glanced over at his dog Rufus. He was becoming agitated; he hated the sound of raised voices.

"Your husband left you. He believes he's owed money. I believe he's getting his own lawyer. My advice, Ms Duchkov, which you consistently ignore, is to lawyer-up before he tries to repossess your house and car which I understand he paid for."

Ms Duchkov impetuously kicked the workbench leaving

an imprint of her Ted Baker sneakers. "He can't do that."

Delaney shrugged. "My contract was to find him. I found him, end of. Go home. Stop bugging me."

Her lips curled with contempt. "I'll ruin you. I'll blast every social media platform what a useless SOB you are Delaney."

Delaney offered a tight smile. "Join the line-up. Dissatisfied customers are my speciality apparently. Go home, our business is done."

He moved towards the boathouse doors and waved her through. "There are no happy endings in a breakup, Ms Duchkov."

She stared daggers at him as she brushed past him to the dockside. "You haven't heard the last of this," she threatened.

Delaney called after her. "I think I have. You return, I will have to get a restraining order. You're angry with the wrong person."

She gave him the finger as she headed towards her Lexus. He noticed she had swollen ankles, probably water retention. He glanced down at the dog. "Thank you for not biting her on the way out."

Rufus came over and nudged his legs as Delaney rubbed the dog's flanks with affection.

"Maybe it's time to consider a different line of business, Rufus. What do you think?"

Delaney stood back and examined his day's work. The last of the sun bathed the timberwork in a golden glow. His arms ached from sanding the old workbenches, but it was satisfying to work up a sweat. He'd always wanted to own a workspace like this. When the boathouse came up for sale it was tied up in an awkward probate situation following a sudden death. He'd known the old man Billy for years – slow, methodical, always ready to bitch about how hard it was to keep a boathouse repair business going. His death was no surprise to anyone who knew him. Turns out being a heavy smoking, bottle of whisky a day man is no defense against old age. He'd died all alone in his back room, forgotten until they came to turn off the utilities for unpaid bills.

He'd gutted his small apartment at the back. Now the building was beginning to look a lot like it did back in 1860's when it started life as a ships' chandlers. The high ceiling oak timbers had been restored, the polished concrete floor and secure doors and windows the only modern touches. He loved the location and old harbor sounds.

Rufus ambled towards the open doors and stretched deep and long, letting out a little yelp as he let go.

"Don't go far," Delaney told him.

Rufus gave him a quick glance in affirmation and wandered outside, nose in the air, sniffing for trouble.

Delaney stared down into his hibiscus tea frowning. This was his partner Asha's latest idea to prevent high blood pressure and he wasn't enjoying it.

Rufus stood at the edge of the dock watching the gulls diving up and around a fishing boat coming in with the day's catch. Delaney watched them tie up and wondered if they'd been successful. There had been a lot of grumbling of late about the paucity of catches and wild theories as to where all the fish had gone.

Delaney sighed, how he was ever going to pay for this place. Business wasn't steady and he needed clients like Ms Duchkov like a hole in the head. It wasn't as if people had stopped being scammed or cheated. The problem was those who needed the help usually had no money left to pay for an investigation to get their money back and too often the scammers hid behind Russian or Asian firewalls, mostly impossible to reach. There were times when he checked his bank account and regretted leaving the safe world of insurance and a regular income.

But these moments of regrets were brief. He'd hated it, even though he'd been paid well. Now he had a responsibility to his partner Asha and the kid Maria to keep the agency going. He was thinking that almost every job has its drawbacks. Keeping the show on the road was not a given. He smiled remembering that Asha had suggested the boathouse would be more profitable as a coffee shop than investigation agency and he had to agree it would be a lot less grief. Definitely a Plan B option.

His phone rang, Asha's number flashed up. "Hey, you must have known I was thinking about you."

Asha laughed. "Good thoughts, I hope. Just reminding you that we're due at Albion's gallery opening tonight. I'll drop Maria at the ice rink. I thought we'd eat after the showing."

"I'm packing up now. I don't have to dress up do I?"

"Smart casual, Delaney, we might meet new clients and god knows we need some."

"Ok, I'll be home shortly. We need anything?"

"Rye Bread. Almond milk."

"Ok. On my way."

Delaney disconnected and headed to the back to check the door was locked. Yeah, a coffee shop made a lot of sense right now. People always wanted coffee.

"Hey Delaney. You in there?"

The unwelcome sight of Harvey Jenks stood in the entrance, unsure of the way Rufus was looking at him.

"Is this dog trained? It's looking at me funny."

Delaney returned and snapped his fingers. Rufus lay down. "Yep, he's trained. Just doing his job, keeping insurance brokers away. You've been out sailing?"

Harvey adjusted the collar on his anorak. "Uh-uh, just inspecting the old tub. Going to need some work before I can take her out again. You've done wonders with this place. I guess you're not going into the boat repair business."

"No, too labor intensive. This is going to be my new office. When I finally get organized."

Harvey chuckled. "Yeah, I heard you were fighting crime these days. Don't see any caped costume hanging up anywhere though."

"Seems I lack superpowers. Sorry to disappoint."

Harvey beamed. "Well in that case you'll be happy I came along. Special deals on indemnity insurance and life insurance this month. From what I read about you; you're going to need it."

Delaney grimaced. He really didn't need this. The years had put a lot of bulk on Harvey. Another guy waiting on his first heart attack he reckoned. "Uncanny how many insurance brokers approach me these days. They must think this is a profitable business or something."

Harvey smiled. "No pressure. I've been watching you get this place into shape so I'm just making a courtesy call. I'm not hustling you. But for the record, do you have liability insurance?"

"It's due for renewal, Harvey. There must be some secret algorithm that goes out to brokers when a policy is due. I'm due to meet my partner about twenty minutes ago but if you want to send me quotes, I'll take a look." Delaney took out his card and handed it over. The great secret to getting rid of insurance brokers was to seem to show interest.

Harvey looked surprised; it was usually harder to sell than this. "I'll do that. Life insurance? I know you have a family now. I've seen your kid polishing the floor here. Nice finish by the way. Can never get my kids to do a damn thing for me."

"Bribing helps," Delaney answered. "I've really got to lock up Harvey. I'm really late."

"Ok, ok. I'll get that quote to you tomorrow."

"And before you ask, I just insured this building."

Harvey was looking up at the heavy oak timbers.

"Got to be worth a fortune now you've restored it,"

"If I thought that I'd put it on the market tomorrow. I'm way over budget on this. But I'm not selling. I've wanted a space like this for years and I finally got it together. Night Harvey." Harvey finally took the hint and departed.

Delaney locked up and signaled to Rufus to get going as he headed for the harbor gates. He looked back at Harvey climbing into his BMW. He remembered him from when he was a scrawny kid with zero social skills. Never figured he'd end up with a yacht and a Beemer.

It was almost seven when they got to the gallery. Finding parking had been a bitch – the mayor's latest idea to make using a vehicle in Berg City damn near impossible.

Delaney tried to calm down before going in. He gazed at the smart young people inside clutching their glasses of wine, all trying to pretend to be interested in what was on the walls. This was the new situation now since Asha had taken charge of their social life. He braced himself for small talk. He had little inclination to discuss 'art'.

His late wife used to drag him to these events in his old life in Paris. It still hurt she was gone forever. Now he had Asha pushing him to be sociable, building up contacts to keep the whole investigation show on the road. She went in ahead of him. He watched heads turn. He always got a kick out of that. She had a great walk, dressed to perfection and a perfect ass. He never tired of admiring the way she could enter a space and own it. You had to be born with it he guessed. He joined her, pleased to see the art was photographic with images he could appreciate.

"I swear this used to be a restaurant." Asha declared, staring up at the roof space. She tasted the organic low alcohol wine offered to her and winced turning to Delaney. "Ouch. Retro music is cool though, who is it?"

"Blue Mondays by New Order," Delaney noted, wondering when he'd last heard them.

"I knew you'd come in handy one day," Asha said, impressed.

Delaney was examining a large black and white print of a bleak American landscape, a part of the collection on display in the room. "Notice anything weird about these images?"

Asha leaned in to stare at a moody study of a Virginia Mansion. "No people?"

Delaney nodded as he looked around the gallery walls. "Forty images, not one person in any of them. I kinda like them. They're obliquely sad. The photographer's got a real eye for dramatic skies. It's very David Lynch."

Asha shrugged. She didn't know about any Lynch. "And prices. That's a lot for a print, isn't it? Even if it's one of twenty."

"Add a zero if these were on show in New York." He suddenly glanced up at the vaulted timbered ceiling and remembered. "You're right, Ash, Juliana's. Italian. I came here when I was a teenager. Spaghetti and meatballs, white tablecloths, authentic Italian waiters. I thought it was very sophisticated."

Asha mocked him. "Dinosaurs came and went in that time, Delaney. But it makes a nice space for a gallery."

Delaney stared at another all-American house image. The perfectly positioned John Deere ride-on mower, the threatening sky overhead, a well-worn Ford 150 pick-up in the drive. A Confederate flag at half-mast for some forgotten person. Iconic stuff. He wondered if it was all posed.

A young guy with a ponytail drifted towards them with open arms. He wore a gaudy waistcoat and high-heeled boots in respective shades of purple and gold to compliment his make-up.

"Darling, you came." He tossed some air kisses Asha's way and seemed happy to see her. "Confess, this is the best gallery space you have been to in this City."

Asha grinned. "Definitely the best." She turned to Delaney. "Delaney meet Albion. The naughtiest boy at Berg City University. Got away with murder. I don't think he ever attended one lecture but somehow got onto the honor roll."

Albion was appraising Delaney with a critical eye.

"This is the 'one'? Full of surprises, Asha, as ever."

Delaney raised an eyebrow. He was getting used to the look of surprise from her friends as they likely wondered why she'd chosen high mileage rather than anyone new.

"Congratulations on your new space, Albion. Asha says you're quite the entrepreneur."

"And artist." Asha chipped in. "Given up on your Mondrian phase I hope, Al."

"Long time ago, sweetie. Don't you just love these images? Can't believe the photographer has been living in Berg City for decades and never exhibited. They're like stills from a horror movie. You know something dark is about to happen."

"I like the empty streets." Delaney remarked. "Very moody."

"Apparently there's over a thousand images stored somewhere – all of this quality. I had a hell of a time editing for this show. Martinet has sold to National Geographic, New York Times, his images from Ukraine after the Chernobyl explosion are absolutely haunting. Next show I think."

"How did you find him, Al?" Asha asked.

"I didn't. His son Brin asked me what to do with some negatives he brought around and I was going to brush him off – then I started to look. I told him I wanted to exhibit, and he let me rent this space for practically nothing. Ten-year lease, Ash. Turns out he owns this whole street. You must meet him, he's here somewhere. I mentioned you to him Asha. He's looking for some help for something. Don't say no. He's loaded." He was keenly watching a couple looking at a price sticker. "I scent a sale. Sold eight already tonight. Don't hesitate if you're going to buy. Got to go and sell, sell, sell, darlings."

Delaney watched him hurry off to hustle. "You spent

four years studying with him?"

"He was in and out of love with so many boys no one could keep up with him. Every heartbreak he'd come tumbling into our place as if it was the end of the world and one day later, he'd have forgotten everything. He has a good eye though."

"I don't think I passed his appraisal."

"You're *my* dinosaur. No one else can have you."

Asha kissed his neck and he put an arm around her with an affectionate squeeze.

"Shame about the wine, though." Delaney muttered. "What time are we supposed to pick up Maria?"

"Eight."

"She's not thinking about taking up ice-hockey, is she? Brutal sport."

Asha wrinkled her nose. "I think it's more about the boy."

Delaney was surprised. "Isn't this the girl who said she'd never date a boy as long as she lived?"

"That was last summer. Keep up Delaney."

"You've talked to her about condoms and stuff, right? I tried but she just went bright red and fled."

Asha laughed. "She's more clued up than you think. And yes, we had a talk."

"I'm not going to enjoy the next phase of her life, am I."

"Probably not. Nor the next twenty years actually."

Delaney sighed. Too late to back out now. He noticed a young guy with a goatee was glancing in their direction. He wondered if it was another of Asha's university friends making a critical appraisal. Sometimes he worried that she'd always be comparing him to young men her own age. It wasn't as if the age gap was going to change any. So far, she seemed happy but there was always a nagging worry that one day she'd wake up and wish she'd made other choices.

"Vintage Air Jordans," Asha whispered in his ear, as if this meant something.

Delaney glanced the guy's worn sneakers and thought he could probably afford new if he wanted.

The young guy approached them asking, "You'd be Delaney and Asha?"

"That's us." Delaney replied.

"Brin Martinet." He didn't offer his hand.

Delaney registered the name. "I'm guessing the nephew of the photographer. Impressive show."

"I'm his son, actually."

"We love the images," Asha gushed. "Albion has done wonders with this space too."

Brin Martinet nodded. His expression remained serious. Delaney speculated that he was not easily impressed or perhaps slightly bored. He was hard to read. He noted the simple gold chain around his neck. Something about him spoke of someone trying hard to fit in and was uncomfortable doing it.

"I have a little problem. It's a bit awkward," Brin began.

"We're happy to help anyway we can." Delaney remarked.

"Perhaps I can come to your office tomorrow?"

"Erm, it's under construction at the moment. Bought the old boathouse down by the harbor, might have bitten off more than we can chew there. Lots of restoration regulations I hadn't budgeted for. We could talk now if that's ok with you?"

His eyes lit up. "Huh, so you're the guy who bought it. I'm glad it's getting restored. I want to preserve as much of the old Berg City as I can. If you need help, I'm on the City's Historic Building Compliance Committee."

Delaney was impressed. "They're tough crowd to please I've found."

"Yeah. We aim to stop as many tear downs as we can."

Asha pointed towards the back of the galley and some sofas. "It's quieter over there."

Brin nodded and followed them over. Asha noticed people staring at him.

They sat opposite him waiting for him to speak. Asha wondered what his little problem could be. Every time she heard the phrase 'little problem' it triggered horrible memories of being fifteen and being seriously embarrassed trying to catch the pharmacist's attention. She tried hard to expunge these thoughts.

"Is your father here?" Delaney asked.

"My father doesn't know it's happening. He's in Summertree."

Delaney winced. Awkward. Summertree was the dementia clinic on Third Avenue. Expensive and inevitably long term. "That's tough on him and you."

"He still recognizes me. Just not all the time."

"How can we help?" Asha asked, feeling a lot more sympathy for the guy now. He seemed to be embarrassed to talk about it.

"I, um – I hired someone to write my father's biography. Paid up front. He was supposed to deliver a finished manuscript three weeks before my father's eightieth on Dec 9th."

"A week away. I confess we're not exactly literary critics if you're worried about the quality of the writing," Delaney remarked.

"That's not my concern. Well, it is because I haven't seen anything from him at all. He doesn't answer any of my calls or reply to any emails. I should have paid just half, but I had put a lot of time pressure on the guy to get it done and he would have had a lot of research to do."

Delaney frowned. "Is it the money or the manuscript you're worried about?"

"The money's irrelevant. $10,000 is nothing, but I wanted it whilst he was still able to function. My father has done so much for Berg City and for me. I wanted a small celebration of that. I know it's just a book and maybe no one will read it, but it would go into the library and schools, there would be a permanent record of his life. He's helped so many children to get a better education. He's raised well over two million dollars for kids to get a chance at competitive sports they wouldn't get otherwise. He gave over half of everything he earned over the years to his sports charity Potentia. It sends fifty kids a year to Europe to participate in international events."

Asha turned to Delaney. "I know that charity. I had school friends who used it to go to Italy for winter sports. They brought back medals. I remember."

Brin smiled. His face relaxed a little. "See? My father made a difference. He was one of the good guys. This writer, Wolfie Sigurdsson, came highly recommended. He was supposed to gather all the details of my father's life, interview his friends. Arnold Martinet mattered, Mr Delaney. Got a shooting bronze in the '72 Olympics in Germany. He wasn't a nobody."

"Does your father know about this biography?" Delaney asked, curious.

"Not really. I made an arrangement with the nursing home. The writer was sent in to pose as a specialist in cognitive memory – ask him about his days at Munich and his passion for photography. Put a camera in Dad's hands and he can tell you exactly about a photoshoot thirty years ago. He nearly got frostbite in one shoot in Alaska and almost got himself jailed in the Ukraine for his Chernobyl series for National Geographic."

"Ok, so you're disappointed that the writer hasn't delivered. Your father doesn't know about it and its obviously time sensitive. So, what do you want us to do?"

"Find the writer. You come recommended by Jonas Everard, the Editor of The Star. He wasn't exactly flattering about you Mr Delaney, but he said you'd be the best."

Delaney grinned. "We go back a long way. Competitive sailors. I'd probably be rude about him as well."

Asha leaned forward. "Just to be clear. You want the money back or the book?"

"The book. I don't care about the money, although if he hasn't done any work, I'll make sure everyone knows he's a crook. I imagine he'd care about that. I don't like to be cheated."

"No one does," Delaney agreed. "This is a missing person case. It takes time and we're not cheap. Expenses can mount up. I need you to be aware of that."

"No limits. I'll pay whatever."

Asha brought out her phone. "I can send you our contract details now on WhatsApp."

Martinet took out his phone and they did a quick exchange. "I'll send you my home address. This is urgent business for me. Call me anytime you have news."

"We will." Delaney answered. "We expect a $5000 retainer to get started. Don't worry, we itemize every cost."

"Money isn't an issue. It's more of a curse actually."

It suddenly clicked for Asha. "I just remembered your nickname. Bitboy." She immediately regretted blurting it out, biting on her lip as he recoiled. "Sorry. I didn't mean to..."

Brin shrugged. "It's hard to escape that nickname."

"Bit boy?" Delaney queried, glaring at Asha. First rule of business; don't embarrass the client.

"I'm the kid who bought ten thousand bitcoins at a dollar each in February 2011. The Star did a feature on me. That's how I know the editor."

"Jeez, you must have been about twelve. How did that happen?" Delaney remarked.

"Fifteen actually. I made a proposal to my dad. Stake

me and I'll never ask for anything again."

"At fifteen? Did he even know what bitcoin was?" Delaney asked.

"No. I begged him for a month. He finally gave in and told me he'd write me out of his will if I lost as much as a penny."

Delaney glanced at Asha, noting her eyes had widened at little as she considered just how wealthy Brin had to be. "Must have been quite a tense ride."

"My father would come back from business trips and start yelling at me to sell when it hit a thousand. He'd scream at me to sell when it hit $19,000, practically had a heart attack when it went past $30,000. But I wouldn't sell. I had a minimum wage job all through college and racked up fifty-five thousand in debt. When I finally sold everything at sixty-nine thousand, he told me I was a fool for selling out so cheap." He laughed. "Almost the last proper conversation we had before y'know..."

Delaney stared at this young guy in his old sneakers and figured he could probably buy most of Berg City and still have change.

"What's it like to have so much money?" Asha asked. "I think I'd have a panic attack every day."

"Yeah, that's exactly what it's like. I made some real estate purchases, but it was so hard to find investments I could trust. I almost put it all back on Bitcoin in the big dip but luckily, I was dissuaded. It's with Goldman-Sachs now. My father always wanted me to understand the value of money but turns out I'm not much interested in it all."

"He must be proud of you, knowing how you stuck it out." Asha remarked.

"Maybe. I just hate the idea of him being forgotten. Hence the biography and this showing of his photos. I wish I had half the talent he had. I really do."

"Send us details on the writer. Any addresses or

phone numbers. We make no promises. I know you have a deadline but sometimes people don't want to be found and go to great lengths to disappear."

"Find him, Mr Delaney. Who'd cheat a guy with dementia? It's disgusting."

"How do you think your father would react if he knew you'd commissioned a biography?" Asha asked.

Brin Martinet looked away a moment to think about that before finally answering. "He'd be deeply embarrassed. He was very modest. Wouldn't even put his name on the charity, although people knew it was him. Find the writer. Let me know your progress."

Delaney offered his hand to close the deal, but Martinet backed off, he didn't do hands. "We'll do our best." Delaney told him after an awkward pause.

Martinet glanced back at the people staring at his father's photographs. "If there's any photo you'd like, tell Albion. I'd like you to have a copy."

Asha and Delaney watched him disappear into the crowd. Delaney turned to her with a sigh. "That's a pretty sad story, don't you think? Kid wants to impress his dad and the poor guy won't even remember him in a few weeks."

"How would you feel if I secretly commissioned a biography about you?" Asha asked curious.

"Angry. Anxious. Probably call my lawyer. I'd have to go into full denial mode."

Asha laughed and pulled him up off the sofa. "Yeah, I think I'd do the same."

"I can understand why he'd approve this showing. They're more than good. A biography is kind of weird. Most people would pay good money to keep all their secrets hidden. Who reads them anyway?"

"My mother. She has the greatest collection of celebrity biographies you ever saw. Even people from Love Island. She actually believes that these sad people write them."

Delaney laughed. "Come on, let's go get the brat."

They waved at Albion giving someone the hard sell and drifted out of the gallery as more people were coming in.

"You think there's a manual for finding missing persons?" Asha asked.

"There's a manual for everything, Ash. The writer probably couldn't believe his luck on getting someone to part with ten grand. But it will run out eventually and he'll be wanting to line up other suckers. He probably advertises in writer's magazines. We can start looking there."

"As easy as that."

"Someone will know him. After all, he lives in Berg City. Everyone knows everyone."

Maria was waiting for them in the car park. She was alone, shoulders slumped. Delaney knew that posture. Things hadn't gone to plan.

She shuffled towards the car, head down trying to avoid their eyes. She climbed into the car without a word.

"We're eating at home. I put a bean casserole in the oven." Asha told her. Maria didn't respond.

"Any split heads at the game? You thinking of signing up?" Delaney asked.

"Never ever going there again," Maria mumbled.

"Was Shannon there?" Asha asked. Maria's new bestie.

"She blew me off."

"Unlike her." Asha remarked.

"New boyfriend."

"Ah."

"He's a creep."

"Did you ask about the skiing trip?" Delaney asked.

"Mr Chapman's off sick and anyway there's a problem with insurance."

Delaney nodded. "Just as well, it sucks breaking your leg. Any school trips that don't involve possible injury or insurance issues coming up?"

"You want me gone that bad, huh." Maria rubbed her cold hands. She'd forgotten her gloves someplace and was annoyed with herself.

"No. I just don't want you to miss out on anything." Delaney informed her.

"I'm not signing up for anything except a transfer to a better school."

"Didn't we do that already?" Delaney remarked.

"This school sucks ass."

"We may run out of schools in Berg City." Asha pointed out.

"Yeah. That's the plan." Maria muttered.

"I'm guessing Avery wasn't ..." Asha began.

"I'm not discussing Avery. I'm not discussing boys, period. Ever. They're gross."

Delaney continued driving. Half of him was happy boys were off the menu, the other half wondered what was coming next.

Rufus was noisily drinking from his water bowl and checking his food dish for the tenth time in case some food had magically reappeared. Delaney was rinsing, then stacking the dishes in the washer as Asha was researching the writer.

"Sigurdsson seems to have written five mystery novels. Last one was six years ago."

"Icelandic name." Delaney noted.

"Is that relevant?"

"Might be to Sigurdsson. Ten thousand to write a biography that no one will read is probably good money for a writer. You have to wonder why he'd stiff Martinet. My guess is he's not the type of guy to let that go easy."

"Brin has already sent the retainer," Asha said as she checked payment details.

"I sense he'll want quick results. Can't imagine how he resisted cashing in on those bitcoins. He's worth how much?"

"Well over half a billion." Asha remarked. "He sent us the writer's details and his own address, which is odd, because I swear St Paul's is a private school."

Delaney frowned. "I think it closed down. Maybe he bought it. If you're going to be a billionaire, that's what you'd buy, I guess. Big old statement mansion you can fix up. Add twenty-four-hour security. I'm guessing he's single. I didn't notice anyone hanging on his arm. In fact, struck me as being a bit of a loner."

Asha glanced up at Delaney. "You think?"

"Every woman in Berg City in his age group will know about Bitboy. Just like you did. He'll never know who to trust. He'll never know if they like him for his personality."

Asha wrinkled her nose. "I'm not sure they'd care about his personality, Delaney. If he has one. I still think it's weird he'd want to commission a biography for a man who won't ever be able to appreciate it."

"It's not for his father. It's for him. He's got the money, the big house but everyone thinks he just got lucky and doesn't deserve it. The biography is a marker. Establishing family history in Berg City. This is proof. Dynasty stuff."

"Pop psyche 101." Asha remarked, rolling her eyes. "Hey, I've found some reviews of the writer's biography work. One four stars, six two stars and two one star."

"One star isn't exactly positive."

Asha read from the screen. "Sloppy research, failed to listen to anything I said. Another one says: 'Disappointed and late delivery'."

Delaney shrugged. "Nevertheless, that's nine customers, Ash. Clearly, he's able to part people from their money. He knows how to do that at least."

"So why screw it all up?"

"That's what we'll ask him when we find him. We'll

go there tomorrow early, after we drop Maria at school."

"He's not going to be there."

"But that's where we start. Missing Person's Manual, remember?"

Asha laughed and shut the laptop down. "I'm taking a shower before bed."

Delaney nodded. "I'll take Rufus for his last pee." He glanced at the fire. "Remind me to order more logs. Winter has definitely arrived."

CHAPTER TWO

Losing the Plot

The rain was easing as they pulled up at 1239 Melbury. Asha stared with confusion at an empty lot, a mailbox leaning at an angle in the garbage-strewn driveway.

Delaney shrugged. "Not only missing, but he's taken the whole damn house with him. You have to say he's thorough."

Rufus was agitating to get out of the vehicle.

"Wait, dog. Ash, check the mailbox. I'll see if the people across the road have anything to say."

"Be careful. This is not exactly a friendly neighborhood."

Delaney climbed out and Rufus practically jumped over him in his rush to flee.

"I guess someone needs to poop."

Delaney surveyed the tumbledown shack across the way, a rusted Chevy on blocks out front on the drive. He ignored the dog turning in circles looking for the best spot and made his way towards a front door that showed many signs of having been kicked in more than once. He knocked and stood well back and to one side in case they were armed.

The door opened a crack. "Yeah? Who is it?"

"Delaney. City Investigations. Looking for your neighbor, Wolfie Sigurdsson."

The door opened wider. A professional beer gut emerged first, the rifle next, Delaney was staring at a massive ginger beard before noticing the torn vest and baggy underwear.

"If he owes money, kiss it goodbye Mister. He drove his motorhome out of here about a month ago. Didn't say goodbye."

Delaney nodded. The rifle wasn't pointing at anything in particular, he wasn't worried.

"I don't suppose you have any idea of where he might go?"

The guy laughed revealing several missing teeth. A woman was calling him from inside.

'Vern? Who is it, Vern?"

Vern rolled his eyes, irritated. "Got to go. Don't bother looking for Wolfie. Right now, he'll be conning some other mark out of their money. You have to give him some respect. He's fucking ace at parting people from their money."

With that Vern retreated and slammed the door.

Delaney looked down and saw a steaming pile of shit had been left dead center of the yard. Rufus was looking all yippy skippy it was out of his system.

Delaney was sorely tempted to leave it but knew his civic duty and withdrew a biodegradable shitbag.

"You had to do it right there, didn't you. What have I said about using the curb?"

He scooped, then dumped it in the guy's stinky bin. He wasn't going to notice any.

Asha was standing by the vehicle with his mail in her hands.

"Lot of red ink – last chance mail."

Delaney nodded. "Figures. Don't open them. Put them back. The law is very clear on other peoples' mail."

Asha did as instructed. Delaney opened the door for the dog and Rufus jumped inside. "Wipe your paws."

Rufus ignored him, of course.

Asha stared at the empty lot. "He just took the money and ran? Doesn't make much sense. Ten thousand dollars would have been good money for a guy living in a motorhome. All he had to do was write the book. I mean, that's his job."

Delaney shrugged. "We don't know his circum-stances. Might have owed at lot of money to someone and didn't want to hand it over. We do know he's getting final notices though. It's a good incentive to get out of town and hope it all goes away. Never underestimate the capacity for a person to fuck up."

"You think he owns the lot?"

"Maybe, but you can bet he hasn't paid taxes on it. Let's go Ash. At least now we know we're looking for a guy in a motorhome. He's got to park it up somewhere. I have someone who can get us his license number. Drop me in town. I'll Uber back."

Asha belted up and drove away. She thought about her own fuck ups in her first year at university, all because of a stupid, inconsiderate boy. She took a deep breath, nope, she wasn't going there again. Not thinking about that at all. She glanced at Delaney who seemed deep in thought. Funny how things turned out. She'd taken that job he'd offered her and hadn't crossed her mind back then that she'd fall for him and now they'd been together for over two years. "You think you'll ever get a beer gut like Vern, Delaney?"

Delaney glanced down at his stomach and laughed. "Feel free to shoot me if that ever happens. Jeez, he couldn't have been more than thirty."

Asha nodded. "No going back from that. Damn, I forgot to tell you. It's Grandma Bunty's 65th. I promised to go up to the farm."

Delaney frowned. "Today?"

"Tomorrow. I promised I'd take Maria. Sorry. You're invited too."

Delaney rubbed his face. "Bad timing. We've just taken on a client." He thought about it a moment. "But go. Take Maria. She looked heart-broken last night. I wanted to hug her, but she slunk away."

"She said that he totally ignored her, then overheard

him calling her his bitch."

Delaney winced. "One thing I'm sure of, she'll never be someone's bitch. I'm so glad I'll never be fifteen again."

Asha rolled her eyes. "Shit yeah, I have no idea how I survived it at all. Thank God for basketball and swimming. It kept me out of trouble."

"Bet you were hot though."

She shook her head. "You'd be very wrong, Delaney. I wore passion killer braces and the worst haircut on earth. I basically prayed to be invisible almost every day."

Delaney reached out and squeezed her shoulder. "Go see Bunty. She'll be so happy to see you."

"You won't come?"

"Let me see how the search goes. If I can get up for one day, I will. Did you have snow tires fitted to your Fiat?"

"Yeah. Can't believe how much that cost."

"Has to be done. It's getting colder. It must snow a lot up there in the mountains."

"Yeah. Hate to say this, but she'll want us for Christmas as well."

Delaney smiled. "I was going to work on the boathouse. But, yeah, a log fire, fine wine, that sounds good."

Asha grinned. "I'm sorry. I keep making plans for family stuff."

"I'm happy you do. Family is important. I want Maria to feel that people care about her too. You don't want to see your father? I know you won't see your mother."

"No, Daddy doesn't celebrate Christmas and let's not discuss my mother. Ever."

Delaney pointed out a stopping point. "Drop me there. I'll get Bunty a gift."

Asha smiled. "I hope you'll come. She likes you. Oh, and if you're getting something for Maria for Christmas, she wants new trainers. Has to be Converse High Tops, size six. Not black or red. Make sure you keep the receipt, in case, you know what she's like." She pulled over.

Delaney rubbed Rufus's head. "Ok. Converse size six. Are her feet still growing?"

"She's still got a growth spurt to go, I think. But I seem to recall my feet have been the same since I was nineteen."

Delaney nodded. "Rufus be good. Take care of Asha. Ok? See you at Harry's in about an hour. That work for you?"

Asha smiled and gave him a thumbs up.

Rufus stared back at him with a worried whine as he walked away from the vehicle. Asha signaled and rejoined the traffic. She wondered what Bunty would like for her birthday.

Delaney entered Bookbank and was happy to see it was busy. Being the last surviving bookshop in the city it was quite a feat. He went up to the first floor where the boss reigned supreme. He seemed happy to see him.

"Mr Delaney, you've been avoiding us I think."

Delaney stared at Mr Abrams astonished to see him standing and looking remarkably well. They shook hands and then sanitized. It was hard to give up on that now.

"I owe you everything, Mr Delaney. That woman you recommended works miracles."

Delaney smiled. "Jasmina is the genuine article, Mr Abrams. I hope you were generous with her."

"Did exactly as you suggested. Had a new front door fitted. She was very hard to persuade to accept it, but I insisted. I have my life back. No pain for a year now."

"Same for me. I keep expecting it will come back but so far, I'm clear."

"It restored my faith in everything. I send her flowers every chance I get. Coffee? Come, we'll walk there. Imagine that. I can walk the floors again. The staff are much more alert now I think."

"And busy."

"Thank God. Sales are up. We are having a good Christmas so far. Is this a social visit or are you investigating another scam?"

They arrived at the coffee counter and ordered.

"One shot, with almond milk for Mr Delaney and some Hibiscus tea for me."

"Hibiscus?" Delany queried. "Asha's got me on that too."

"Supposed to lower blood pressure. I aim to stay well, Mr Delaney as long as I can."

"You ever hear of a local writer called Wolfie Sigurdsson?"

Mr Abrams pinched his nose like he'd discovered a bad smell. "Terrible writer, awful person. How he ever got published I'll never know."

Delaney accepted his coffee and moved to one side to let a customer through.

"Seems he specializes in writing paid-for biographies."

Mr Abrams shook his head in sorrow as he took his tea to a tall table near the window.

"I heard about that. Sad fact of life. There really is a sucker born every minute. I blame social media. Everyone with the slightest following thinks they're so important everyone wants to read about their sad little lives."

Delaney sipped his coffee. "He's been doing this a good while. I've got a client who paid ten grand up front. Seems Wolfie took the money and vanished, took his home with him too."

Mr Abrams held a hand over his steaming cup to ease his joints. "You know how many writers actually make ten thousand in a year? You could probably count them on your fingers. I suspect he's quite the salesman."

"I think so."

"I take it your client didn't like the finished product?"

Delaney shook his head. "There's no product.

Client's highly aggrieved."

Mr Abrams nodded. "I should say so. But if you knew Wolfie, you wouldn't be surprised.   There were rumors about him killing his wife until she turned up with a new lover. Sort of man people hate on sight. Can't believe people pay him up front."

"So, you wouldn't have any ideas about where he might go?"

Mr Abrams took a slug of his tea and thought about it. "He used to run a workshop at a writers' retreat up the coast at Bridgetown. It's pretty remote. I sponsor a course there once a year. They might know where he is or where he goes. It's a long shot. I'll get you the address."

Delaney smiled and drank off his coffee. "Thanks. It's a start and it's great to see you looking so well."

"You too, Mr Delaney."

"Oh yeah, I need a couple of good crime novels. A present for a woman who likes them pretty hardboiled."

Mr Abrams eyes lit up. "I will find you some personally. There has been quite a good crop of new titles this fall. Funny how people never tire of murder mysteries. You'd think after Covid and Ukraine everyone would want happy stories."

Delaney shrugged. "I heard misery loves company."

CHAPTER THREE

Harry's

Harry's Bagel and Beanz was buzzing as ever. Asha waved him over to the undercover veranda where dogs were allowed. Rufus greeted him with his usual enthusiasm.

"Settle down. Sit. Wow, it's packed in here."

Asha leaned in for a kiss. "Rufus has been guarding your chair. I don't think people dare go to the bathroom in case they lose theirs. We may have to find ourselves another hide-out, Delaney. Harry's has become way too popular."

Delaney squeezed in and gave Rufus a treat to reward him.

"I may have a lead."

Asha held up an almost new paperback. "Me too. *Sheep's Clothing* by Wolfie Sigurdsson. Found it in a second-hand bookshop."

"Any good?"

"Who knows. Starts with someone baking an apple pie. Couldn't get past the thrilling moment she finished rolling out the pastry and pops the whole thing in the oven at 356 Fahrenheit."

Delaney laughed. "You have something against apple pies?"

"Life's too short to bake – actually life's too short to read about someone baking."

"You don't know what you're missing."

Asha stuck out her tongue. "When did you last bake a pie, Chef."

Delaney smiled. "That might be never. But I am a connoisseur of apple pies. Especially with sultanas. Pastry has to be slightly soggy under the filling and the top flaky but not too flaky you get covered in crumbs."

Asha stared at him in astonishment. "You have to use shortcrust pastry for apple pies. Flaky sounds wrong somehow."

"See, you're a secret pie expert too. We'll ask your grandma."

Asha snorted. "Yes, we will, Mr Delaney. Flaky, flaky, flaky, I think not."

Delaney put up his hands in surrender. "Ok, enough. Seems there's a writers' retreat up the coast at Bridgetown. I tried calling but they didn't answer."

"Hey you cheated. That's my info." She flipped to the inside cover page of the book. "With thanks to Bridgetown Writers' Retreat for all their support and feedback."

"So, I guess I'm headed to Bridgetown tomorrow." Delaney remarked. "Did you order?"

"Spicy pumpkin soup and rye toast."

"Sounds good."

"Bridgetown is only about sixty miles from Ciderbee. You could make it to Grandma's after seeing them."

Delaney thought about it. "If I can, I'll try. Narrow twisty roads up there."

"But pretty. Bridgetown is kinda cute, but they had terrible floods last winter I recall."

"Yeah, I wonder if that's why the retreat doesn't answer their phones. Could be out of business. When was that book published?" He took the paperback from her. "Bloodclot Books? 2018."

"They went out of business during Covid. I checked. I was hoping someone there would know Wolfie."

"It's never that easy, Ash. Bloodclot? Horrible name."

"But perfect for crime fiction I guess."

"Not so perfect apparently. Bridgetown would be a good place to disappear this time of year. No tourists. Pretty bleak I should think. Lot of forest to vanish into. But he'll need to drink and eat – someone might remember him." He picked up the book again examining the back cover. "And now we have a photo. Hmm, not what I was expecting. He looks more like a trucker."

"Truckers read. I read about one who listened to a thousand audiobooks driving Coast to Coast."

"Well let's hope our trucker needs company up there in Bridgetown. Looks like the kind of guy who might seek company of strangers. Eyes a bit close together, like Putin's."

"That's a bad sign."

"Never a good sign, put it that way."

The waitress arrived. She looked harassed. "Two spicy pumpkin soups with rye toast?"

Asha looked up and smiled. "That's us."

"I don't think we'll find another place as good as Harry's," Delaney mused. "It's good to see it full again." He slipped Rufus a bit of toast which he snatched out of his fingers.

"What are you going to do if you find our trucker?" Asha asked.

"Make him see the error of his ways."

"Sounds ominous."

"I'm sure he'll understand. Maybe I can persuade Rufus to growl at him a little."

Asha giggled. "I don't think I've ever heard him growl."

"He's the strong silent type. Eat your soup. We have stuff do after lunch."

CHAPTER FOUR

A Writer's Reputation — is a precious thing

Delaney rubbed his eyes and squirted the windshield again, flipping the wipers to clear the mud away. He was exhausted. One hundred and sixty miles in driving sleet and rain. Rufus whining for the last thirty miles.

"We're nearly there. Cross your legs."

Rufus nosed his neck. He was getting desperate. Delaney turned off the coastal road onto a muddy track and came to a stop. He reached over, opened the passenger door and Rufus bolted.

Delaney unfasted his seat belt and got out of the vehicle to take a leak. He'd known about the flooding, of course, but had not reckoned on the extent of the damage in the area or the size of the potholes. Not much had been done to make good either the roads or the wrecked vacation homes perched on the ocean side of the route. Made him all the more certain he was going to find Wolfie Sigurdsson somewhere up here. No one with any sense would come in this weather.

"Rufus?"

Rufus came bounding out of the woods. He looked spooked. Moments later a stag appeared angrily snorting, looking for trouble. Delaney beat a retreat to the car. Rufus had already spread his muddy paws on the front seat and probably wished he knew how to close the door after him. His eyes looked scared.

"Got a little surprise, huh. Let's go. You're not in the city anymore dog. This is where the wild things are."

He drove on down the muddy track and prayed the sat nav had been correct. One thing was for sure, no one was going to find this writers' retreat by accident. It was well and truly off-piste.

Fifteen bumpy minutes later they emerged into a large misty clearing with wide lawns and well-spaced trees. He slowed again as a large white 18th Century clapboard mansion revealed itself complete with a large stone portico and one elaborate central tower. It was nestled into a sheltered spot with the mountain looming behind it.

"Was kinda expecting wooden huts, not Tara. Jeez, we'd better mind our manners and wipe our feet, Rufus."

The rain had stopped but the mist closed in behind him. He noted a red-faced stout woman in shorts chopping wood at the side of the mansion. She had a good rhythm going and a healthy stack of firewood at her side.

Delaney climbed out and Rufus quickly followed. He didn't stop him. He needed a run around. He was about to approach the woman in shorts when the front door of the mansion opened with a distinct creak. A tall bony woman wrapped in an overlarge coat stepped out in sturdy boots. She seemed surprised to see Delaney.

"Delaney. City Investigations." He flashed his ID, not that she'd be able to read anything at this distance. "Investigating the disappearance of a writer."

The woman seemed almost amused.

"That's a new twist. Usually, writers make everyone else disappear."

Delaney moved a little closer. "Wolfie Sigurdsson. I heard he ran a workshop here."

"In the past," the woman replied. "That your dog running wild?"

Delaney turned to glimpse Rufus running after some unfortunate squirrel.

"Shouldn't those things be hibernating already? Rufus, leave. Come here."

Rufus decided his tone wasn't definitive. He stayed at the base of the tree sniffing the ground.

"Trained him well, I see."

Delaney shrugged. "It's a long way from the city. Dog needs to stretch his legs. Noted a stag as we came through."

"We have deer. They have been known to trample a dog when annoyed."

Delaney noted that detail.

"If you came looking for Wolfie Sigurdsson you have wasted your time, Mr Delaney. He's banned. Odious little shit."

"Seems he accepted ten grand to write a biography but chose to take the money and run."

"That someone actually paid him is nothing short of a miracle. Running away from his responsibilities is his specialty. A biography?"

"Seems he has found a little niche."

The woman's lips curled. "Yes, everyone needs a niche but that bastard – no way."

"I detect you didn't exactly rate him as a writer."

"No, Mr Delaney, I don't rate him as a human being. His workshops were a disaster. All the feedback was dire. Doesn't listen, talks over people, doesn't read the work."

Delaney shrugged. "Any ideas where I might find this piece of shit?"

"What will you do to him?"

"Either make him pay the money back or drag him back to Berg City to apologize to my client. I'm afraid I'm not really permitted to do any lasting damage."

"What a pity." The woman looked over to where the wood chopper was working. "Berenice? Bernie? Where did Sigurdsson used to go?"

Berenice rested a moment on her ax wiping some sweat from her brow. "Cold Rock Beach. Good luck finding him sober." She spat.

Delaney figured this Sigurdsson had made quite an impression on these women.

"You got any writers in residence here now?"

"Next week. Ten-day novel-in-progress marathons. Women only. Sorry if you wanted to join."

"That's ok. I'll let someone else write my memoirs. Maybe not Wolfie though. By the way, Mr Abrams from Bookbank sends his regards."

He called Rufus and this time he came bounding back.

"Mr Abrams is a good patron. Tell him Janine sends her best to him."

Rufus jumped up into the vehicle and Delaney made his way back to the driver's seat. "If Sigurdsson should pay a call…"

"I'll put a stake through his heart. Good afternoon, Mr Delaney."

Delaney turned the vehicle around as Rufus licked his legs. "Good boy. Sorry Rufus. We've still got a few more miles to go."

He was about to set off when Berenice approached wheeling a barrow full of logs.

"There's a motorhome park overlooking the beach. A lot of people like him winter there."

"People like him?"

"Restless, angry at the world. It's where conspiracies are born and sail forth anew in the spring."

Delaney nodded. "I always wondered where those conspiracies came from. You actually know Wolfie?"

"They say he killed his wife."

"I heard that. Almost a shame she turned up alive, huh."

Berenice shrugged. "I prefer the first draft."

She picked up her barrow and set off with her load towards the back of the mansion.

Delaney drove into the mist. It would be at least an hour's drive to Cold Rock. He remembered it was a pretty bleak spot. He hoped there would be somewhere to eat when he got there.

CHAPTER FIVE

Cold Rock

It was almost twilight when Delaney paused his vehicle on the ridge overlooking Cold Rock. He wound down the window to breathe in the ozone. Waves lashed the shoreline driven by a fierce cold wind. Rufus was already excitedly sniffing the ocean air. He loved the beach more than anything.

"This place doesn't look in good shape either, dog."

Abandoned homes with shattered roofs littered the coastline. Someone had recently scraped drifting sand off the road, but it was already building up again. The once lush cedar forest that lined the shore was mostly gone; the burned-out stumps all that remained from the fierce heat dome of the summer. Cold Rock was supposed to be a surfers' paradise like Narragansett, but it had never really taken off, too remote, too darn inhospitable. Rhode Island had the best waves he recalled. He stared at a timber lodge where kids used to go for wild weekends in his student days. That too was a burned-out wreck.

Rufus whined. He wanted to get out. Sick of being cooped up in the car.

Delaney moved forward, looking for the Lobster Pot Bar and Grill. He had to abruptly swerve, narrowly missing a hooded figure riding an electric scooter without helmet or lights. The rider gave him the finger as they sped on, oblivious to how close they had come to being crushed.

He no longer expected to find the winter nomads parked up on the bluff overlooking the rock. He knew some of the coastline had been washed away in the floods that followed the fires. Many main street stores were still boarded up or for sale. Some diehards would tough it out of course.

A few homes up on the slope had lights on, so at least there was electricity.

"Better hope the Lobster Pot is open Rufus, or we aren't going to eat tonight."

He drove around a traffic circle with a scruffy Christmas tree in the middle strewn with a few working lights, several bulbs having burned out. Be hard to get the Christmas spirit in this spot, he reckoned. He was briefly cheered by an illuminated sign outside the Lobster Pot which flickered 'Open'.

He pulled up outside an old red barn overlooking the fishing harbor below. Rufus leapt out, making sure he wouldn't be left behind and quickly peed on someone's electric scooter. Delaney hoped it belonged to the idiot on the hill.

Fishing boats heaved at anchor in the harbor. He counted six small vessels. Fishing was probably the only way to make a living in winter in this area without the summer visitors. "Come on. Let's try their hospitality."

He decided to ignore the faded 'No Dogs' sign by the door.

Rufus was already there, anxious to get out of the cold wind. Delaney closed the door behind him with a heave against wind resistance. He brushed back his windswept hair, pleasantly surprised to find the place was half full and warm. An open log fire burned at one end and several old boys had parked their beer guts on the bar as they openly stared at a rare stranger entering their domain.

"Kitchen open?" Delaney asked as he approached the bar. "You ok with the dog? He needs to eat too."

The bartender was emptying the dishwasher and stacking clean glasses. "Better be, this is the only place to eat in twenty miles. That dog well behaved?"

"Yeah. He's very civilized."

The bartender shrugged an ok. Delaney felt relieved and took off his jacket, placing it on the back of the bar stool.

"Any wine?"

"White or red?"

"Any actual list?" Delaney asked, disappointed to see box wine on the back counter.

The bartender looked back at the old boys who were still staring at Delaney.

"Well now, finally we have a discerning customer. The apocalypse must be over."

Delaney smiled, taking it in good spirit. "Apocalypses are overrated. Any water for my dog? We've come a long way."

The bartender found a bowl and filled it as Rufus momentarily jumped up to investigate the bar.

"Nice looking hound, some Ridgeback in there, I'm guessing. I'm Raymond and you are?"

"Delaney." He pushed Rufus's paws off the bar. "Manners, dog. Some obsessive Collie in there too. Doesn't like to be ignored."

Raymond handed Delaney the water bowl and he set it down for the dog.

A waitress appeared from the kitchen area and took a burger and fries to a waiting customer. He noticed she had a plaster cast on her right arm.

"White or red?" Raymond asked again.

"Red."

"We've got a Shiraz, but I'd choose the Malbec if I were you."

"If you recommend it, then the Malbec. Anything you'd suggest we eat? We're pretty hungry."

"Catch of the day. Yellowtail tuna. Done any way you like it with lemon rice or fries."

"Sounds good to me. And something for Rufus here?"

"I feed my dog dried food mostly, but tonight its beef mixed with some grains and greens for his gut. No preservatives. She seems to thrive on it. That's her hogging the fire."

Delaney glanced over at a black Labrador soundly sleeping in front of the open fire. He looked down on Rufus and ruffled his head. "He's never interested in other dogs. Beef sound good to you Rufie?"

He nodded back at the bartender. "We're sold. Tuna medium with fries for me."

The bartender disappeared under the counter a moment then reappeared with a dusty bottle. "Argentinian." He glanced at the returning waitress. "My wife, Giselle."

Delaney nodded to her as she made her way to the kitchen. The bartender followed her to place the order. Some of the beer guts were still staring at Delaney, unasked questions hovering over their heads. Delaney nodded towards them. "Anyone seen Wolfie around here?"

He could see their faces were immediately troubled as they wondered if he was friend or foe. "I was looking for his motorhome. I guess with all these floods he must have parked up someplace else this winter."

One of the beer guts decided to answer. "Murdo's. We're all parked up at Murdo's. Son of a bitch charges an arm and leg for water and power but it's the only place to go right now."

"Ain't that a bitch," Delaney replied. "As if Cold Rock doesn't have enough problems."

The bartender returned and opened the Malbec. He poured a large. "You'll like this." The liquid was bright with a glossy finish.

"Looks healthy."

"It is. 2018. Before Covid. I try to avoid anything from 20 through to 22."

"You having one?" Delaney asked, offering.

"Too early. I'm on till late. Have to stay sober to toss these guys out into the cold dark night."

"Tough schedule. It gets busy later?"

"It's Friday. It will be packed by eight. You a cop?"

Delaney shook his head. "Private."

"I should have guessed. Cops don't drive Range Rovers."

Delaney shrugged, interested that he'd taken the trouble so see what he drove.

"I'm looking for one of your regulars. Wolfie."

The bartender seemed surprised. "He's one step away from being blacklisted here."

"Blacklisted?"

"He gets very argumentative when loaded."

"I'm guessing you wouldn't want to be banned from the only place to eat for twenty miles either."

The bartender laughed. "Most of these guys eat in their motorhomes, then spend all their money here on beer. Fortunately, we have regulars who come for the seafood."

"Must have been your lucky day this place survived the flood."

"God intervened I reckon. The water surge swept right past us down into the harbor. My old Jeep is still underwater. Been waiting on a crane to lift it out."

Delaney sipped some of his wine and was impressed. "Good, very good. I have to say that I think luck plays a big part in life. It's not something you can buy."

Raymond poured two beers for another customer. "What did Wolfie do? Must have been something bad to drag someone all the way from Berg City."

Delaney took another sip of the wine. He looked at the label, made a mental note to get some. "Wolfie failed to complete a contract. Clients hate that kind of thing, especially if they have paid in advance."

Raymond glanced at the guys at the far end of the bar. "Hear that? Some idiot paid Wolfie up front."

They dutifully laughed. Delaney felt it was a tad forced. He guessed they all had to be on best behavior for Raymond. His bar, his rules.

"He was pissed at lunch." One of the beer guts admitted. "You won't get much sense out of him."

Delaney nodded. "I can but try," he said, raising his glass at the old boys.

"Up on the ridge." Raymond told him. "First turn-off on the left. Broken sign says Murdo's Leisure Park. I guess some of those people he bummed money off will be surprised he had up front money."

"I expect they will. I'm told he's a bit of a writer."

Some of the old guys laughed.

"He can barely hold a pen. Never seen him write a thing," one of the beer guts declared.

"He says he's going to rock the world with his next book," another remarked. "I saw him working on his laptop last month. He was mostly sober too."

"Good to hear. Maybe the situation can be rescued after all," Delaney said.

"Five minutes. Just waiting on the fries. Giselle has set up a table for you. I'll bring the dog's dinner over in a moment as well." He handed Delaney a knife and fork wrapped in a paper napkin, pausing to add, "You might want to take whatever Wolfie tells you with a pinch of salt."

"Yeah?"

"He's a bit paranoid. Claims people are watching him."

Delaney frowned. "And are they?"

Raymond shrugged. "If they are, they've never been in here to eat or drink. Can't think of why anyone would hang around Cold Rock in winter unless they had to. I imagine he has debts back in Berg City. Half the people here are running away from something."

Delaney understood. "Better here than sleeping rough there. But I can't imagine debt collectors being shy, can you?"

Raymond nodded. "Take the bottle to the table."

"Can't. I'm driving. It's 14 percent. Don't worry, I'll pay for the whole bottle. I know you wouldn't open it normally. I might return later."

Raymond nodded. "Do that. I might have a glass with you after all."

Rufus needed a walk after supper. Delaney was in no rush to sober up a drunk. He pulled his collar up and walked the beach as the dog had a mad moment dashing along the sand. The air cut like ice. He didn't need to worry about the wine in his system, he was wide awake now. He held his phone up to the sky but couldn't get a signal. Asha would have to wait. Same went for his client. No need to tell him he'd found Wolfie just yet.

It was interesting that Wolfie had no friends up here, despite being one of the winter regulars. Several of the guys at the bar admitted to helping him get back to his motorhome from time to time, but none admitted to being a 'friend'. Two of them confirmed that Wolfie claimed he was being watched, but none believed him or cared. Drunks get paranoid all the time. It was just one more strike against him. One thing was for sure, he'd told no one he had money.

"You happy now?"

Rufus came running and Delaney removed some seaweed from his back. "Please tell me you didn't roll in this stuff." Rufus wasn't going to admit anything. "Come on, let's go pour a guy some coffee."

They walked back to his vehicle and were finally glad to be out of the wind. Delaney pulled on his gloves, fired the engine up and they went to find Murdo's Leisure Park.

The motorhome was dark, parked a little away from other vehicles. One dim streetlight served the whole park and Delaney figured there were about thirty assorted vehicles gathered here.   Wolfie's was old and shabby but had new tires which told him that Wolfie wasn't entirely irresponsible.

He knocked but didn't wait for a response and entered the cabin. He couldn't find a light switch and flicked on the flashlight on his phone. Wolfie was lying prostrate on the floor with his trousers at half-mast completely out of it. Looked like he'd fallen straight after leaving the can. It didn't smell so good in there either. Rufus stood guard outside with orders to bark if anyone approached.

He looked around for the light switch and eventually managed to get the overhead light on. He looked around expecting chaos but found a neatly made bed, a laptop open at the small foldaway table, and everything shipped away tight, as you would expect in a cramped space. There was a half-finished bottle of Glen Moray on the sideboard. Wolfie wasn't the kind of guy to drink rotgut then. Only the finest ten-year-old whiskies for him.

Delaney put the kettle on and boiled some water. Couldn't find any coffee but instant and shook his head in disappointment. "No self-respecting writer drinks instant Wolfie, you're letting the side down."

He pulled the writer up off the floor and propped him up against the bulkhead. His photo on the paperback portrayed him as a tough trucker, not the short stocky guy he actually was. He looked older too. You can never believe an author's photo. He lit a match right under his nose and only blew it out when Wolfie's eyes popped open in shock.

"Little trick I learned in Paris. Wake up Wolfie, it's confession time."

Slowly, with the aid of blistering hot coffee pushed down his throat, Wolfie returned from the dead. Delaney didn't allow his head to sag, he wanted him lucid enough to tell his story.

"Let's start at the beginning, shall we? The day you couldn't believe your luck some sucker gave you ten grand in cash. You must have thought Brin Martinet was a total sucker. Tell me, what did you do next, Wolfie? Apart from get drunk."

Wolfie blinked, then kept on blinking. He struggled to get his voice working. It was a huge effort and he urgently needed to piss. He stared at Delaney scared out of his wits.

"Are you going to kill me?" He rasped.

"I think you're doing a pretty good job of that yourself, Wolfie. By the way, the lovely ladies at the retreat send their – well let's just say they wish you were already dead."

Wolfie's eyes darted left, then right, clearly hoping there was some way out of this situation. "You're going to kill me."

Delaney frowned. "That's not my orders. I want the book you're supposed to be writing. Remember that? You signed a contract to supply a biography. A contract with a guy who can afford the best lawyers in the whole wide world. You weren't thinking of stiffing that guy, were you?"

Wolfie gulped. "They told me to stop."

Delaney looked momentarily confused. "They told you to stop? What? Your demons? You're hearing voices in your head? Who are 'they'?"

Wolfie suddenly twisted around and launched himself towards the can as he threw up with a spectacular surge of vomit, then did it all over again. Eventually he rolled back sweating like a pig and collapsed completely, out cold again.

Delaney had to step outside; the smell was overpowering. Rufus stared up at him expecting to go.

"Not yet, big guy. Lie down. I need to look at a laptop."

The laptop fired up but was password protected. He sighed. Get this wrong and he'd be looking at a brick.

"Now Wolfie, are you a 123456 man?" He entered the numbers, but the laptop shook him off. He knew he'd only get three chances at this. He looked around for clues wishing Asha was with him. She had a good instinct for this stuff.

There was a photo hanging skew on the wall of Wolfie standing next to some smug celebrity he vaguely remembered. He seemed to be handing Wolfie an award in the shape of a dagger. Delaney dimly recalled this was an accolade for crime writers but found it hard to believe Wolfie had ever won anything. It was a longshot, but he entered 'dagger' and it burst into life. His triumph was short-lived, however. There was absolutely nothing on this machine. No folders, no works in progress, it was like he'd hit factory reset.

Delaney looked down at Wolfie's body on the floor and shook his head.

"You don't fool me for a minute, Wolfie. I know you backed everything up. There's a memory stick somewhere in this little kingdom of yours and I'm going to find it."

It was lucky the writer was anal retentive and kept the place so neat. He began a methodical search, cupboard by cupboard, drawer by drawer.

"You can wake up at any time and tell me where it is, y'know."

Wolfie remained lifeless. For a moment he worried he'd died, but a quick check of his pulse said otherwise.

Rufus whined out there in the cold, curled up under the vehicle to get out of the wind. "I hear you, dog. Pity he didn't bury it outside, you'd find it in a flash."

Delaney wondered why he'd wiped his laptop. It's a drastic measure at the best of times. A flash of headlights swept through the motorhome as someone arrived back on site. It was enough to reveal something stuffed at the underside of his bunk. Delaney reached in and dragged out a flight bag. He unzipped it and stared at a bundle of cash. He didn't count it, but Wolfie was smarter than he'd given him credit for. He reckoned there was at least nine of that ten thousand bucks he'd been given. "You're a man of surprises, Wolfie."

He left it there. Martinet wasn't interested in his money; he wanted the damned book or whatever Wolfie had managed to write before he grew paranoid.

And there it was, stashed in the toilet bag, one tiny purple 6 gigabyte memory stick. He pocketed it; Martinet was entitled to something for his money after all.

"Time to wake up, Wolfie. I can't stay here all night and I don't have a room booked."

He shoved the flight bag back where he'd found it and opened the fridge. He took out a bottle of sparkling spring water, unscrewed the cap and poured the contents over Wolfie's head. He needed cleaning up.

Wolfie stirred, then fearing the worst forced himself up to a sitting position clutching his sore head.

"What's going on Wolfie? All you had to do was write a boring biography. It wasn't as if you had to do much research. I looked him up on Google. His whole life is there. Old guy's a genuine hero, won a bronze medal at the Olympics, got lucky with his investments, took some great photos, had an adventurous life. All you had to do was color in the pictures."

Wolfie stared up at him, blinking, questions coursing across his face.

"Olympics?" he croaked.

Delaney laughed. "What? You didn't know he was on the American shooting team at Munich? Did you do any research? They said you were sloppy but hell man, you could have Googled the guy."

Wolfie looked confused. Struggled to get his mouth working.

"Or did you find something you didn't like. He beat his wife maybe. The client thinks he's a saint, so best to leave out that stuff, I guess. Is that why you stopped?"

Delaney didn't think much would bother Wolfie, but he was puzzled he hadn't spent the money. He poured a glass of water into a dirty mug and handed it down to him.

Wolfie gulped it down, closing his eyes again, but Delaney kicked his legs, and he rejoined the living.

"It started at school," he mumbled.

Delaney pulled up the only chair and leaned over him. "What started at school?"

"I can't tell you."

"Who told you to stop writing, Wolfie?"

Wolfie shook his head. "I can't tell you."

"What can you tell me? What do I tell Brin Martinet? You remember there was supposed to be a deadline for this thing?"

"Can't write it."

"Can't or won't?"

"Can't. They took it. Made me wipe my laptop."

Delaney wasn't convinced. "They again.   Who? Some literary critic who doesn't like you much? Makes no sense, Wolfie."

"They said they'd kill me if I told anyone."

Delaney could sense his fear was genuine, but they weren't getting anywhere. "I know you backed it up, Wolfie."

Wolfie's eyes briefly darted towards his bed, he couldn't help himself. Delaney didn't reveal he'd already found the bag.

"Let's say you're a man with integrity. You signed a contract. You didn't want to let the client down but then these other people came along telling you to stop. Must have been after you interviewed someone – otherwise how would they even know about you?"

Wolfie nodded, still clutching his throbbing head.

"Did this happen before you left Berg City? I know you left in a hurry. Vern confirmed it. Your neighbor."

Wolfie coughed and shuddered a moment. It was hard to think.

"This 'they'. You think they followed you to Cold Rock? Not exactly a hospitable place these days. Except the Lobster Pot. Your drinking pals say hi, by the way. Probably a bit surprised you got cash up front for the contract. They might be asking for their loans back tomorrow."

"I've got no pals."

"Brutal, but true, I think. So, before you left Berg City, these guys, I'll assume they're guys, came to see you and told you what exactly?"

Wolfie looked up at him. "Take the money and run."

"And that's exactly what you did. You didn't think you could drop an email or even post a letter to your benefactor to say you wouldn't be delivering the manuscript. A little courtesy goes a long way I find."

"No. They were very specific. I was to disappear, no traces."

"Moot point, Wolfie. You left a lot of traces actually. After all, I'm here. But now you think they're still watching you. Was it something you discovered? You can tell me. I'm not writing anything down. What's so special about an old man with dementia?"

"I can't say."

"Sure, you can. You think they've got this motorhome bugged maybe? It's 200 miles to Berg City. I'm betting there's no one sitting in any car measuring your keystrokes on the laptop or listening to you talking in your sleep. What the fuck did you find out that's worth threatening you?"

"I swear I found out nothing. Nothing."

"You know I can't buy that. You interviewed him at the care home, what did the old man tell you?"

"Nothing. He talked about his camera. He was very passionate about his Olympus camera, and he said it all began at school. He's been taking photos all his life."

"But someone wanted you to stop writing because of what he told you."

Wolfie nodded. "They watch him. Believe me. The nurses are informers. They watch him all the time."

"This might come as a surprise to you, Wolfie, but nurses are supposed to watch their patients, aren't they?"

Wolfie shook his head. "The old man told me nothing except about his camera. Shit he couldn't even remember the names of his wife or his son."

"So, in your opinion, whoever are watching him, or you, are wasting their time."

Wolfie smirked. "Now they'll be watching you. Anyone who comes near this."

Delaney doubted it. "What do I tell Brin Martinet? You want to give him his money back, or what's left of it."

"It's gone. I spent it."

"How? You don't exactly live the high life, Wolfie. Grant you, Glen Moray here is beyond my budget. You don't even eat at the Lobster Pot. I checked."

"It's all gone. I have debts."

Delaney smirked. "So, all that cash under your bed is definitely not Brin Martinet's money, right? Must be about nine thousand there, I'm guessing."

Wolfie looked crestfallen.

"I'm not here to take back the money, that's on your conscience, not mine. I want the book you wrote about an old guy who raised money for disadvantaged kids and made a mark in his city. What the hell did you write that could possibly upset whoever 'they' are?"

"I swear I don't know. I spoke to several people, civic leaders, school principals. Everyone liked him, no one said anything bad about him. He lived like a monk. Couldn't find a single place where he ate or drank, not one friend turned up. His son was raised by his sister after his wife died suddenly. The old man didn't pay a dime towards his son's college tuition. I don't think they ever socialized. You know how hard it is to write a biography if there's nothing there."

"What about his photographs. The son is pretty proud of them."

"Sure, but he doesn't remember taking them or the road trips. He doesn't remember anything except his damn camera. That he remembered down to the last screw."

"But 'they' think he does, or that he told you something."

"I don't know anymore that you do, but yeah, obviously they think he told me stuff. I know nothing, I wish I'd never seen him."

"You know who 'they' are?"

Wolfie shook his head, then regretted it, pressing fingers to the die of his head. "I just know they're scary people."

Delaney cocked his head. "CIA, FBI, that kind of scary?"

"I don't know."

"Here's what I'm thinking, Wolfie. You're alive. If it was criminal, you'd be dead. Only the government is inclined to give the benefit of the doubt, that, and the fact you have a very wealthy client who might, I stress *might*, kick up a fuss if your body washes up say on Cold Rock beach."

Wolfie stayed silent, trying to process this.

"Did you they give you a number to call?"

"No."

"You sure? They told you to get out of Dodge and no further contact?"

"They just wanted me to disappear."

"And you wiped your own laptop?"

"In front of them. Factory reset. I'll have to buy all the fucking software again."

"But you backed it up first."

"No."

"You're a bad liar, Wolfie."

"I didn't. I was going to, but ..."

"But?"

"I just didn't."

"And none of your recent work is in the cloud?"

"You think I'd pay for that? Besides there's no wi-fi here."

"I think it costs about a dollar a month. You're too cheap for your own good, Wolfie. You found absolutely nothing bad in his past?"

"No. Forget him. Walk away."

"Unlike you, Wolfie, I respect my clients. That thing he told you at the care home: "It started at school."

"What of it?"

"Which school?"

Wolfie shrugged. "I don't know. It must have been in the early fifties."

"But you didn't query it?"

"He said something that sounded like Scimitar, but there's no school called Scimitar or even similar in Berg City."

"So, you did check."

"I asked a teacher. He's big on local history in Berg City."

"You get one gold star for effort, Wolfie. Did you perhaps ask where Mr Martinet was born?"

"Brooklyn. His son told me. He couldn't remember where he lived when he was a kid. His father moved around a lot. In the end who gives a shit about an old guy with dementia."

"His son. His son cares a lot."

Delaney was satisfied he'd got enough. "I suggest you clean up; it's not going to smell any better in the morning."

Wolfie looked surprised. "That's it? You're leaving?"

Delaney paused at the doorway. "I'll be telling Brin Martinet where you are, Wolfie. You can either contact him or keep running, but like you say, you know nothing. Begs the question as to why the Government would want you to disappear. I'm guessing they made a copy of your stuff before they made you wipe it."

He could see from Wolfie's face that he was right.

"Clean up, try and eat something. No one is watching you."

Rufus leapt up and yawned as Delaney stepped outside. Delaney kept moving, happy to breathe in fresh air again.

"Good boy. Time to get out of here." He pulled out his phone, held it up high, but there was still no signal. He looked at the time: 10.33. If he went via the mountain route, he could be with Asha in two hours. He hated the thought of driving those narrow, twisty single-lane roads but at least at night he'd be able to see if anyone was coming towards him.

He opened up his vehicle and waited for Rufus to jump up. He flopped down on his blanket with a sigh. Delaney gave him one of his favorite pumpkin biscuits to chew on.

"You driving?"

Delaney turned to see a vaping white-haired woman in a green quilted dressing gown and slippers walking her tiny dog nearby. She stopped to stare at him as she exhaled a cloud of smoke into the chilly air.

"Thinking about it." Delaney answered her.

"Going to snow. It was on the radio just now. Two inches they say."

Delaney's heart sank. The mountain route would be foolish but then again, his Range Rover was supposed to be all-terrain.

"I'll try a hotel ..."

"Nothing left since the floods and all the Airbnb's closed as well."

Delaney looked back down at the small harbor in the distance. Even from here he could hear the waves crashing against the shore. "Maybe I'll take the coast road."

She nodded. "Yes, that's safest, snow doesn't stick to the coast road. It's the salt." She pulled her dog away as it tried to piss on his tires and shuffled back towards her well-lit motorhome.

Delaney drove about a mile before thick snow started falling and looked like it would settle. That decided it. He turned around and headed back to the harbor. Maybe the Lobster Pot would let him sleep on a bench or something.

Too darn cold to sleep in his car, even with Rufus to keep him warm. Worryingly when he got there the 'open' sign was switched off.

Raymond, the bartender was stood outside, smoking a cigar, watching the snow fall.

Delaney parked up and climbed out of his vehicle.

Raymond smiled. "I was thinking you probably wished you'd booked a room for tonight."

Delaney shrugged. "Any room at the Inn?"

Raymond blew smoke into the falling snow. "Two hundred bucks a night. That's what we're supposed to charge."

"And what are you charging?" Delaney asked, fearing the worst.

"Nothing. Giselle's kid is staying in the only spare room, she's got a cold. I can fix you up a futon by the fire."

"Deal."

"And we've got a bottle to finish."

Delaney smiled. "That we have." He grabbed his overnight bag and let Rufus out.

"Did you find Wolfie?" Raymond enquired.

"He's a bit worse for wear. Drank half a bottle of Glen Moray and let's just say it didn't agree with him. Can barely function."

"Anyone watching him, you think?" Raymond asked, turning back towards the door.

"Might be an old biddy in a quilted dressing gown. She looked very alert."

"Sounds about right. Everyone watches everyone here."

Delaney followed him inside, Rufus dogging his heels.

"You got a phone signal?" Delaney asked closing the door behind him. The bar was empty.

"They keep promising to repair the mast but nothing for a month now. There's a landline."

"Good to know you have at least one link to civilization."

Raymond went to the bar and hauled out the bottle, still three-quarters full. He found two glasses and brought them over to the fire as Delaney gave a log a shove. Sparks flew up the chimney.

"I thought you were open till midnight."

Raymond shrugged. "We had a rush between seven and ten and that's it. It's cold, everyone gets anxious when it snows."

"Where's the dog?" Delaney asked.

"Betsy's gone to keep my wife warm in bed until I get there."

"Thanks for taking us in. I hadn't realized how bad things were up here."

"It'll come back. People will still want to surf and go fishing. However, we definitely expect five stars when you write us up," he added with a wink, pouring them both a glass of wine. He grinned and sat himself down on a bench.

Delaney smiled as Rufus curled up at his feet, it was way past the dog's bedtime.

CHAPTER SIX

A Turn of Events

It was a bitter cold and heavy clouded morning at the beach. Rufus, wary of the freezing Atlantic backed away from the incoming waves. Behind him Delaney fought the wind and snow. He shouted for Rufus to stay close and stay dry.

The cleaners had arrived at eight, and he was obliged to get out of their way. He couldn't grumble, he'd had a bed to lie on, fresh coffee to wake up to. A shower would have been good, but he didn't want to disturb them upstairs. He'd left fifty bucks and a note of thanks in the tip jar.

As he turned to go back, he heard a loud crunch up by the main road and someone blast their horn. He ran towards it. "Rufus!"

He climbed the dune to discover an angry woman in a massive winter coat standing in the snow staring at the side of her VW Golf. Rufus arrived moments later sliding between his legs.

"Did you see that? Fucking motorhome came out of nowhere and sideswiped me. Didn't even stop. I can't believe it. I just bought this car."

Delaney gathered his breath and surveyed the damage. There was a long scrape of silver paint along both doors but no dents. She'd been lucky. He could see tire tracks weaving away in the crisp snow.

"It's fixable. Don't bother claiming on the insurance. They might be able to polish the scrape out or do a small respray. You're lucky no dents."

She wasn't so easily consoled. "I didn't get the license plate, but it was definitely one of those damn nomads. No one drives that fast in the snow. No one. I am so angry right now."

"It sucks, could have been worse," Delaney told her. "At least you weren't hurt."

The woman made a mean face at him, she'd expected more sympathy maybe. She reluctantly got back into her car and drove off, spinning her wheels until it found traction.

Delaney watched her go but he had a bad feeling about this as he walked back to his vehicle. He looked down at Rufus. "We'll get breakfast later, ok? Bound to be somewhere open eventually."

He walked back to his vehicle and drove back up the slope to Murdo's Leisure Park.

He didn't need to investigate beyond the gates. Heavy tracks in the snow led from where Wolfie's motorhome had been parked to the road. He'd chosen to run. Delaney shrugged. Had he been too hard on the guy? Either way, he'd woken up sober and chosen the paranoid route. He didn't give that clapped out motorhome much of a chance in the snow. He'd already sideswiped that woman's VW.

He turned his car around and stared up at the sky. It had stopped snowing for the moment. "What do you think, Rufus? You think we can risk the mountain route? Be a good test of these all-terrain tires. We'll gas up and give it a try, huh?"

Rufus made no comment. He didn't want to be blamed for any wrong decisions.

Twenty minutes later Delaney noted that he wasn't the first person on the mountain road that morning. He was grateful for someone giving him tracks to follow. Had to be a local farmer. Or someone with a 4x4 who lived up on Porcupine Ridge.

Snow drifts were piled up on his left covering the hedgerows. It was 21F outside, the snow clouds briefly parted to reveal a hint of a cold blue sky. He was looking forward to seeing Asha and Maria at the farm and tasting some of her grandma's famous pies.

Moments later he had to brake abruptly on a blind bend as the tracks ahead veered off through a snowdrift. Whoever had been driving ahead of him had failed to see the bend and careened right through the snowdrift. Must have been driving way too fast.

He switched on his hazard lights and killed the engine. He turned to Rufus. "Stay. Guard."

He regretted not having boots to put on. He pulled up his hoodie and slipped on his gloves. He checked his phone. Still no signal.

He followed the wheel tracks into a field that sloped down towards a ravine. One flashing indicator light showed him the way and he waded through deep snow to where a motorhome had met its end. A fog of fumes surrounded the vehicle, the motor was still running. The vehicle was pitched at a 45-degree angle into a dip. The front cabin was buried deep into the snow.

Delaney banged on the side, covering his mouth and nose against the fumes. "Hello? Anyone still in there? Wolfie? I'm guessing this is your vehicle. Can you hear me? Turn your engine off, man. Turn it off."

He tried the side door, but it wouldn't budge. He walked around it, eyes smarting, but there was no easy route to the driver's seat. The motor abruptly coughed and died. The toxic fumes hung around the vehicle like a shroud. He had to back off a moment to wait for the fumes to disperse.

"Wolfie? I know it's you in there. You didn't have to run."

Wolfie didn't reply. Delaney sighed. He'd have to dig his way to the driver's door with his hands. His leather gloves weren't ideal for the job. He began to scoop out the snow, struggling for a foothold on the slope. The motorhome appeared to have slammed into solid rock.

It took almost fifteen minutes. He was already sweating, and his hands were frozen, the gloves saturated. He regretted leaving Rufus in the car, he would have loved digging this out.

Finally, he reached the door handle and swept enough of the snow aside so he could open it some way and look inside. He had to hold a hand over his nose as exhaust fumes spilled out of the vehicle making him cough.

A snow-covered body was slumped over the wheel. A spray of blood covered the partially smashed windshield. He pulled it back and did a double take. The green quilted dressing gown should have alerted him. The white-haired woman with the little dog had been driving. Her lifeless face drained of color. Delaney looked back into the cabin and saw Wolfie slumped against the side, his mouth taped over, and his hands tied, eyes bulging. He'd been asphyxiated. There was a little dead dog in there too stuck halfway out of a carrier.

Delaney had to step back, falling into the snow, gasping for breath. He took several deep breaths, rubbing his stinging eyes with the snow. He thought back to the previous night. Of course, it was always the little details you neglected to register. He'd been trying to get Wolfie to talk and totally dismissed the idea of him being watched. He shook his head. Wolfie couldn't have possibly guessed it was the woman with the stupid little dog who lived right across the way from him. She probably said hello to him every damn morning.

Delaney sat up and studied her. She wasn't so old either. Her hair was white, but she couldn't have been more than forty. So, who the hell was she? More importantly, who the hell was paying her to watch Wolfie? Why had she snatched him right after he'd left?

He didn't think he was ever going to find any of those answers.

He trudged back to his car, shook off the snow and headed on up the road. He'd like to pretend he hadn't seen anything but a whole lot of people would know he'd been to see Wolfie. Someone might even think he had something to do with this, given he was on the same road and all. He swore. He couldn't ignore it. He'd stop at the first place with a working phoneline and let someone know. Either way Wolfie wasn't going anywhere.

Rufus nudged him. He was cold. Delaney rubbed his head. "I know, the heating's back on now. Rufus, next time someone tells me they're being watched, make sure I listen."

It took an hour to go barely ten miles – the snow was falling again. The Range Rover dug in and there were several hairy moments when he nearly stalled, but he finally made it to Porcupine Ridge and parked outside the General Store. He was amazed to discover it had a working charging point and he hooked the vehicle up before heading inside.

Faces turned with surprise as he stomped his feet to shake off the snow. Some locals were all gathered around a small coffee shop counter. Rufus wasn't fazed one bit and headed up to them wagging his tail.

"Where the hell did you come from?" The waitress demanded to know.

Delaney peered at her name tag and smiled. "Cold Rock, Beverly. Don't even try to go there. The snow's deep the whole way down. Dog ok to come in?"

"Sure, we like dogs here."

One guy went to the window to look at his vehicle. "You made it in that?"

Delaney smiled. "All-terrain tires. A vehicle left the road back aways. I need to report it."

A guy in John Deere overalls swiveled in his seat and stood up. "No one's going out in this. You check the driver?"

"She's dead. Smashed head on into a rock. Must have been going one hell of a lick."

The waitress checked the clock. "The Deputy Sheriff will be here for his coffee soon. If he can get through. You can tell him then."

Delaney nodded. "Anything to eat. We're both in need of breakfast."

She looked over the counter at Rufus sitting patiently on his haunches. "He like sausages? I got some leftovers."

Delaney nodded. "I'm sure he can find a space for one or two." He looked up at the chalkboard. "Oatmeal, rye toast and jelly and coffee for me."

She smiled. "Coming right up. Sit yourself down. You aren't going anywhere for a couple of hours; radio just said the snow will come back." She poured him a cup of coffee and hollered his order to someone in the back.

The John Deere guy was still interested in his Range Rover. "How much are those things?"

"I just pay what the lease says. My old one saved my life when I plunged off a cliff, I kind of felt obliged to stick with the brand."

He could tell the John Deere guy wanted to know more about that, but the deputy arrived, beating snow off his hat as he closed the door. "I might be here for a month from the look of those snow clouds," he announced to no one in particular. "That coffee best be hot, Beverly. Who's the guy driving the Range Rover?"

Delaney nodded towards him. "That would be me."

The deputy took up a nearby seat and stared at him.

"You had to have come up from Cold Rock, road's blocked further up until the snowplows get there."

"It was a struggle. You need to know there's a motorhome that went off on a sharp bend about ten miles back. I checked. Driver's dead. No signal, I couldn't call it in."

The deputy looked at him as if he was talking nonsense. "A motorhome? In this weather? What kind of moron would try that?"

"It had to have been driving way too fast. Went clear through a hedge and sailed half-way across a field until it hit a rock."

The deputy frowned as Beverly poured his coffee. "Dead you say?"

"Very. It will be hard to tow out of there in these conditions."

"And I ain't about to ask anyone to do that either. The snow will keep the body frozen. Motorhome? What the hell were they thinking?"

Delaney nodded. "That was my thought too. It had to have happened about half an hour before I came through. No other tracks on the road."

His food arrived and some sausages on a paper plate for the dog. Delaney set them down and they were gone before he'd even turned back to his coffee.

"Cold Rock's pretty miserable in winter," the deputy stated. "Why were you there?"

"I heard the seafood was good."

The deputy laughed. "You must be from Berg City."

"Yeah. Got a client thinking of buying some land there now it's cheap. But I dunno; it's going to be hard bringing it back to life."

"It'll take a few years. Used to surf there when I was younger."

Delaney sipped his coffee and added honey to his oatmeal. "You need any details from me?"

The deputy thought about it. "Name and phone number will do. Consider it reported. I'll inform Cold Rock. Maybe they can get out there tomorrow. I can't believe you got this far in that."

"I think you'll find it would give whatever you're driving a run for its money."

The deputy drank some coffee. "They'd never let me have one anyway. Got to drive American."

"We've got winter blankets on special." Beverly informed him with an encouraging smile. "You should buy some water too if you're thinking of driving on."

"Good idea, Beverly. Dog was complaining earlier about being cold."

"Where are you headed?"

"Ciderbee Farm. You know it?"

She grinned. "Best cider in the State. Nice country up there."

"Hoping to get there for a birthday party tonight. You may have to wrap up a snowplow as well. You have any birthday cards?"

"Back of the store. Next to the Christmas stuff."

The sky darkened outside, and the snow fell a little harder. Delaney didn't hold out much hope for any birthday party.

CHAPTER SEVEN

The Art of Peeling Shallots

Asha pulled the duvet up around Maria and brushed her hot forehead. "You'll feel better in the morning. Remember what the Guru told you, most pain is in your head."

Maria screwed up her face. "Most of the pain is in my ass, actually."

"You're lucky you fell in the snow. You aren't the first to fall off a horse, but you are very fortunate not to have broken anything."

Maria had to acknowledge that. "I'm so cold," she moaned.

"That's the shock. You were out in the snow too long, girl. It's freezing. There's a hot water bottle beside you. Let the painkillers do their work. Try and sleep."

"Will Delaney come? I know you're worried."

Asha reassured her. "I'm hoping he's holed up somewhere warm with Rufus."

"He'll miss Bunty's birthday dinner."

"A whole lot of people will miss it thanks to the snow. You want to me to bring something up to you later?"

Maria shook her head and hugged her hot water bottle. "Not hungry."

Asha left her to it, aware that the kid had been incredibly blessed to injure nothing more than her pride. A bruised coccyx wasn't easy, but it could have been worse.

Grandma Bunty was baking in the kitchen, fretting over a huge chicken pie she'd put in the oven. She looked up as Asha entered.

"How is she?"

"Cold, feeling very sorry for herself."

"She was out there too long. She has a chill."

Asha nodded. "She's tough. She was scared she'd broken her back again. Hopefully it will serve as a warning. She's a bit ambitious to prove herself, y'know."

Bunty laughed. "Pot, kettle, black. You were just the same. You and Zuki used to come back with so many bruises." She frowned remembering something. "My first husband, your grandfather, had a terrible fall one spring. Had to have stiches in his head. Never rode a horse again."

"That's not what killed him though."

Bunty shrugged. "Might have contributed. Who knows? He was gone two years later."

"I'm sorry I never met him."

Bunty checked on her pie. "But then I wouldn't have met Mr B. I was so lucky. I was widowed at thirty-one with a difficult child. He swept in and changed my life. I might have stayed a doctor's receptionist for the rest of my days. Instead, here I am, helping to run a cider business and now writing a baker's cookbook. Never would I have dreamt of that when I was your age." She glanced at a bunch of vegetables yet to see the oven. "I'm making a root vegetable pie for your little family. But if you want to sneak in a bit of chicken, I won't tell."

"You were going to show me how you do your caramelized shallots."

"So, I was. Best you get peeling some. And some carrots and parsnips too. They're all there in the basket."

Asha sat down on the stool and got to work. "Did you roll out the pastry already?"

Bunty looked at her with surprise. "All done. Who does the cooking at home?"

Asha looked guilty. "Delaney mostly. I do pasta, but he likes to cook."

"Then I better give Maria some lessons. I still remember those scones you made."

Asha winced. "God yes, they were like rocks. Mr B laughed his head off. I remember that. I cried buckets."

Bunty grinned. "You're still alive and here with me on my birthday, that's the main thing. One day this will be yours. Mr B is still hoping you'll take some time to learn the business. You can't run an apple farm without knowing all tricks and problems. There's always something that needs urgent attention, or you lie awake worried about the weather."

"One day, Bunty. I promise I'll spend a whole summer here learning. Delaney keeps saying that I should. But right now, I couldn't abandon him for so long. We have a business to run. It's not making much money but I'm using my research skills. And oh yes for your information I make great soups. Delaney and M both love them. Nothing goes to waste. You taught me that." She wiped her eyes as she backed off from the shallots she'd peeled.

Bunty slapped her hand before she could rub her eyes again. "Never touch your eyes when peeling onions, girl. I'm going to warm up some stock. Maria tells me that you want to start a coffee shop. Is that true?"

Asha started on the carrots. "I was, y'know, thinking about it. Just a dream. Delaney bought this boathouse to be our office, but I think it would be a very cool space for coffee. Get a lot of people walking down by the harbor and there's the Art Museum nearby."

Bunty smiled. "Then I'd better make sure you know how to make scones."

Asha laughed. "God yeah. And cake. People always want cake."

She glanced out of the window. She was disappointed to see it was snowing hard again. "You still think Delaney will make it tonight?"

Bunty glanced out of the window and nodded. "He's on his way. Don't ask me how I know, I just do." She took Asha's hand and squeezed it. "You still love him?"

Asha squeezed back. "More than ever."

Bunty was satisfied. "I'm happy for you. It's the finest feeling in the world to know someone loves you as much as you love them."

Asha laughed. "Aren't you the lady who once told me the only thing you can be certain will make you happy is hot bread straight from the oven."

Bunty grinned. "That remains true, young woman. Is it too early to have a little sherry and some hot English mince pies? Your great grandfather grew addicted to them when he was working there for the Army. He brought back recipes for all manner of things although I could never take to his pork pies. A definite acquired taste I think."

"It's your birthday and I love your mince pies."

"It is. I do hope some people will come. Always the same. I plan a party and the snow does its worst to stop them coming."

"They'll come. Even if they have to use tractors."

Delaney was following a tractor at that very moment, his wipers barely able to shift the falling snow. Rufus was wrapped up in the blankets in the back. Delaney almost wished he was wrapped up with him. He'd been driving in fits and starts for four hours now. His unexpected passenger was staring out at the snow and sighing.

"You think my car will be safe back there?"

Delaney snatched at glance at her. He'd dug her out of her stranded vehicle about an hour ago. She had a broken arm and had been trying to get to the nearest doctor.

"It might be buried under snow the next time the snowplow comes through. Getting it started will be an issue – I hope you belong to the AAA."

She looked at him and nodded. "Got no signal. Couldn't get through."

"I don't know how you thought you could drive with one arm." Delaney told her.

She sighed. "I wasn't thinking straight. I just didn't want my arm to set wrong, y'know?"

Delaney nodded. "You sure the doctor will be there?"

"He lives right next to his practice."

"Well, I hope he knows someone who'll take you home after."

"Yeah. I hadn't thought about that either."

"Is it like this every winter up here?"

"Pretty much, although it rains a lot more now in the spring. It affects the tree roots. That's why the wind brings so many trees down." She suddenly pointed. "Next house up ahead."

Delaney saw it. "You want me to wait till you get inside?"

She was about say no but then hesitated. Delaney smiled.

"I'll wait. I hope he can fix your arm."

"Me too. Not the first time either. They say I've got brittle bone disease, but they don't say how to fix it."

Delaney wasn't sure there was any fix for that. He slowed down to a gentle stop.

"Don't slip," he told her as she left his vehicle.

She didn't have to wait long. Delaney waved as he drove off, praying there would be no more delays.

Five guests had made it for the dinner and then happily driven off in a 4x4 to the next farm. Bunty was happy some had made the effort and of course they'd all enjoyed the pies. Mr B had told stories they'd all heard before and their closest neighbor had definitely drunk too much but Bunty had turned 65 with friends and that was what mattered.

Asha checked on Maria. She was sleeping but restless with a slight fever. She prayed she wouldn't develop pneumonia. Getting any medical attention would be difficult in this weather.

Headlights brushed the ceiling and Asha rushed to the window, heart in mouth. It had to be Delaney, it just had to be. She raced down the stairs. She was trying to put on her boots when the front door burst open and Rufus ran in, his helicopter tail spinning and snaking from side to side with happiness to see her.

"Rufie. You're here. Thank God."

She heard Delaney stomping snow off his shoes on the stoop. He called out, "I hope there's some pie left. Been thinking about it for the whole darn day."

He entered and Asha launched herself on him, hugging him tight. He did the same, kissing her, eyes closed, so happy she was safe and well.

Bunty appeared behind from the kitchen all smiles. Delaney turned to her grinning.

"Happy birthday, Bunty. Rufus apologizes for being late to the party."

Bunty greeted the dog with pleasure. "I knew you'd come."

Delaney handed her the birthday card. "Sorry, couldn't find flowers."

"Who needs flowers. I got those books you sent. Mr B was upset I read the first one until about two am last night. Couldn't put it down."

"Am I too late to eat?"

"It's all ready for you. And Rufus, I made you something special too."

Asha couldn't stop holding his hand. It wasn't as if they'd been parted for long, but she'd worried about him out there in the snow all day.

"Where's M?" Delaney asked, pulling off his coat.

"Unwell. She fell off her horse and is pretty sore. Nothing broken but she caught a chill in the snow. She's sleeping."

Delaney nodded. "I'm happy nothing broken." He heaved a sigh. "You have no idea how relieved I am to be here. I am seriously thinking about moving us to Miami."

"Miami? I read it would be under water soon," Bunty told him.

"But no snow." He leant over and gave Bunty a kiss. "Sorry I missed your party."

"Go wash up. Asha and I will join you in the dining room. We haven't had cake yet. Mr B's opening up a special bottle of wine for you."

Delaney grinned. "Thank god I made it in time for the cake."

Asha watched him go and Bunty took her arm. "You're a lucky girl, you know that? Remember when you were nineteen and that boy broke your heart? You said you would never love anyone again."

Asha closed her eyes. She hated being reminded of that horrible year of her life. "You told me I'd find love when I least expected it. I, of course, thought you were totally wrong."

They walked to the kitchen arm in arm.

Asha snuggled up to Delaney in bed happy he was finally back at her side. "Can't sleep?"

"Still driving, I think. Staring for hours at falling snow in my headlights is kinda hypnotic. I was thinking about our business model."

Asha frowned. "It's one o'clock in the morning, Delaney. I didn't even know we had a business model."

Delaney turned his head towards her and kissed her on the nose. "That might be the problem."

Asha nuzzled his warm neck. "I hope it involves a coffee shop. It has to be more profitable than finding lost writers."

Delaney smiled. "Can't disagree with that. I started out wanting to help people from being scammed. Not sure how we ended up searching for lost dogs."

"Actually, I read that's big business. People pay a fortune when their precious dog's get stolen."

"I wasn't thinking of getting into dognapping either."

Asha grinned. "It's a business model. We could save pooches from overindulgence. It's a mission."

Delaney wrinkled his nose. "Perhaps it could be your side-hustle. We could get Rufus a superdog costume."

"We could call it 'Off the Leash'."

Delaney lay back on the pillow with a smile on his lips. "Maybe a coffee shop might be better. I need to sleep."

He put a hand out to her and stroked her stomach.

"Missed you so much, Ash."

"I'm so happy you're back, babe."

"Me too. And you're wearing such sexy bed socks too."

Asha laughed. "Aren't they just? Believe me, you do not want to know how cold my feet are without them."

Delaney snuggled ever closer – how much he loved this woman, even with cold feet. He never ever wanted to be parted from her.

CHAPTER EIGHT

Life Story

"It has to be one of the worst life stories ever written," Asha declared. "There is literally nothing in it. I don't know what he liked, who he liked, what he ate, how he got on with his son. It's so bland it could have been written by some generic biography software program. Nothing about his childhood, friends, zilch. He got paid ten grand for this? Listen, *'The Olympus OM10 SLR was my constant companion. It's compact with a good action, the standard 50mm lens is particularly adaptable, although I used a telephoto lens quite a lot. The trouble is you get some distortion on the outer edges. So, if I can get close to my subject, I prefer the 50mm lens. I develop my own photographs, and this allows me to correct any flaws or exposures. I still look for my camera every day. I use Fuji black and white ISO 100 mostly. It's the grain I prefer. When I first started out, I used a Rolliflex, but it wasn't suitable for my needs, so I switched to my first Olympus in 1973, then my last camera was the OM10. I tried a Pentax but found it too heavy when on location.'*

"Gripping stuff," Delaney commented.

"Hate to say it but there's something about grips too. Wolfie had to have taped the conversation."

"Martinet took photographs for decades; stands to reason it's still stuck there in his memory."

"There's nothing about his time in the Ukraine though. Or his photo series on Chernobyl. I mean that's what he's famous for isn't it?"

"I don't think Wolfie researched his subject at all. In fact, I know he didn't. He wouldn't have asked the right questions to trigger the old guy's memory."

Delaney's phone tinged. He stared at a text message on his phone and frowned. "Brin Martinet is in Italy on business. Back next Friday."

"Did you tell him the writer is dead?"

Delaney shook his head. "Only told him I found him, and he ran away."

Asha narrowed her eyes. "Interesting. Why not tell him the truth?"

He picked up his coffee cup, thinking hard about his choices here. "Because Wolfie wasn't paranoid. I misjudged him. Someone was watching him and if they are watching him, they might be watching Martinet Junior or reading his texts and emails."

Asha set aside her laptop. "I really don't get it. There is absolutely nothing of interest in this biography. Nada."

Delaney stared at the window as snow slid down the glass. "We're going to be here a few days, I think. How's Maria this morning?"

"I made her have some breakfast, but she's gone back to sleep. She still has a temperature, but it hasn't got worse."

"Good to know. I'll catch up with her later."

Asha rubbed his arm with affection. "You're very edgy. What's bugging you?"

"Everything. I wish I hadn't reported the accident, but I ran it through my head and couldn't avoid it. Too many people in Cold Rock knew I was looking for Wolfie. When they hear about his death in suspicious circumstances, they're suddenly going to remember my name with clarity, what I looked like and what I drove. The Cops will definitely connect the dots and figure I'm involved somehow."

"But you didn't kill him."

"I told the deputy that I'd seen a dead woman at the wheel of the motorhome. I didn't identify that it was Wolfie's home or that I'd opened it up. It snowed so much I think that would cover any evidence of me digging snow away from the door."

"You said it was half buried in snow."

"It was and I'd only seen his motorhome in the dark so I couldn't be certain."

"What are you worried about specifically?" Asha asked, curious now.

"Being connected. When they finally recover the bodies, they'll find Wolfie taped and tied up. Technically he was abducted, not murdered. The exhaust fumes killed them both I should think."

"Which an autopsy would reveal."

Delaney nodded.

"You leave any fingerprints?"

"No, but at least six people at the Lobster Pot know I went to see him."

Asha shrugged. "I really don't think there's anything to worry about. Our client will confirm he sent you to find him. You'd have no motive to kill him. Or tie him up."

Delaney drank his coffee. "I can't understand why she'd abduct him. Why the hell was she watching him? I pressed him hard, Ash. He'd been slowly drinking himself to death for weeks. It was difficult to get him to focus. I don't think he even discovered Martinet was an Olympian he was so useless."

"Definitely not in the book, that's for sure."

"He was genuinely scared."

Asha frowned. "So, we assume the old guy had a secret."

"Which maybe Wolfie knew and wouldn't reveal to me, but whatever this is, I don't think its crime related. It has to be government. Martinet must have witnessed something important, and they feared he'd told Wolfie. Criminals would have taken him out long ago. Government is more likely to watch and listen."

"Nothing like that in the book. Not even a hint. Maybe it's a conspiracy thing. Like he knows who really killed President Kennedy."

Delaney laughed. "Yeah, maybe. We'd need to know where he was when he was about twenty years old. Seriously, I can't make sense of it. If the FBI or CIA didn't want the biography to be written they should have talked to the son, don't you think? He was the paymaster. That's where the pressure should be. Wolfie interviewed the old man but got nothing out of him. There's something else. A woman got sideswiped by the motorhome as it fled Cold Rock. She was really pissed about it. I'm pretty certain any investigation would find her."

"Why's that important?"

"It puts me in Cold Rock at a specific time, about ten to nine. Gives me an alibi of sorts."

Asha gazed at him a moment. "You really are worried."

"I'm being careful. This kind of thing can really bite you on the ass."

Asha leaned over and mussed his hair. "So, what are we going to do on our snow day."

Delaney stood and drew her to him for a hug. "I promised Mr B I'd chop wood."

Asha smiled. "Ah yes, men bonding time."

"And you?"

"I promised to update Bunty's computer and proof her 'Country Baker's' book. She has a publisher interested already."

"Excellent. We're both going to be making ourselves useful."

"Bunty is making a special spicy vegetable soup for her cold. How am I going to persuade her to drink it?"

"Hmm, good luck with that. My mother used to give me raw onions for a cold."

"I think that ranks as child abuse."

"It kinda worked though. Tell M, hot soup or raw onion. See which one she chooses."

"Devious, Mr Delaney."

He shook his head. "Straight from the Parenting Handbook."

Asha smiled and kissed him. "Catch you later. Do not have an accident with an ax."

Mr B was already togged out in his warmest work clothes. Delaney found him out by the barn putting in fresh hay for the horses and cleaning out the stalls. It stank of ammonia, but it didn't seem to worry Mr B any.

"Hi. You look a bit fresher than last night."

"I slept like log. You seen Rufus?"

"Dog is curled up by the kitchen range. He isn't stupid."

"He had enough of snow yesterday. "

Mr B closed a stall and shoveled the old straw into a barrow. "I reckon the snow's all my fault. I was only saying last week that we never get cold winters like we used to and wham, that cold North wind buried us."

"You worried about the apple trees?" Delaney asked.

"Snow doesn't worry them. Frost is the killer."

"It's pretty up here, I'll say that. Come to think of it, when I was sailing and got into difficulties, there was always someone who would tell me how much worse the storms were twenty years ago."

Mr B smiled. "I heard the opposite. Certainly, the hurricanes are stronger."

"A lot more frequent. I got caught in one off Costa Rica. Never want to do that again. There's nothing romantic about drowning."

Mr B dumped his barrow load on a well-established stack of waste. He pointed to a large wood pile. "If you want to get started, the saw is hanging up by the birdhouse there. We had so many trees down in the storm last July, it's a battle to keep up with it all."

Delaney put on the work gloves Bunty had given him and set to work.

Mr B joined him once he'd finished his stable duties.

"You got no help with the stables?" Delaney asked finishing off an awkward branch.

"Stable boy is nicely tucked up at home I reckon. It's a hard slog to get down here from where he lives. Can't blame him. Not sure I'd trek through this snow for minimum wage either. Or even double the money."

Delaney continued to saw, and Mr B stacked a pile of wood ready for splitting.

"Asha tells me you're working on something to do with Arnold Martinet."

"Yeah. It's kinda odd. Writer got hired to write his biography and then refused to complete it. Said he was forced to stop work. Wouldn't say who stopped him though."

"Asha tell you I met him a couple of times?"

"Martinet? Really?"

"I used to be on the Sports Panel for Berg City when I lived down there. We chose people who got the awards or sports scholarships. I don't know if Bunty mentioned it, but back then and I'm talking thirty years ago, I was a State Champion showjumper."

Delaney straightened up and looked at him with surprise. "I didn't know."

"I don't think Asha knew. Not something I ever talk about now. That's how I met Bunty. I had an accident; a horse gave me a good kicking when I rode too close. Could hardly walk for three months, let alone ride.

"Bunty was on reception at the medical center. I fell for her immediately. Didn't mention anything, I didn't know if she was married or single but when I found out she was widowed, I made my feelings known and she burst into tears. I thought I'd insulted her, or she hated me, but turns out she liked me and hadn't dared say anything as I was a patient." He laughed. "We got married two months later. She got a shock to discover I was younger than her."

"Well, you both seem indecently happy, if I may say so."

"Never got Asha's mother to like me though. She was a very annoying kid with firm dislikes. Not one thing I could do right."

Delaney smiled. "Asha has done a good job of keeping me well away from her."

"Take my advice and keep it that way. She has a very mean streak. Asha's father is a nice man. I know some people don't like races mixing but not me. He never deserved the treatment he got from her, and I don't blame him one bit for finding someone else."

Delaney finished off a log and started another. "I met him last Christmas. He has an excellent sense of humor."

Mr B grinned. "Yes, he does. Bunty stays in touch with him. Anyway, I was going to say something about Martinet."

Delaney wiped his brow. He was sweating but his feet were freezing in the borrowed boots. "When was this?"

"First time I saw him I was a kid. He came to talk at my school in Berg City. St Paul's"

"You're Catholic?"

"Not anymore. He came to talk about sports shooting and the Olympics. His team won Bronze at Munich a year earlier. Of course, all we wanted to ask about was the terrorists and if he'd seen any planes blown up. There was a lot of that kind of thing going on back then."

"Must have been a strange time. I don't know much about that period."

"Funny thing is, he wasn't what I expected. A bit overweight, about five-foot-six. Not much good at public speaking, if you know what I mean. He knew his stuff but us kids weren't impressed."

"It's hard to impress kids at the best of time. Maria is quick to dismiss anyone over twenty-five."

"She'll grow out of that, I hope. Anyway, I met Martinet for real at a dinner for athletes in City Hall. He was giving an award to a new generation of shooters and Olympic hopefuls. I remember he was making a name for himself as a photographer back then."

"There's an exhibition of his work in Berg City right now."

Mr B looked interested. "I'd like to see that."

"So, what was he like?"

"That's the funny thing. Remember I'd seen him when I was about eleven years old. Now I was twenty-five, a showjumper and studying apple farming. My father worked this farm for decades. He was very keen for me to take it on but wanted me to study the science. Of course, his holding was half the size it is now. When Bunty came along, she bought the adjoining property and that's how we got into the cider business. The thing is, Martinet had changed. My younger self remembered the tubby guy with no personality.

Thirteen years later he was older, of course, but taller and thinner and had, what do you call it, gravitas. He weighed his words carefully and people listened to him."

"People change. He lost weight, that might make him seem taller."

"Hmmm, maybe. Truth be told I wasn't the most attentive child and inclined to mock the weird collection of teachers and priests that taught us back then."

Delaney stopped sawing. "All I can say is that you did more to bring Martinet to life than Wolfie Sigurdsson did in two hundred pages."

"Got to be a hard job to write a book about someone who doesn't remember anything about his life."

"I hear you." He looked at the wood pile. "I'm going to split a few logs. Stand back Mr B."

"Put your goggles on, Mr Delaney. Not a good time to be having any accidents."

Delaney slipped them on, grateful for the reminder. He swung his ax.

Maria sat up in bed and blew her nose. She looked properly poorly.

"Whose idea was it to try and make me eat raw onion."

Delaney grinned. "Did you try?"

"No. I drank the soup." She stared at him wondering how to ask what was on her mind. "Is it true you saw two people die in the snow?"

"I saw two people dead in a vehicle accident. Didn't see them die."

"What's Cold Rock like? A kid at school surfs there in the summer."

"Bleak. A bit like surfing at the edge of the world. The forest burned in the freak hot summer and floods washed away most of the town after it. It couldn't have been much of a town to begin with. Rufus loved the beach though."

Maria smiled. "He loves any beach. I heard you get forty-foot waves there."

Delaney nodded. "I suspect even higher during the storms. You want to come down and sit by the fire?"

She shook her head. "I'm going to listen to my music. You can send Rufie up though."

"He chased a squirrel up a tree just now. I bet that squirrel is regretting it's not snug in bed like you. I guess the snow caught a few of them by surprise. I'll send him up when I've dried him off."

"Is Mirabelle ok?"

Delaney frowned. "Mirabelle?"

"My horse. It lost a shoe. He went limp just before I fell."

"I'll make enquiries. You were lucky to survive unhurt."

Maria protested. "I am definitely not unhurt. I have a huge purple bruise to prove it."

"Better a bruise than a plaster cast. Make sure you're better tomorrow. We're planning a visit to the Monastery for their Medieval Festive Fayre. Open fire roasts, liquor tastings and craft stalls. The one day a year the residents make contact with the outside world."

"Roastings – dead meat, ugh."

"There will be cake."

Maria weighed it up in her mind. "I might be well enough for cake."

Delaney grinned. "I'll go find the hound."

CHAPTER NINE

Without A Trace

The log fire was still throwing out a decent heat. Rufus was spread out on the hearth, his paws twitching with dreams of squirrels not yet caught.

Asha was staring at her laptop as Delaney brought in a bottle of Mr B's apple cognac. "Thought we might try this."

Asha wrinkled her nose. "You might want to go easy on that, I think it's 80 proof. He wants me to come up with a name for it. Naming it Firewater is cultural appropriation I discovered."

"Try 'pomme de feu', sounds less threatening in French." He extracted the cork and sniffed the aroma. He winced, glancing back at Asha. "Only 80 proof? I think we could run the Range Rover on this."

He poured two small glasses. "Any luck with finding any photographs of Arnold Martinet?"

Asha shook her head. "Not only has he lost his memory, but it's like someone scrubbed the entire internet of any images of him. I found a Martinet in France around 1800 who published lithographs of Napoleon's Army."

Delaney shrugged. "Well almost everything he did predates the internet."

"I can't buy that. Press photos are digitized going back to the beginning of photography. Millions of photos were taken at the Munich Olympics. There has to be at least one photo of the American team that won the bronze medal. There are photos of the Russian teams that won silver and gold."

Delaney sipped a taste of the cognac, he swallowed fast, eyes watering. "Wow, not as smooth as I was expecting."

"Mr B said it would need to age ten years before he could sell it."

"Meanwhile he could market it as rocket fuel. Wow." He rubbed his chest. "Just what you need when you're out in the snow."

"Your face has turned bright red, Delaney."

He laughed pulling a face. "Ouch, I think my whole body is glowing right now." He wiped tears from his eyes.

"Two things I remember from my chat with Wolfie. One: it started at school. Whatever it was, that's where it started. Two: Scimitar."

Asha exhaled, drumming her fingers on her laptop. "We have no idea where he went to school and scimitar is going to throw up a million images of blades and swords."

Delaney rubbed the dog's belly, couldn't believe how hot his fur was. "Try Team Scimitar. This dog is cooking. Rufie you sure you're ok?"

The dog barely moved; he was in bliss mode.

Asha sighed as she saw what came up. "Sportswear, football and rugby clubs, blades you can buy for the metaverse. Not exactly helpful." She reached for the cognac. "Here goes with pomme de feu." She winced as she forced herself to swallow. "Jeezus." She protested, feeling it slip down to burn her innards. She could barely speak. Delaney laughed again as he watched her face turn red.

"Dangerous stuff, hey?" He put the cork back in the bottle.

"Lethal."

Asha recovered after a moment and modified her search to include Rifle and Shooting Championships. She smiled as a link turned up. "Ithaca College Rifle Team - The

Nocton Scimitars - win a gold medal at a State Championship Event - The Ithaca Journal, July 10[th,] 1961."

"Any photos?"

Asha shook her head. "But that would be about right. Martinet would be about eighteen in 1961. College kid. Bad vibes, Delaney. I dated a guy who went to Cornell when I was seventeen. I caught a bus, several buses to surprise him and when I got there, he pretended he didn't know me. One for my many 'greatest disappointments in love' catalogue."

Delaney leaned in and kissed her. "I can't believe anyone would do that to you."

"It taught me a lesson, I guess, but I was just glad no one I knew saw my humiliation. Zuki rescued me and we got very drunk at a bar by one of the lakes. They didn't even check our IDs. Second great lesson was that a hangover does not improve a desperate situation."

Delaney stared at her laptop screen. "We have names, look."

Asha stared at the screen. The Nocton Scimitars. G. Zolloff, B. Kinnerson, R. Calhoun and A. Martinet.

"Now check the names of the Bronze medalists for shooting at the 1972 Olympics."

Asha searched then squeaked. "Gus Zolloff, Bennet Kinnerson, Regie Calhoun and Arnold Martinet."

Delaney smiled. "No photos, but I bet there are plenty somewhere, not yet digitized. Makes sense, a shooting team at college stays together and ten years later are selected for the Olympics. They're friends. Wolfie really didn't try very hard did he. What happened to these characters? They'll all be about eighty now."

Asha began to search. "Gus Zolloff was killed in a road accident in 1975. And looky here, we have a photo of Bennet Kinnerson..." she whistled. "Olympian, soldier, a

Colonel and former Deputy Director of Logistics at the Pentagon."

"Yeah, he'd be exactly what they look for." Delaney remarked.

She read the caption. "Regie Calhoun, former Olympian shooter is the billionaire CEO of Blackwand. Blackwand was a major supplier of equipment and logistics to the US Army in Afghanistan from 2001 to 2021." She frowned. "He looks very pugnacious. Is that the right word?"

Delaney nodded. "Agree with me or I'll punch your lights out, type of guy. So, we have photos of two of the team when they're older and successful. Zolloff, we don't care about because he's dead. So, what's the great mystery about our guy? Why no photos of Arnold Martinet? I mean, he's not a nobody. He's an Olympian, he's raised a ton of money for kids to have a better life, he's a photographer..."

"He's either very shy or someone went to a lot of trouble to scrub him out existence."

"But all the information too? We know that he won two medals. Wolfie was right, it began at school. Or college to be precise."

"But what began?" Asha asked. "Shooting we know, but what else?"

"Martinet traveled extensively. He's celebrated in minor circles for his photos on the aftermath of Chernobyl."

Asha nodded. "Not a trace of those online either, at least not by him. But that means he had some influence to be able to travel to the Ukraine when it was hostile territory, right?"

"He had friends in high places, Ash. He could probably go anywhere he wanted."

Asha stared at him narrowing her eyes. "My Kennedy assassination link is looking better all the time."

Delaney grinned. "I think they got the right shooter on that one. But yeah, we have to assume Martinet knows something about the other two they would prefer was kept secret."

"And both could afford to 'watch' him if they wanted to."

Delaney sighed. "If they're watching him, they'd know he's lost his memory and couldn't hurt them, let alone tell Wolfie anything useful."

"But they couldn't be sure about that. So, they started watching Wolfie."

"And then I turned up." Delaney pointed out.

Asha nodded. "It's definitely crazy conspiracy stuff, Delaney."

"Sort of low-level conspiracy. Martinet was a great photographer, could be he witnessed something he shouldn't have, or they think he photographed it."

Asha stretched in her chair. "You're forgetting Mr B told you Martinet changed from short and fat to tall and thin. That's a conspiracy right there and someone made sure all the photos are gone so no one can prove it."

"And what? We think Martinet isn't Martinet?"

"Maybe." Asha shut down her laptop. "His son probably knows more about that. We should ask him." She glanced at the clock on the wall. "Enough for one night. Rufus needs to pee, and I need my bed. Arnold Martinet is a good mystery, Delaney. Bunty would probably solve it by page 75 if it was crime fiction."

He smiled. "We might have to set her to work on it. What's our call here, Ash? We found Wolfie, but now he's dead. We walk away, give the client the manuscript, which is pretty useless, but fulfils our contract. Job done."

Asha studied him a moment. "I hear what you're saying, but I can tell you don't want to walk away."

Delaney woke up the reluctant dog and placed the fireguard up in front of the fire. "I guess we won't know who else was standing on the grassy knoll unless we look, right?"

Asha took another sip of the brandy and shuddered. "Ouch, it's truly evil stuff. Mr B needs to work on the recipe a while longer I think."

Rufus stretched his legs back and forth, his eyes still half closed.

"It'll be hard getting him to go outside," Delaney remarked. "I'll take him. Check on Maria when you go up, she has a habit of kicking off the duvet."

"I'm kinda excited we're going to the Monastery tomorrow. I remember going there when I was a kid. They had a hurdy-gurdy man there and I was fascinated."

"Well, it is a medieval fayre. We should probably wear bells on our toes."

Asha laughed as she headed towards the stairs. "Yeah, hell there might even be some bells in the loft."

CHAPTER TEN

Connections

Mr B hitched a trailer to the tractor and tossed in some rugs. Seemed like another foot of snow had fallen overnight, and it was the only way to get to the Monastery. Maria was trying hard not to be excited. Bunty made sure they were suitably attired to survive the cold. No actual bells on toes but she had found them an assortment of warm hats that set the tone for the day.

Delaney was grateful for the warmth of Rufus huddled up beside him and Asha, Maria and Bunty shared a rug and a flask of coffee as they made their way up the mountain tracks.

"Who exactly are these monks or residents as you call them?" Delaney asked.

Bunty offered him the coffee flask, he passed on it. "They're just people who needed to follow a different path. Not everyone can cope with modern life. Did you know they have a waiting list? So many people gave up their jobs after Covid and craved living in a supportive community. The monastery is very picky though. They can give people support but it's not easy hiding away and growing your own food and practicing meditation. Some of the people there feel they have to make amends for their misdeeds – the vetting committee doesn't judge but they do look for compatibility and certain skills."

Delaney was impressed. "You seem to know a lot about them."

Asha leaned in on Bunty. "She's the mediator. If they can't resolve a situation between themselves, they have three outsiders come to weigh the options. Bunty expelled someone I remember. Can't remember why."

Bunty shook her head. "Never tell. But sometimes people do things that can't be forgiven or ignored."

Delaney looked at Bunty with a new appreciation. "It's a different world up here."

"We solve our own problems mostly. You never know who might come knocking on the door seeking sanctuary, but their job is to protect the harmony of those already inside."

"Sounds harder to get into than Berg City Country Club." Delaney remarked.

Asha rolled her eyes. "Money, money, money. That's all they care about, and they're not interested in how you made it or who you crushed on the way."

"I detect some resentment, Ash." Delaney said, curious she'd spoken with so much venom.

"My mother's a member. Husband number two is a slum landlord."

Bunty kissed Asha's cheek. "Let's not spoil the day thinking about them. I'm helping with the bread making class today. You think you might be interested in that, Maria?"

"I'm definitely going to join that session, "Asha said. "I really want to be able to make my own bread."

Maria was staring out at the snow-laden trees. "I love being here. I don't ever want to go back to the city."

Bunty smiled. "If you ask Mr Delaney nice, maybe you can stay for Christmas."

Delaney held up his hands. "Don't you have exams or something coming up soon?"

Maria made a face. "Yeah."

"Maybe if you're isolating with 'flu with you could do them online. You know how strict they are now about not letting people into school with infections."

Maria began to brighten. "And I am sick."

Delaney glanced at her. "You might want to remember to blow your nose and cough from time to time to convince them."

"I will." She beamed, already scheming to make this happen

"But not today, Maria," Bunty insisted. "We don't want to be refused entry to the fayre."

Asha was surprised at how many people had made the effort to come out in this cold weather. Tractors, 4x4s, Skidoos were all lined up outside the huge wooden gates. They entered the inner courtyard arm in arm, happy to see so many people laughing and generally have a good time. Mugs of hot mulled wine was pressed into their cold mittens, and it was good to be embraced by the welcoming residents who greeted them in medieval costume.

Delaney kept Rufus close to him and watched as Maria gravitated to the demonstration of glass blowing and seemed fascinated by it.

Food stalls boasted genuine 17th Century choices and tastings and he looked forward to trying the homemade liqueurs the monastery was famous for. Asha brought him some hot roasted potatoes to try. "Cooked in rosemary and something. They taste amazing."

Delaney looked around him impressed. "You'd never guess from the outside just how interesting this place is."

"I know, right? I always wanted to live in a place with a courtyard and vines. You going to take me to Spain one day?"

Delaney nuzzled her. "Sounds like a plan. You've never mentioned this before."

"I like to slow drip my fantasies, Delaney." She spotted he had a paper cup of something. "What are you drinking?"

Delaney wrinkled his nose. "Mead. It's too sweet for me, too much honey I think."

Asha reached over and tasted it and her eyes lit up. "I'm confiscating this. Oh, by the way, someone wants to talk to you. Bunty mentioned Martinet and well just be warned."

Delaney inwardly groaned; Bunty had a bad habit of sharing things that ought to be private. He bit into the potato. "Hmmm, these taste great."

"I know. Got to go. Maria's going to try the glass blowing, keep an eye on her."

"I am. Enjoy the baking thing."

Delaney watched her go as a snowflake settled on his nose. He glanced up at the sky and frowned as more snow was incoming.

"Don't let a little bit of snow upset you," a woman said from his left side.

He turned to face a woman of about sixty dressed in a period green velvet dress and an elaborate headgear. She looked very regal.

"Mr Delaney?" She asked as Rufus greeted her. She stroked the dog's head.

"Stay Rufus."

"It's alright. I happen to love dogs. He has a very noble face. I'm Joyce. One of the mad residents."

"I hope not too mad."

"I haven't resorted to howling yet, but occasionally feel like it."

"I love the atmosphere here."

"It's quite a contrast to how it is normally. We've been preparing for it for months."

"You should charge entry."

"Not quite in the spirit of Christmas though. We make enough on what we sell."

"You spoke to Bunty?" Delaney remarked.

"She's quite a character, isn't she. And you're with that lovely niece of hers."

"I am a lucky man."

"You are, Mr Delaney. I wanted to speak to you about Arnold Martinet. It was probably indiscreet of Bunty to mention him, but she wasn't to know I know him. Or know of him, to be more correct."

Delaney stamped his feet. He was getting cold standing in the snow. "Talk to me nearer the fire perhaps. I can see your hands are frozen too."

She smiled. "I'm used to it, but yes, let's walk over there. Brother Mike loves his bonfires."

They made their way past laughing visitors and a demonstration of impressive wood carving. Delaney wondered what she was going to say or how it was even possible she knew Martinet.

"My late husband was in finance in Berg City. He used to handle Mr Martinet's investments and the disbursements to the various charities he was involved with."

They stood close to the warmth of the log fire; Rufus practically stood on Delaney's feet watching events unfold around him. Delaney sneaked a glance at Maria attempting to blow glass from the corner of his eye.

"I'm curious how a not very famous photographer made so much money he was prepared to give most of it away," Delaney remarked.

Joyce smiled at him. "I suspect it was nothing to do with photography, Mr Delaney. My husband got in early on the first dot com boom and took his clients with him. Mr Martinet allowed him free rein. Several millionaires were made, not all of them grateful. My husband also called the top of that boom and made all those who would listen sell before the crash. Mr Martinet I suspect felt guilty that he'd made so much money without any effort."

"Interesting. Did you meet him?"

She shook her head. "My husband rarely saw any of his clients in person and I never did."

Delaney was disappointed. "How long have you lived here?"

"Nine years. Many resented me coming in and were skeptical I'd last. But as I do the accounts, I suspect some would be disappointed if I left."

"How many women live here?"

"Eleven right now. There should be more. Thirty-two souls in need of repair including the men."

"Well, I'll know where to come if I need repairing."

She smiled. "It's not as arduous as you might think. The communal dining is the secret, or rather, having no secrets. Tell me, why are you so interested in Mr Martinet? He must be quite old."

"Who handles his investments now?" Delaney asked. "You said your husband had passed."

"Very passed. I served ten years for killing him."

She searched Delany's face for a reaction. None came. She might have been disappointed.

"And then you came here. Interesting you chose another incarceration, Joyce."

She shrugged. "It's very hard to be accepted by your peers when you reappear in society. I had money but I knew long before I was released that this was where I wanted to be. If jail was like this, no one would ever leave."

Delaney nodded. That he understood. "You didn't mention who handles ..."

"His son. The crypto boy wonder. I might be incarcerated here, Mr Delaney but we do have the internet. I do wonder how much financial luck one family can possess. Father and son self-made millionaires."

"I try not to be jealous." Delaney said. "Did you know Martinet senior is in a home with dementia?"

Joyce expressed sadness. "Oh, that's too bad. I suppose his luck had to run out sometime." She frowned. "So why are you interested in him?"

"His son hired a writer to write a biography of his father."

"Oh, that's doubly sad."

"Unfortunately, the writer did a pretty poor job, and his subject remembers nothing anyway."

"I shall do a special prayer for Mr Martinet tonight."

Delaney spotted Mr B bidding at an auction in the far corner of the courtyard and Maria talking to some women in costume getting ready to dance. He glanced at Joyce. "Did your husband go to Ithaca College by any chance?"

"The great Mr Hardle never went to college I'm afraid. He was just good at making money and meeting dancing girls. Especially young dancing girls."

Delaney suddenly knew exactly why her husband had met his untimely end.

"Thanks for talking to me, Joyce. I'm not sure if it helps but it certainly rounds out the picture."

"Bunty told me you also killed a man. I was interested in how you internalized it."

"I killed a man who had just killed about six others and was intending on killing more. I have not yet faced my demons, nor have they come calling, if that's what you mean."

Joyce leaned in and kissed him on the cheek. "I never regretted killing my husband either. I think that's why they refused me early release. No remorse. That's me. No one likes someone who doesn't repent."

Delaney didn't quite know how to respond but smiled and gave her a little bow. "I appreciate you seeking me out, Joyce. May you be happy here for a long time."

She waved and disappeared into the crowd. Rufus began to walk in circles looking for a place to go. Delaney got him out of the courtyard quick before he had an opportunity to embarrass him.

Mr B was climbing out of the tractor cabin as he returned from the woods.

"Problem, Mr B?"

He grinned. "Bought a little something for Bunty, wanted it to be a surprise."

"I'm hoping to taste their liqueurs now. There seems to be quite a choice."

"Brother Deacon is the specialist. He's going to take a look at my apple brandy and see if he can make it smoother."

"At the risk of offending you, it does need work."

"That's the problem of making something that can't be drunk for ten or twenty years. I'll be gone before you can open it."

"Asha will appreciate it when she's forty. Think of it as a legacy."

"What did Joyce Hardle want with you? I saw you two talking."

"Her husband used to manage Martinet's money. Sadly, she never met his clients."

"Hmmm, she tell you she killed her husband. Self-defense mind. He used to beat her. Left loaded guns around the house. One day she couldn't take it anymore."

"Ten years is a lot to reflect on that decision."

"She should never have gone to jail. Hard to get true justice in this world."

"Come on, let's go taste some firewater." Delaney said putting an arm around Mr B. "If I haven't said it already. Thank you for making us feel at home with you all."

"I love it. You are very welcome."

Maria curled up with Rufus on the way back. The tractor made easy work of a new layer of soft snow, and everyone was happy with full stomachs. Bunty clutched the antique copper cauldron that Mr B had secured in the auction. She was trying to decide whether to use it for jam making or to put on display. Asha slept on Delaney's lap as Mr B navigated by the stars with confidence, despite the quantities of cognac he'd imbibed.

Bunty smiled at Delaney. "You've done a good job with that girl, Mr Delaney. I told Mr B after you left last time that you were a good person and Asha was lucky to have met you."

Delaney shook his head. "I'm the lucky one. Believe me."

Bunty sighed. "I definitely drank too much of everything. It beats me why they only do this once a year. You can see how the residents like to talk with everyone."

"Perhaps it works because it's only once a year. Like Thanksgiving or Christmas. Best to limit good things so we don't become indifferent to them."

Bunty pondered on that as they continued on, Mr B breaking into an off key 'Come all you faithful' that ran the risk of waking slumbering bears.

CHAPTER ELEVEN

A Change of Plan

"You sure you want to do this? You'll miss Christmas with us."

Maria frowned. "I know but I love being here, Delaney."

"You haven't got your books or anything. You can't revise for your exams."

"I can. We've got wi-fi. Ton of stuff on-line I can use. Bunty's got me on a schedule. The school approved it, Delaney. I'm sick. They really don't want me there. Might be a new variant.'

Delaney narrowed his eyes. "I think you tried that last year remember?"

Maria laughed. "I have to go back by January the second. Don't forget to come back and get me. If you ever get out of there that is. It snowed again this morning."

Delaney smiled. "Mr B made a track for us. And we'll be back for New Year's Eve. Make sure you're a good guest. Keep your room tidy, help with cooking and cleaning. Did you decide what you wanted for Christmas."

"World peace, remember? I've signed up to the Buy Nothing thing."

"So does that mean we don't have to buy you anything?"

Maria gave him a mean stare. "I signed up, not you. Anyway, Asha's ordered me a new coat. Do you think I'm still growing?"

"Of course. You're only just fifteen, M. I fully expect at least four inches from you by next year."

"You'll regret it. I'd have to replace all my clothes and shoes."

Delaney looked thoughtful. "Hmm, I might have to sign up for this Buy Nothing thing myself."

"Ha Ha. Bunty's going to teach me a whole lot of vegan recipes I can try. Hell, I'll be MasterChef by the time you get back."

"Great, so you'll be doing all the cooking at my house from now on, right?"

Maria quickly realized her error. "Oops."

Delaney turned as Asha entered the bedroom. "All ready?"

She glanced out of the window at the whiteness in every direction. "You sure we can make it to the highway?"

"We've got Rufus to dig us out if there's a problem."

Asha went over to Maria and hugged her. "Don't fall off any horses and make sure you help with mucking out. Don't leave everything to Mr B. I'll miss you at Christmas."

Maria held on tight for a moment, reluctant to let go. Asha broke free and looked momentarily dazed. Delaney took her hand worried. "You ok?"

She shook her head. "God, had a real déjà vu moment. Me in this room, twelve-years-old saying goodbye to my mother. Had no idea she'd dumped me here and was leaving forever."

Delaney pulled her towards him and held her tight. "At least she left you here."

"I know. She drove straight to the airport and went to Paris with her lover. My father had already gone from my life with his new girlfriend. I was suddenly Little Orphan Annie. Took me longer than it should have to realize that I'd been left with the best people in the whole world."

She looked back at Maria staring at her open mouthed.

"Mr B and Bunty saved me, M. I'm afraid they're going to spoil you rotten."

Maria gave her a broad smile. "I know. I told you already I don't want to go back to the city."

Delaney pulled Asha out of the room. "Reality kicks in January the second, Maria. Be ready and good luck with your exams. I left your present with Bunty. It's well hidden so don't go looking for it."

Maria's eyes widened. "I'll find it. Hard to keep a secret from me."

Delaney laughed and waved his hands in the air. "It's out of my hands now."

Asha was deep in thought as they drove towards the highway. Delaney drove slowly, sticking to the ruts in the snow made by others.

"You alright?" he asked.

Asha sighed. "No. Didn't like remembering what my mother did, that's all. You should know I'm from a broken family, Delaney. I should come with a warning sticker."

"Half the world is from broken families. Besides, you get on with your father ok. I never got on with mine."

She tilted her head back and forth until she heard a bone crack. "I'm twenty-five. I shouldn't be caught by surprise by this emotional stuff now."

"You're not your mother. You're the best person I know. Maria loves you; I love you and Rufus adores you. Nothing else matters."

Asha turned to see Rufus sprawled on the back seat swaddled in rugs. "He's had a lot of fun."

Delaney skidded on a bend and half spun but swiftly brought the vehicle back under control. "Wow, that was close. Coffee at the Inn on the Pass? If they're not snowed in."

Asha was looking at her phone. "Sounds good. I forgot to say we had two work enquiries yesterday. I pushed them back to the new year. That's ok with you?"

Delaney frowned. "Yeah, I guess, we might lose them, or at least one, but we have enough trouble on our hands. Remind me I have to get some lumber organized for the boathouse. It's not going to finish itself."

"I forgot that's your Christmas project."

"Yours too. You were going to measure up for the blinds."

She wrinkled her nose, she'd forgotten. "Oh yeah, so I was."

Delaney's phone began to ring. He looked at it and sighed. "I guess we have a signal back." He tapped a button on his steering wheel.

"Morning, Delaney here."

"Brin Martinet." His voice sounded hoarse.

"Hi. How was Italy?"

"Warmer than here. I have another problem, Mr Delaney. It's going to sound crazy, but my father has disappeared."

Asha glanced at Delaney puzzled.

"How? I thought he was in a secure facility."

"So, did I. They just called me. Happened last night, some staffing issue they say. He wandered off."

"Wandered off?"

"More than wandered. He managed to get out of a locked care home and the locked gates. They have CCTV of him leaving. No coat. It's sleet outside. He has to be freezing. I've told the police, but you know they aren't going to make it a priority."

"Does he still have a place to go to?"

"Maybe. I haven't sold his apartment. Didn't feel right until..."

"Have you checked it?"

"No sign of him. He'd need to remember the entry code to the lobby and know the new six-digit code to his front door. I had to have it changed as I couldn't get in my-self."

"I can see why you're worried. Can you send me the address and the codes? Any other places you know he might go to?"

"Denny's on 5th Avenue, two blocks over from his apartment, he used to read his newspaper there."

"We'll check them out. We're about two hours away from Berg City at the moment."

They could hear Martinet hesitating with a question.

"Did I hear right that Sigurdsson was found dead in his motorhome?"

"I'm afraid so. I'd like to discuss this with you later and ask that you don't talk to anyone about it. I'll explain when I get there."

"Ok. I should warn you I'm starting a bad cold."

"I can hear that. I'll check in with you as soon as we get back to the city."

Delaney disconnected, glancing at Asha. She shrugged.

"Did he leave on his own or was he taken?" She asked.

Delaney was thinking about it. "My guess is he woke up suddenly, recovered his memory or he was taken. But if so, by who and why? If he's out there without a coat he's mostly likely going to die of exposure. We should check hospitals."

"It's so weird, Delaney. What the hell would anyone want with a guy with dementia?"

"That's the question. Pity Wolfie never asked it."

Asha took an Uber to Martinet Senior's apartment block, the famous Beatie Building. She was annoyed with having to leave her car back at the farm. The elaborate old money mansion block was built in 1890. Ten floors, four apartments to each corner. She reckoned each one would be worth two million or more. The lobby was lavishly paneled in redwood, the mailbox was highly polished brass. The floor was a classic varnished herring-bone pattern. She stepped back in time as she entered and looked for an elevator. It was ancient, she decided not to risk it. She mounted the elegant wide staircase and wondered who else lived here. In her experience the rich didn't like stairs – unless of course it was part of their ten thousand steps regime. Certainly, Martinet senior wouldn't have relished mounting the ten floors to his apartment. She wondered about that, did dementia stop you from walking up or down stairs? Had to be a hazard.

She noted the security cameras on every floor. No way was he getting in or out of here without being noticed. But then again, she hadn't found a managers apartment listed, so who was watching and where?

It took two tries to activate the six-digit key code. Another reason a man with dementia might not master it, even if he knew it. She entered and paused taking it all in. Parquet flooring, very expensive Persian rugs, beautiful, but definitely worn four-seat rose pink damask covered sofas, a rosewood dining table to seat twelve with chairs to match. A perfect example of a gentleman's apartment circa 1935. She looked around the huge thirty-foot living room and was surprised to find not one family photo. Certainly not a photograph of himself. A photographic triptych of the ruins around Chernobyl filled one section of the dining area wall. She wondered why a man who allegedly had no friends needed such a vast dining table.

Filled with curiosity she ventured room to room. No televisions, no sound systems, no wi-fi hub, there was a landline (she picked it up) disconnected. She found a radio and switched it on. It was tuned to NPR, and someone was discussing climate change.

"So, who are you, Arnold Martinet? Did you actually live here or was it primed for a magazine shoot?"

The kitchen was quaker style, not the original 1890 kitchen, but definitely old. She figured the Electrolux fridge/freezer was from the 70s. The 60s electric Frigidaire Flair range was in perfect condition. She guessed he never ate at home much. There was a modern Maytag washing machine and dryer in the scullery (how the word scullery popped into her head she had no idea). She'd figured he liked to keep clean.

The main bedroom was pristine. The king-sized bed a surprise and there was a dog basket in the corner. So once upon a time he had a dog – that probably liked to sleep by his bed. This was the only personal touch she'd spotted.

The walk-in closet had seven perfectly preserved suits, mostly black or grey. Seven pairs of leather shoes, two snow boots. Two of the shoes had shoe trees in them to preserve the shape and leather. The shirts were neatly folded in racks, as were the sweaters. The ties, all but one quite forgettable, were draped from a metal rod just behind the suits. Martinet may have given much of his fortune away, but he had lived well.

Her phone rang.

"Where are you?" Delaney asked.

"In his apartment. Where are you?"

"Waiting for the gates to open outside Martinet Junior's house. I say house but I think it's just about half the size of the White House. It really is St Paul's College."

"Think of the power bills, Delaney."

"Yeah, I just counted almost thirty windows along the top floor."

"See, don't be jealous. It costs a lot of money to be rich."

He laughed. "Any sign of the old man?"

"No. I'm looking for clues, but this place is tidier than Marie Kondo's house."

"I called the hospitals. Nothing. People keep asking me for a description. I have no idea what he looks like."

"No photos here either. Not of him anyway. He's a very private man."

Delaney drummed his fingers on the steering wheel as he waited at the gate.

"Oh yeah, Ash. I heard from the Sheriff's office at Cold Rock. I was right, a whole lot of people remembered my name, my vehicle, the dog and that I went to see Wolfie. Luckily for me, two of his pals dropped by at eleven and got him drunk again. The Sheriff's on the ball. He found the woman whose car got sideswiped by the motorhome at 8.45 am and there's a camera at the gas station showing me gassing up at 9.15 am."

"This means you're not a suspect?"

"Preliminary investigations say that Wolfie died between 8 and 9.30 am. He was already dead when that woman crashed his home."

"Jeez. Does anyone know who this woman was?"

"Jennifer Yeaver. Ornithologist. She arrived at the leisure park one month after Wolfie."

"A twitcher?"

"I know, weird huh. Apparently, there's some rare species of bird that arrives there in winter."

"How many bird watchers go bat crazy, steal motorhomes, and kill writers; do you think?"

"Just about one."

"Could be she had a thing for Wolfie. Might be a crime of passion."

Delaney shrugged. "Beats me, that doesn't exactly fit with our conspiracy theory though. But you're right, maybe he spurned her, and she wanted to teach him a lesson. Ok, gate's finally opening. I'm going in. Wow, it's really huge for one guy, how I wish I'd invested in Bitcoin, hey." He laughed and disconnected his phone.

Asha was about to leave when she realized she needed the bathroom. She chose the guest bathroom admiring the granite floor and black and green marble tiling. She had a brief fantasy about what it would be like to live in such an apartment, then came to her senses, she knew she'd miss Delaney's house and harbor view. She looked up at the skylight window and thought it odd. Surely anyone up on the roof could look down on someone using the can or the shower. In fact, the more she looked around the room the more puzzled she got. The bathroom should be the same size as the one next door. Why was it smaller? Why no window to the outside? She knocked on the tiled wall behind her, but it felt solid enough.

She heard the doorbell and hurriedly washed her hands feeling guilty she'd been wasting time. She raced to the front door and opened it. There was no one there. The elevator wasn't in action and there was no one going back down the stairs. Puzzled, she turned to go back inside, only then noticing two wet footprints outside the door and some muddy dog pawprints.

She turned back to the stairs. No wet footprints. She ran to the elevator. She pressed the button and the doors opened. There was a puddle on the floor of the elevator. A sudden sound behind her made her turn sharply. A woman was standing there wearing a long overcoat, raindrops on her shoulders and beanie. She wore stout muddy boots.

"Did you just call on number thirty-nine?" Asha asked.

The woman smiled brightly. "Is Mr Martinet back home? I heard the radio."

Asha figured this woman had to have super hearing. It wasn't on loud.

"His son asked me to check his apartment was ok."

"Oh, you don't need to worry about that," she trilled. "He always kept everything immaculate. I live next door. I have an envelope for him. Can I give it to you? It was too big for the mailbox, and I took it in for him."

Asha smiled. "Of course. When did you last see Mr Martinet?"

Her eyes looked up to the ceiling a moment as she tried to remember. "Not for several months now. But he's always going away. I wish I had a place in Florida. St Augustine sounds about perfect right now."

"That's the old Spanish town, right?"

"Must be so lovely there. I'll fetch the envelope. If I don't give it now, I might never remember. I forget so many things these days."

Asha smiled sweetly and followed her squelching boots back to her apartment. "Pretty wet out there today."

"Just awful but Snookie needs her walks."

Snookie, a sodden labradoodle, was sitting in a puddle by the front door patiently waiting to be let in. She greeted Asha enthusiastically and shook the rain off.

Asha tried to be polite about it as the woman unlocked her door and entered. The dog raced inside with her, but Asha waited on the threshold. It looked chaotic inside, crammed full of furniture and all kinds of walking hazards.

The woman returned having shed her wet coat at last. "It's here somewhere ... ah yes, under this." She lifted a small box of dog treats and slid out the large envelope.

Asha took it from her and backed away. "Thank you for being a good neighbor."

"We should all be good neighbors my dear. I hope you've got a coat; it's set to rain all day."

Asha nodded and smiled returning to Martinet's apartment, closing the door behind her.

The envelope was from Sorakin and Partners – Accountants. She grimaced, she wondered if that old goat had ever found someone to live in his penthouse. She still felt hot anger remembering Sorakin's outrageous offer to her to be his mistress, right in front of Delaney. Total sleazebag.

She wasn't about to open it. But it was probably useful to know who his accountant was. Doubly useful to find out about the winter place in Florida. No way an old guy with no money or coat was on his way there – even if he did suddenly recall where it was.

The more she thought about it, the more convinced she was that there was a secret to be discovered in this apartment. She stood there and surveyed the room, thinking aloud.

"You're nearly eighty. You probably know you're losing your marbles. Maybe you're worried a secret is going to come out one day and you need to protect yourself, your reputation. Some kind of defense. You're a neat freak, like me. Is it about money? No, you gave most of it away, you don't really care about money. But you saw something, someone do something, but now you're scared of forgetting and losing your leverage. You want to protect your son from scandal maybe. You've hidden it here. Where is it Mr Martinet?"

Nothing was out of place. She doubted it was hidden behind the big photo frames. That only happens in movies.

She went back to his bedroom walk-in closet. Seven suits, seven pairs of shoes. Was that a prompt to help him remember? She removed the suits and laid them on his bed. She studied the closet. Nothing was out of place she could see. Nothing in any of the suit pockets. There was a small safe recessed into the wall behind the sweaters. She recalled something her father once told her. 'Never put anything really valuable in a safe, so they can't steal it.' She used to think it was stupid advice, but maybe not. She wasn't exactly a safe cracker anyway. It would have to be ignored.

She was about to return the suits to the racks when she looked again at the boring ties. Eight ties. Eight. That's wrong. One of the ties was blue, the rest were black. She examined the blue tie, it had nothing hidden in it. Hmmm, wrong call. Maybe he had no secrets at all. She felt deflated.

She replaced everything just as it had come out of the closet and closed the doors. Then, remembering the guest bathroom anomaly, she inspected Martinet's bathroom more closely. It was equally grand but twice the size. She went towards the window and began tapping the adjoining wall. A thick white monogrammed dressing gown hung from a hook. Nothing in the pockets. She was pushing it to one side when the hook moved a little. She blinked. Hooks shouldn't move. She pushed it to one side some more and heard a click. The wall opened up and she stepped into a windowless room. She searched for a light and found a pull cord.

The red light welcomed her to his darkroom. Of course, the old man was a photographer. The clue had been there all the time. Albion had told her that there were at least a thousand more photographs stored somewhere. Boxes of photos and negatives were stacked floor to ceiling, all neatly labeled with time, place, and year. An enormous enlarger stood on a bench with all the dishes and bottles of chemicals needed for developing his prints. A wire hung across the room with prints still attached. This was strictly old school stuff. She found lenses and a row of assorted cameras and different attachments on a shelf. There was also a stack of receipts, a ledger with columns of numbers and dates. Martinet had taken his photography seriously. Asha sighed. Ok, she had a lot of work to do here. If there really was a secret, it had to be in this room.

She briefly wondered if the old man remembered this space even existed. She could see writing scrawled on one wall – passwords? He must have known his memory was failing. A laptop cable lay there. Not so old school after all.

Two hours later Asha walked away from the building carrying one heavy purloined shopping bag. She headed towards Denny's situated two blocks over. She had a great deal to think about now and reflected on a man who'd made so much money but probably ate in Denny's seven days a week. How many single old people lived like that she wondered?

She texted Delaney to meet her there. Wondered how he'd got on with Brin Martinet.

The restaurant was full of seniors having the meat-loaf special. Any one of the men could have been Martinet, she still had no idea what he looked like. She felt sorry for him. If he was still alive and that was a big if at this point, he was probably terrified, unable to work out why he wasn't back in his comfortable room. Was anyone feeding him?

She looked around the restaurant, contrasting it with her regular haunt Harry's. It was like discovering a parallel world. No one under sixty, including the waitresses. She wondered when it was exactly that you realized you couldn't be cool anymore and learned that shiny vinyl upholstery and whipped cream from a can was exactly what you wanted.

"I'll have a low-fat blueberry pancake and coffee," she told the waitress. "No whipped cream. Do you have any almond milk?"

"Huh?"

"Make the coffee black. Thanks."

He'd stood across from his apartment building for hours watching, trying to keep dry in an empty building porch. The building behind him had been due for demolition years ago but here it still stood with the lower windows all shuttered. He'd watched Alice and her dog Snookie walk back from the park, both of them soaked to the skin. Hours later he'd seen a young women he didn't know depart carrying a shopping bag. Too young to be a resident, maybe a home help. He'd observed a young man in his government issued vehicle parked one block over, his bored gaze fixated on the comings and goings of his building. Saw him take photos of all those who entered or left. Had to be FBI. But why? Why now? He hated not being in the loop. He wasn't sure how long he'd been gone. Six months maybe, or was it more?

He gambled that there was only one person watching and was pretty confident they didn't know about the service entrance. Built at a time when staff and deliveries all had to come to the back of the building. He was chilled to the bone but knew never to take risks. Never assume anything.

A delivery truck arrived. He took the opportunity to cross the road whilst the observer's line of sight was obscured. He alone had used the back stairs over the years to come and go unobserved. The internal surveillance cameras were all focused on the front stairs and elevators. He'd made sure no camera was facing his front door.

The back stairs were narrow and mean. They served every floor. He struggled a little, ten floors would be a challenge. He'd lost his strength after all those months in the care facility. He wished he could remember exactly when Brin had sent him there. He had a total blank to that period. Something had obliterated that period from his memory. It had been a shock to discover he'd grown a beard and lost weight. He could barely recognize himself in the mirror. One minute he was a zombie lost in a fog and the next being woken by 'care staff' that had zero interest in who they were looking after. The humiliation of discovering they intended to spoon feed him baby food had been a shock.

It had taken three whole weeks to get his legs working again, days and days of mentally recording staff comings and goings and their security arrangements, keeping up the pretense of imbecility all the time. They'd allowed him to walk the corridors to get exercise, seemingly pleased that he wanted to move around again. He'd lengthened the time of his 'exercise' sessions to measure how long it would take to take to reach the front of the building.

The moron who turned up for night duty didn't even notice when he'd swiped his security pass. He'd gone to bed like a 'good boy' and they'd shut him in his cell as per usual. Only it was the moron who was tucked up in his bed having imbibed two weeks supply of sedatives in his coffee.

He hadn't left straight away. He'd finished the moron's rounds, tucking up the inmates, wishing them sweet dreams. They were all happy to swallow the drugs, didn't mind going down at seven pm. He'd even mopped up piss and changed nappies of another. Took two hours to get the moron's section bedded down.

He left during a disturbance when some woman began shrieking in the other section and all staff were requested to attend. He had a clear run out of the building. They probably didn't notice anything was amiss till the morning shift arrived.

He climbed the back stairs slowly, resolving with each leaden step to get fit again, go swimming, anything to build his strength back. He had to pause to gather his breath on each floor. Finally, he made the top floor making sure no one was in the corridor as he slipped out of the door. He approached his own front door searching his mind for the six-digit combination he'd need to punch in. He knew he'd only have three chances to get it right. Brin's birthday.

Nothing happened. He put in the numbers again. Nothing. He tried one last time and a red light started blinking. He'd be locked out now permanently. Someone had changed the numbers. He was angry now. He needed dry and warmer clothes. He needed money. He had no way of contacting Brin. He hadn't been able to find a working payphone. How long had he been gone?

He heard the elevator start up. He quickly moved back to the service access door. He needed a friend, needed food. He started down the stairs again trying to figure out what had happened. He wanted to know exactly why the FBI was watching the building for starters. Had the moron been speaking the truth when he was teasing him about his biography. He'd thought the man was mocking him. Told him someone had been to interview him twice about his life story when he was ill. He had no memory of that, of course, wondered what he could have possibly said. But why would anyone want to write his life story? There was nothing to tell. Nothing anyone could ever know anyway.

Where was Brin? It suddenly occurred to him that he had no memory of him ever visiting him at Summertree. Not since he'd woken up at least.

The FBI guy was asleep in his vehicle when he walked by on the other side of the road. He badly needed a friend. He tried to think. It was pitiable that here he was at almost eighty and he couldn't think of a single person he could go to. Maybe one. Sorakin. His accountant. Was he still alive even? Maybe it was true what the moron had told him, Summertree was full of people who had outlived their friends and family. 'Got people here who've never had a visitor in five or six years. This my friend is the dumping ground for the rich.'

Brin clearly had no more use for him. Never really had. His own damñ fault for never being around. Kid was bound to grow up independent.

He turned left and headed towards the suburbs, said a little prayer that Sorakin was still with the living and at home.

CHAPTER TWELVE

Cold Reason

Delaney was annoyed. He'd had to wait over an hour to see Martinet who'd apparently taken some pills earlier and couldn't be disturbed. He stood by the window, a good twenty feet away from Martinet who lay on a giant seven-seater sofa well wrapped in a rug. At least he had the grace to look sick. He was red-eyed, nursing a bad cold and pressed his fingers against his forehead and the bridge of his nose to ease the sinus pressure. He took a swig of a strong-smelling liquid to suppress his cough.

"I swear it's just a bad cold, Mr Delaney. Seem to get them every time I fly long distance."

"You're sharing germs with four hundred people. I avoid air travel now if I can."

"Doesn't help flying business class either, the air is still the same. I wish the hell I'd never gone."

"Why Italy?"

"Invited to give a speech and an award to some tech advance that will probably turn out to be a scam of some kind. I'm still 'Bitboy' over in Europe. Everyone loves someone who made a fortune out of crypto. Not as if I actually developed an app or anything."

"I suppose you're a role model, like it or not."

"Not. The world is full of kids now who feel a complete failure if they're not a billionaire by the time they hit twenty-one."

"And live in a mansion like this I suppose."

"It's not what it looks like, Mr Delaney. I only occupy the East Wing. This used to be my old school. It went bust in 2010 and was left to rot. I rescued it and restored it to how it looked back in 1915 when one of the Vanderbilts owned it. The rest of the place is an incubator hub. About a hundred people develop ideas here in any given day."

"I wondered why you have so many beat up cars outside."

"The facility is free – my way of giving back, but if they need seed money, I can put them together with investors and take a stake in the company."

"Interesting, an incubator campus."

"Exactly." He coughed, wincing with pain as he grabbed the tissue box. Delaney didn't like the sound of his chest. This was more than a cold. He waited patiently for Martinet to recover.

"I shouldn't have gone out to look for my father in the rain. You said you called the hospitals?"

Delaney nodded. "I've been calling around. It would help if I could describe him, but no one has reported an elderly man with dementia being brought in."

Martinet nodded. "I've got people checking the homeless shelters. I don't get it. How the fuck did they let him leave?"

"You might want to get your lawyer onto that."

"Believe me, I already have. It's supposed to be secure. Now tell me what happened. Why is Sigurdsson dead? The news is very sketchy."

"The writer had a very paranoid personality. I don't know if you picked up on that."

Martinet blew his nose and shrugged. "I don't think I paid much attention to him at all. I took him at face value."

"He stopped writing; told me he'd been told to stop by an unnamed party. I've got a copy of what he wrote for you but it's practically worthless. I've learned more about your father in a week than Sigurdsson discovered in months." He dug a memory stick out of his pocket and placed it on the mantlepiece, making sure Martinet knew it was there. "You won't be impressed."

Martinet nodded and tried to suppress another bout of coughing.

"You should be in bed. Do you have anyone to look after you?" Delaney remarked.

"My P.A. Sheena. She's out looking for my father."

"Do you have a photo of your father? It would help if I knew what he looked like."

Martinet's head drooped. He was struggling to stay awake. "He's intensely private. He loved making a difference to people's lives with his money but didn't ever want any publicity about himself."

"No photos at all?" Delaney pressed.

Martinet thought about it. "Bathroom wall. Framed newspaper clipping."

Delaney headed towards the bathroom, taking care not to come in contact with anything. He really didn't want his cold.

The bathroom was almost the same size as his entire home. Black and white tiling, a huge walk-in shower and separate bath and his and her basins. A wall-length mirror seemed to double the size of the space. The framed newspaper clipping was from The Star. A young Brin Martinet sitting by a computer with a towering older man wearing dark glasses standing behind him. The headline read, 'Bitboy says Cyber currencies will take over the world.' It went on to say 'Berg City Philanthropist Arnold Martinet wants his son to cash in his chips, but young Brin Martinet (17) has refused. Threatens to go to court to prevent forced sale.'

Delaney understood why this clipping was framed. Not many kids threatened to go to court to protect their pocket money. He wouldn't have adult legal majority rights till 18 in this State. His father could have forced the issue.

Brin would have had to claim emancipation rights in court at seventeen.

He took a photo of the clipping. It wasn't very revealing of Martinet senior. He looked formidable and stern, but both seem to have willingly posed for the photo, so perhaps the article was more provocative than the real situation.

He went back to the living room and found Martinet on the phone talking to someone about his father. Delaney resumed his remote stance by the window and checked his phone for any messages from Asha.

"Negative at the homeless shelters," Martinet told him as he put the phone down.

"Negative at his apartment and Asha's in Denny's now. I've just sent the photo, but I don't think it helps much."

Martinet nodded. "We've both changed quite a lot."

"Did you actually go to court?"

Martinet almost laughed but it turned into a cough. "Never...." He coughed again. "Never believe what you read in The Star. My father and I had an agreement. I would decide when to sell. Of course, that was December 2017. Bitcoin hit $19,000 dollars on the 18th. My father had been talking to finance people and they all told him I had to sell, this was the top. It was a crazy time and I'll admit we had a big argument. I may have remarked to the editor Jonas that I would take my dad to court to prevent a sale, but never meant it. He was supposed to be interviewing Dad about his charity which had just paid out two million dollars to young people for sports development. He really didn't want to be in that photo. I distinctly remember overhearing Jonas telling my father that I might be mentally ill for not selling out and that cyber money would soon be totally worthless.

"Dad was even angrier with me a week later when Bitcoin crashed to $12,000." He smiled remembering. "Even at $12,000 I was technically worth $120 million, Mr Delaney. But I was aiming higher. Sheer stubbornness. I had no idea what I'd do with the money once I cashed out. I think that's why I waited so long. Having money young is terrifying. So much could go wrong."

"Jonas is a newspaperman. He knows zilch about money. But I confess, I wouldn't have had your nerve. I would have sold out at nineteen."

Martinet swallowed two pills and struggled to get them down. "The secret is not to be interested in money. Who do you think was telling Sigurdsson not to write my father's biography? That's what I want to know."

"That's what intrigues me. If I was to make a guess, your father has a big secret. Perhaps something he did in his past or something he witnessed that someone wants to keep secret. Who that might be, criminal or governmental, I've no idea. I was hoping you might know."

He watched Martinet carefully as he digested this. "And whoever it is must think that he told Sigurdsson this." Martinet suggested.

Delaney shrugged. "Sigurdsson said he got nothing out of your father. I put him under some pressure, I don't think he was lying."

Martinet nodded. "I told him he wouldn't. He barely knows me these days."

"Nevertheless, Wolfie Sigurdsson is dead. Driven away by a crazy white-haired ornithologist who tied him up and gagged him in the back of his own home, then crashed the motorhome. Sigurdsson died of asphyxiation."

"That bit definitely wasn't on the news," Martinet said, looking surprised.

"Asha thinks it's about a woman spurned. I'm not convinced. Sigurdsson was genuinely terrified. He thought I'd come to kill him. He'd already wiped his laptop."

"Did you kill him?"

Delaney smiled. "I'm an investigator not an assassin. I could ask you if you sent a crazy ornithologist to kill him. Do think your father had a secret? Is it possible someone in Summertree casually mentioned to him that they were looking forward to reading his biography and this triggered an event? Got him so distressed he left in a panic?"

Martinet considered this. "No. He was a philanthropist and a photographer. He did nothing but good for this city. No fucking secrets. His life was an open book."

Delaney was going to ask more but he could see Martinet was failing.

Martinet sank back into the sofa with a look of pain.

"I'm sick, I'm stressed, can we deal with this later Delaney? Please keep looking for my father no matter what direction it goes in. I'm still paying you right?"

"We'll invoice at the end, but I can't promise we'll find him. You can't predict where someone without a memory might go."

"That's what's making me ill. He doesn't deserve this, Delaney."

Delaney made his way to the door and paused as he pulled it open. "Get a doctor to see you, Mr Martinet. That cough sounds like it could easily turn into pneumonia."

Martinet wasn't listening, he was doubled up in pain, coughing his lungs up.

Delaney called Asha as he let Rufus out to stretch his legs. "Talk to me, Ash." He could hear a hubbub of noise in the background. "Did you get the photo I sent?"

"Yeah, but it's useless. I'm showing it to the waitresses now. You joining me?"

"I'll be there in," he checked his phone, "fifteen minutes. Maybe order me some soup and toast. I'm starving."

CHAPTER THIRTEEN

A Feat of Memory

Asha put her phone down and laughed. Delaney was feeding a very impatient Rufus.

"Poor Maria. I think she's regretting staying up at the farm."

"Already?" Delaney asked. He watched the dog devour his supper.

"Bunty made her revise for four whole hours and then Mr B made her help him muck out the stables. She says she's exhausted."

Delaney grinned. "She'll adjust. We indulge her too much here. Bunty's old school. It will do her good or cure her of the countryside forever."

"Definitely. Wait till Mr B hands her a shovel and gets her clearing snow."

Delaney laughed. Maria was probably going into shock. He put on his coat and wrapped a scarf around his neck. "Got to walk the hound. You made sure that the staff at Denny's will call you if he turns up there?"

Asha nodded. "My number is out with a whole bunch of people. I may have to change it after this, I foresee a whole tidal wave of scam calls heading my way."

Delaney winced. "Yeah, not good. We need to have a special work phone maybe."

"Sure, then I'll lose two phones at a time."

"You really think Martinet is heading to Florida? How would he get there without cash?" Delaney asked.

Asha tilted her head. "My guess is that he's not taking his meds. He's got some of his memory back. He hasn't shown up at his apartment yet, so we need to know about his friends. He might remember one special friend, right? Maybe not enough to tell a cabbie to take him there, but he'd know where it was by habit and walk there."

Delaney agreed. "Sounds plausible, assuming that some other party hasn't actually abducted him."

"No sign on CCTV of anyone else being involved, Delaney. I called Summertree and they have no idea how he got out. He'd need key codes."

"Maybe someone helped him. Which gives us back the abduction theory."

Delaney grabbed the dog's lead and called Rufus over. "You said he got mail from his accountant Sorakin. I wonder if he's still looking for someone to fill his penthouse."

"Don't remind me about that. It still makes me nauseous. That old goat should be shot."

Delaney thought about it. "He's close to the same age as Martinet. He's likely to have been his accountant for many years. People stick with him a long time once they're clients. He might know who his friends are. You think you can find his home address for me whilst I'm walking Rufus."

Asha wrinkled her nose. "I will, but I'm not going there with you."

Delaney smiled. "Wouldn't expect you to. If you find it, text me. I'll go tonight. The sooner we find the old man the better for him."

"Meanwhile I'm going to try and makes sense of the photos and stuff I took from his apartment. I don't really know what I'm looking at, but I've got a gut feeling it's important."

"I'm just proud of you for finding his darkroom."

"Dumb luck really. He's meticulous with his records. There's a significance to every photo, but as to what that might be, I haven't got there yet. I'm hoping I can open his memory stick. He wrote random passwords down on the wall, I guess he knew he was losing his memory for quite a while before it happened for good." She smiled. "Go walk Rufie, I'll call with an address as soon as I find it."

Delaney put on his coat and wrapped a scarf around his neck. He attached the lead to Rufus. He opened the door and a gust of cold wind swept inside. "Feels like it might snow later."

"I sincerely hope not." Asha drank her coffee as she watched him leave. She glanced back at her screen as she searched for Sorakins in Berg City. It might have helped if she'd known his first name, but she dismissed any that were obviously female. That left four possibilities. She didn't want to call any of them. The very idea of the man still creeped her out. She called the first one. 'We are closed for the night. If your pet has an emergency, please call ...' She quickly disconnected and dialed the next number. No answer. She was about to dial the next when she noticed another Sorakin at the bottom of the screen. Seth Sorakin, CPA. Definitely not a penthouse address, more like a ranch house on Placid Lake, not so far from her father's place. She reached for her phone.

"You got it?" Delaney asked. "That was quick, we've only got to the top of the hill."

"5901 Placid Lake."

"That's not quite penthouse territory. Lots of wealthy seniors live out there."

"And my father. You're going there now?"

Delaney checked his watch. "Yep. It's only nine o'clock. I'll catch you later."

"You think he ever had a penthouse?" Asha asked.

Delaney laughed. "I think that old guy had a rich fantasy life. Laters, Ash."

Sorakin was surprised and took a minute to register who it was standing at his front door.

"Delaney, isn't it? Killed anyone lately?"

"Not lately." Delaney stared in some astonishment at the husk of what once was. The man had definitely shrunk and looked a hundred years old. He'd lost weight and all his hair. A lot can happen in two years apparently.

Sorakin noted him staring. "I've seen that look a hundred times since I retired. Come on in, you're letting the heat out. Dog coming as well?" He looked behind Delaney and seemed disappointed Asha wasn't there. "Where's your lovely partner? She left you for a younger man? Was bound to happen y'know."

Rufus barged in; he wasn't going to be left out in the cold.

"You've been ill." Delaney remarked, shutting the door behind him.

"Covid in '22. Didn't think I'd recover. Three damn months on a ventilator. I was too darn smart, too busy to get the vaccine. My mother, bless her soul, always said I'd outsmart myself one day. You think it'll come back?"

"What?"

"The virus, another variant. They say my immune system is shot. I wouldn't stand a chance."

Delaney shrugged as he followed the old man into the living room. "I just get the boosters whenever they tell us to." Rufus flopped down on the carpet.

The room was cluttered, the sofa covered in files. Sorakin hobbled over to his leather comfy chair and sank into it with a huge sigh. He waved at the room.

"No criticism. I had to sell the Penthouse to cover the medical bills. They hit me for a quarter of a million dollars. Can you believe that? My health insurance only covered

treatment, not the time spent on the wards. So now everything that was stored there is stored here."

Delaney noted the piles of magazines and unwashed
empty coffee cups surrounding his chair. He also noticed
another coffee cup beside a dining chair. He played a hunch.

"Was he here?"

"Who?"

"Arnold Martinet."

Sorakin looked surprised. "That's why you're here?"

"He escaped from his care facility last night. His son
has got half the city looking for him."

Sorakin settled back in his chair looking confused.
"He never mentioned anything about a care home. Frankly I
can't believe he was in one. Martinet is the least likely person I know to want care. He's got that apartment all set up
for him in his old age."

"When did he come here?"

"Early this morning. He was cold, said he'd left his
jacket in Denny's. Walked here, can you believe it? It has to
be eight miles from the city. His shoes were soaked. I made
him have a hot bath and fed him scrambled eggs."

Delaney was puzzled. "And he was lucid?"

Sorakin stared at him as if he was mad. "Same as he
ever was. Talked forever. Ate lunch too. Seemed to me he
was on a mission. How the hell did you connect him to me?"

"You recently sent some financial documents to his
apartment."

Sorakin shook his head. "Not me. My secretary
maybe. She's clearing my office. I'm retired. By law we have
to return any legal documents or papers to our clients in case
the IRS gets curious."

"Then you had no idea his son stashed him in Summertree for the last six months with advanced dementia."

Sorakin scoffed. "Garbage. No way. Not Arnold. There's not a chance he ever forgets anything. First question he asked was if I'd done his taxes."

"Who does his taxes now?"

"His son. I passed everything over to him or at least my secretary did. I was six months in recovery. Had to re-learn to walk. It still kills me to read for more than ten minutes." Sorakin frowned. "Summertree? For real? No one comes out of there except in a box. They know how to charge. Arnold is worth a lot of money mind. All those tax breaks I got him for giving away his cash. Do it right, you make back more than you give."

"You think the son might be up to something? Slipping his father some drugs and then when he's fuzzy, call in Summertree?"

"Why? The son is worth ten times what his father is. No reason to do that. Besides, I know he respected his father. Didn't often agree with him, but he respected him."

"His son told me his father was so far gone with dementia, he could barely remember him some days."

"Not possible, Delaney. I listened to him for hours. He was a bit out of date on the news, but now I know why. Come to think on it, he has a red scar on his scalp I don't recall, but then again, I've never seen him with a shaved head. He was always proud of his hair."

"Where is he now?"

"I gave him cash. He's got a place in Florida. St Augustine. I've been there; Charlotte Street in the old Spanish town. It's pretty with a nice shady backyard."

"You think that's where's he's headed?"

"I thought it might be. He always goes there in winter. Snowbird, y'know."

"Did you know there's an exhibition of his photography at the Z&A Gallery downtown until next week?"

Sorakin looked skeptical. "Exhibition? Does he know?"

Delany shook his head. "For all his son knew, he was never going to know anything ever again. He commissioned a biography. Did he mention that?"

Sorakin nodded. "He was very upset about it. He said someone had been asking questions about his life. He was going to talk to Brin about it first chance he got to stop it. He never ever wanted publicity. Of course, he got the wrong son if he wanted privacy. Brin always has a way of getting into the news."

Delaney worried about Sorakin, he looked so frail. "You got someone coming in to look after you?"

He nodded. "Some Mexican woman comes in, yells at me, and then cleans up around me twice a week. She sometimes cooks me food so spicy I can't swallow it. A nurse comes in and checks my blood pressure every ten days and also yells at me to tidy up and take the pills. It's a life of hell, Delaney."

"Pills?"

"To protect my immune system. Not supposed to let anyone in, or dogs."

Delaney frowned. "Sorry. Martinet didn't specifically mention where he was going next. Or why he wasn't heading to his apartment for that matter."

Sorakin squeezed his eyes trying to remember. "I asked him about that. He said his son had changed the key code. He didn't seem to know where his son was."

"He moved into St Paul's. Remember the Catholic college? He's restored it to its original design. Must have cost a fortune."

Sorakin looked surprised. "He couldn't find anything smaller, huh? I guess that explains why he couldn't find him. I gave Arnold all the cash I had the house. Nine hundred bucks. He borrowed a sweater and ordered a cab. He said he'd be back in the spring, so I assumed he was going to Florida. He's probably at the airport. He's not the type of man to use Trailways."

Delaney stood up. There was a chance Martinet was still at the airport. He doubted there was a red-eye to Miami or Jacksonville.

"What I don't get is, why would a man as smart of Martinet allow himself to be put into Summertree? The doctors there must have known he wasn't suffering from dementia. They had to be running tests all the time. I have to confess, I hope you don't find him Delaney, but if you do, at least talk to him first. Don't hand him over to his son."

"Yeah, that's my plan. I'm sorry you ended up like this Sorakin."

He waved a hand dismissively. "All my own stupid arrogance. I'm not the only one but there's days when I wish I hadn't survived. Darn blood pressure is off the charts now."

Delaney nodded; looking at his red face he could well believe it. He glanced at the dog. "Don't get up, I'll let myself out. Rufus?" The dog stood up and stretched.

"What do I say if he calls?" Sorakin asked as Delaney reached the front door.

"Nothing. I don't want him to know I'm looking for him and to be honest, I have no idea what I'm going to say if I do find him."

"You need to know that he's not good at trusting people. Night, Delaney. Don't shoot anyone."

The temperature had fallen to 15F when he got to the airport. Didn't take him long to discover the last remaining flights were all canceled due to ice on the wings. None were headed to Florida in any case. A few people were still milling around, hoping against hope that incoming flights would land. None of these people were Arnold Martinet. It was close to eleven pm, time to call it a night. Martinet was not the vulnerable person he thought he was. He had money, a coat, he'd eaten. He was experienced. If he couldn't leave town, he'd probably seek out another friend to spend the night with or check in to a hotel.

Delaney's head had been spun around after speaking with Sorakin. Was this yet another conspiracy, but this time the son was responsible? The ever-loving son who was exhibiting his dear father's photos and commissioning a heart-warming biography. Had he put his father into Summertree and paid to have him sedated? So many bewildered old folks in there dribbling on their meds, who would notice or care there's another?

Delaney was well aware that he'd been hired to find the old man, not pass judgements and he'd not get paid if he went outside his remit. But Sorakin had said he was lucid, and he was inclined to believe the guy. He had no reason to spin anything.

He got back into his vehicle and headed home. "You ok, dog?"

Rufus lifted his head a fraction, but quickly snuggled back into the rugs. He wanted his bed.

Asha had passed out on the sofa when he got home surrounded by Martinet's black &white photos and the post-it notes she'd stuck on the back of them. The fire was out. Delaney scooped her up and carried her to his bed. She didn't wake. He didn't try to undress her, just removed her beaded moccasins, and laid her out on the bed and covered her up. Rufus staggered to his bed in the corner and flopped down with a huge sigh.

Delaney went to the bathroom to brush his teeth. He felt conflicted. He didn't know his next move and that worried him. He looked in the mirror and wasn't sure he liked what he saw. He looked tired and pale. Maybe a trip to Florida wasn't such a bad idea.

"Delaney?" Asha called out sleepily.

"Go to sleep. It's late."

"I've got something important to tell you."

"Wait till morning. I've got stuff to tell you too."

He joined her in bed, switched off the light and snuggled up to her. He thought back to Sorakin's catty comment about how she was bound to leave him. He wasn't sure he'd ever be able to cope with that. She'd become the biggest part of his life, helping him understand Maria's moods and ever-changing ambitions. He loved everything about her.

She reached back and brought his arm over her. He kissed her warm neck and pulled her tight into him. Moments later he fell fast asleep.

CHAPTER FOURTEEN

On A Roll

Asha shoved a reluctant Rufus outside into the cold and then showered. She let Delaney sleep in. She had no idea what time he got in, but she knew it had to have been late.

She made coffee and let the dog back in who scarfed up his breakfast in record time. Then she quickly made an inventory of things they needed to buy, which from the look of the empty cupboards and fridge was damn near everything. She was about to call Delaney for breakfast when he appeared from the shower toweling his hair. He smiled.

"You look like a girl in organizing mode." He approached her and gave her a kiss and a hug.

"I don't know what you mean?" Asha said defensively.

"Hair tied up, that certain look in your eyes. I love it."

She growled, then kissed him. "I am in working mode. We're out of food, again. There's a ton of post-its reminders from Maria in every cupboard saying we're out of stuff. We're down to year-old oatmeal and our last packet of coffee."

Delaney let her go. "Well, I'm definitely hungry. I had the weirdest dream; we were eating waffles in a sunbeam. Neither one of us could leave that patch of sun though."

"Definitely weird, I bet you haven't eaten waffles in years."

"I know. I'm not even sure I like waffles. Anyway, I have a lot to tell you."

Asha nodded. "Me too. Get dressed, I have something to show you."

Delaney looked interested but quickly backed off as Rufus came over to lick his bare legs. He headed back to the bedroom, pausing in the doorway. "I tried calling Brin Martinet but he's not picking up. He hasn't left a message with you?"

"No. He's in hospital. It was on the local news. Bitboy has pneumonia. You or I get sick or shot at, nada in the news. He gets a cold and its headlines. They said it was caused by exposure when out looking for his father who disappeared from his care home."

"Which is more tear jerking than 'caught a cold in business class on his return from Italy'. I guess now everyone will know Arnold Martinet is on the loose out there."

"Which might just complicate things. I'll explain after breakfast. Hurry, I'm making oatmeal now. There's no maple syrup, will honey do?"

"Fine by me, Ash." He disappeared into the bedroom.

He dressed quickly, trying to collect his thoughts. Martinet junior being in hospital was an interesting development, but inevitable given the sound of his hacking cough the night before. It bought him some time to consider the situation. He checked his phone. Just gone eight am. If Martinet senior was serious about Florida, he'd need to be on the eleven-fifteen flight to Jacksonville. The only alternative was to coach the 1560 miles and God knows how many stops and changes on the way. He had plenty of time to get to the airport to watch who might be checking in. The problem was he wasn't sure this was his priority now. He needed to discuss it with Asha.

Asha was serving up as he returned to the kitchen, fresh coffee in the cafetière.

Delaney glanced into the deep freeze section in the fridge. "We have any blueberries?"

"Uh-uh. I told you, we have zilch. You like blueberries in your oatmeal?"

"I read it was good for you."

"Wow, Mr Delaney finally thinks about his gut. Maybe we could buy some fresh fruit today."

Delaney looked hurt. "Hey, I buy fresh fruit every week, but Maria steals it all for her smoothies."

Asha smiled. "Only kidding. I know we eat healthily. It's weird being just the two of us not trying to guess what mood she's in every morning."

Delaney glanced at Asha and reached out to her, squeezing her shoulder. "I think this is about the first time we've ever been together without her between us."

"Yeah, I'm super nervous, we'll have to talk to each other. How will we cope?"

Delaney rolled his eyes and ate his oatmeal. Asha grinned and affectionally rubbed her bare feet on his legs.

"I'm going to burst your bubble today," she told him. "Our loveable wonderful Mr Charity might not be the wonder boy everyone thinks he is."

Delaney nodded. "He's not missing either. I mean, he's out there, but not missing his marbles, that's for sure."

"Ooo, now I'm intrigued. Oh yeah, go sparingly on the almond milk, there's only enough left for our coffee."

Delaney tossed a treat to Rufus so he wouldn't feel left out.

"Mr Sorakin asked after you." Delaney remarked, knowing this would annoy her.

Asha's eyes narrowed. "I bet he did."

"Seriously he did ask, but you wouldn't recognize him now. He had Covid some time ago. He seems to have shrunk to nothing and looks at least a hundred. You'd go nuts seeing him sitting there on his leather chair surrounded by garbage."

"Gross, I'm eating, Delaney."

"Anyway, your tip was right. He's an old pal of Martinet. Spent most of yesterday with him talking over old times and feeding him."

Asha poured coffee for both mugs. She looks puzzled. "Talking. Actual conversation stuff?"

"Sorakin wouldn't believe me when I said Martinet had been in a care home with dementia. Said he was completely lucid, exactly as he remembered him."

"So, he doesn't have dementia? But he was in Summertree, that's their specialty."

Delaney looked at her. "Curious isn't it. Son puts his father away in a supposedly secure nursing home. You have to think some debilitating drugs were involved and someone or some people at Summertree colluded to keep him gaga."

Asha was appalled. "That's evil."

"But not uncommon, I hear. Next question is, why? Why did he want his father out of the way? Can't be money."

Asha shrugged. "If he wanted his father to disappear, why have the photo exhibition? Why commission a biography?"

Delaney picked up his coffee mug. "Could be a way of showing the outside world how much he loved and cared for his father but in reality, he hated the bastard and put him away forever."

"Sounds plausible but I think you might change your mind when I show you my stuff. I finally worked out his password. Odesa. His father was born there. It was on Wikipedia."

"Hmm, ok, interesting. According to Sorakin he didn't know about the photo exhibition, nor did Sorakin. However, he knew about the planned biography. He must have played dumb when Wolfie came in to question him about his life and began planning his escape then."

"That fits. Maybe he stopped taking the pills and it took some time to clear his system."

Delaney sipped his coffee considering the point. "Could be. So now I have a dilemma. Do I go to the airport in the next hour and apprehend Martinet as he checks in for a flight to Jacksonville, if he has somehow acquired ID. Or do I let him go? Sorakin gave him cash, enough to get to his Florida home anyway."

Asha looked confused. "Why didn't he go to his apartment?"

Delaney smiled. "His son changed the key code remember."

"Hmm, conspiracy deepens, Delaney. Evil son syndrome."

"And as he's regained all his faculties, you're going to have to put back that stuff you took from his darkroom, Ash. You're the only one who had access, so they'll know it was you. I don't want us to be in any deeper than we are."

Asha winced. "Too late. I already opened Pandora."

Delaney's heart sank. "Ok, tell me the worst. Grassy knoll?"

Asha shook her head. "I've set it up for you so can see. It's worse, Delaney. At least I think it's worse."

Delaney checked the time on his phone. "Worth delaying my trip to the airport?"

Asha nodded. "Definitely. Keep an open mind. I'm making a leap here. If you think I'm wrong, say so."

Delaney took a deep breath. "Ok, show me."

Asha went over to the table and activated both computers. "Some time ago he had all his photos all backed up digitally. I found the memory stick in one of the boxes from 2015. Must have taken a long time to do it, they're all high-res. His photos go back to the late seventies. His records are meticulous, and I found a logbook recording times, dates, locations, film used, exposure times."

Delaney sat down in front of his computer and stared at the black and white image of a colonial homestead on his screen. His heart sank. "More Americana homestead photos?"

"Years and years' worth, by location, date, and time. At first, I thought I'd have to go through every box and haul them back home. Luckily, I found his memory stick."

Delaney sighed. "Jeez, I have to look at them all?"

Asha shook her head, pulled up a list and opened a series of photos. "Sample one. 1979. November 14th."

Delaney stared at a series of black and white shots of a house in San Francisco on 21st and Dolores Street. "What am I looking at? I mean, what's the significance?"

"The house, the funny looking car outside."

Asha moved the roll on. The car, a Ford Pinto was moving ahead of the camera, the photographer was shooting from behind from another vehicle. There was a series of still shots as it moved along the street.

"Ford Pinto, terrible car. So what?" Delaney asked.

Asha pulled up another window. "I cross-referenced every date with the local newspapers. They're all digitized, it's not so hard. Check this. November 15th San Francisco Examiner. 1979 - Congresswoman Imogen Pike in fatal auto accident.

"Same car, same registration, happened on the 14th, one hour after he took these shots."

Delaney frowned. "The Pinto had a problem with bursting into flames after an accident. I remember reading something about it. But this could be a coincidence, Ash. Doesn't prove he had anything to do with it."

Asha said nothing. She pulled up another photo sequence.

"1985 – Seattle March 30th."

Delaney stared at a pretty house, an empty street, some cars but no people. It was all very beautifully shot, like stills from a movie. Two shots later it showed the home on fire.

Asha brought up a clipping from the *Seattle Times* – 'Tragic house fire kills Marcia Hillgate a day before she was due to give testimony before Senate Committee. Hillgate had alleged massive fraud in US Navy budget allocation ...'

"Shall I go on?" Asha asked.

Delaney stared at the screen. He was developing an uneasy feeling about this. He glanced at her. "You're saying what exactly?"

"I matched every photo and date with whatever was significant in the news at the time. Get this, Delaney, those photographs on the wall in Albion's Gallery aren't 'art'. They're reconnoiter shots. He was casing the joint, so to speak. He's a great photographer. He covers every angle. Turns out he was looking for the best way to cause a fatal accident. From 1977 to 2014, he's documented every single 'accident' by date, time, and location. These are just random samples. *This* is why he fled Summertree. It's not art, it's *evidence*. Wait till he finds out these shots are on public display. He'll totally flip out."

Delaney stared at the screen with growing apprehension. "I'm not sure whether to congratulate you or tell you to pack and we need to get out of here pronto."

Asha was rightly proud of herself. "This is how he made his fortune, Delaney. He was a paid assassin. You have to think, how many assassins want a public exhibition of their handiwork on show? Or a biography of their fake life? Something in him woke up and he hit the panic button. He knew he was at immediate risk of some random official seeing a pattern in his work."

Delaney doubted that. "You saw a pattern because that's your superpower, babe. Me, I would never have figured out a pattern. I just see random, excellent, but somewhat repetitive photos. What made you match them to the dates?"

"I'm a sucker for 'on this day so and so discovered radium' stuff."

"You found this memory stick where?"

"Stuffed into a 2015 box."

"You would have thought he'd keep it in a safe."

"He's got a safe, but sometimes things are safer left out of it."

"Oh yeah, your dad's theory." He rubbed his head trying to think about their next move. "You think anyone else would find this connection?, Maybe the CIA or FBI?"

Asha shrugged. "If they were looking for it, maybe. I knew he was hiding something, but not this."

Delaney rubbed her back. "Only you would find it, I think."

"There's more. This is the worst one."

"The worst?" Delaney queried, hard to believe things getting worse.

She flashed up some shots of a pretty young woman in cut-off jean shorts hanging out what looked to be tie-dye sheets to dry on a line in her back yard. The location looked military standard housing. There were other shots of a truck and a military officer arriving in a '67 Mustang.

Delaney was surprised. "People shots. He doesn't usually include his targets. Nice car. I hope he's not going to blow it up."

Asha pinched him. "That's what you notice, the damn car? You don't see the pram?"

Delaney looked more closely. "What year is this?"

"1996. This one stood out because of the people."

Delaney wasn't sure where she was going with this. "And the big reveal?"

Asha pulled open another window from a Nevada Local paper. 'Tragedy strikes local couple as treasured Mustang explodes killing both occupants. Colonel Metz and his fiancé Bettina Haslet killed instantly. Colonel Metz was leading an investigation into alleged fraud in Gulf War Military supply contract."

Delaney glanced at Asha. "No mention of the baby in the pram."

Asha was glad he finally got it. "No mention of any baby."

"26 years ago." Delaney stated.

"About the time Martinet moved to Berg City with a baby after his 'wife' died in childbirth." Asha added.

"There's no way you can prove this," Delaney said.

"Maybe not, but I'm guessing there's no Arnold Martinet DNA in Brin Martinet."

"So, you're saying he suddenly developed a conscience and decided to raise a baby. A hitman and a baby. Sound like a very bad premise for a movie."

Asha sat back and stared at him. "We already know Brin Martinet was raised by Martinet's sister, who is conveniently now deceased. I'm betting whoever she was, she was well paid for it and why not? Maybe he did develop a conscience. Maybe he realized after the fact that there was a baby in the photo, and he didn't mind killing targets but not children. We know he likes kids because he gives money to them all the time. I'm guessing he didn't want to kill the mother either. The photos of her are very intimate, there's a whole roll of them. He was watching her for days. I can tell he liked her but had a job to do."

Delaney shook his head trying to process this. "And he's probably at the airport right now heading to his hideaway in Florida."

"Let him go, Delaney. He's not coming back here. He won't be in Florida long either, just long enough to pick up cash and clothes and a change of ID then sail away to Costa Rica or someplace."

"You've been thinking hard about this."

She nodded. "Your Wolfic was terrified you said. He thought he was going to be killed."

"He was killed."

"By a crazy white-haired ornithologist. It makes no sense unless he really did find out what we now know. What really doesn't make sense is why didn't the people who want his silence just kill Martinet? Why did they let him live?"

"We're still missing something. The son put him in the care home, convinced his father has full on dementia."

"Or the father faked it so he would be stashed there. Something happened, suddenly he feared exposure, so it was his way of hiding in plain sight."

Delaney mused on that a moment. "All this time he felt protected. He'd done the jobs they asked him to do without questions and then he retired. If hitmen are allowed to actually retire."

"Maybe the people protecting him also died or retired. Remember his Olympic shooting team. They all went into incredibly high-powered jobs and used Martinet's skills to eliminate problems."

Delaney thought that entirely plausible. "The photo exhibition is the main risk for him. If anyone with knowledge of a trail of horrible fire incidents walked in and recognized any one of these targets, his name is attached to every single photo with date, time, and place. Shit, you think he even knows about it? He didn't yesterday."

Asha's phone vibrated. She glanced at the screen. "Someone has burning ears. It's Albion at the gallery." She put him on speaker. "Hey Al, what's up?"

Delaney heard sobbing. "They burned the gallery, Ash. The whole thing's gone. I lost fucking everything."

Delaney suddenly knew where Martinet had been last night, taking care of business. And Sorakin had given him gasoline money to do it. "Shit." He looked at the time. He shot a glance at Asha. "Airport."

She watched him go as she made sympathetic noises to Albion. "Did you save any of the photos? What about the negatives? Were you insured?"

Al wailed – she heard a no in there. "Shit, really? That's awful, Al. Tragic. This was supposed to be your break-through gig."

Delaney sat in his vehicle a moment to think. What was he doing? If he found Martinet at the airport, what would he say or do? Admit to him he knows he's an assassin and arsonist? Ask him why he didn't use his shooting skills to execute his victims? Make a citizen's arrest? He didn't think so. The security cops would be more likely to arrest him for causing a problem.

There was no doubt in his mind that Martinet had burned the art gallery. That was logical, although coincidently it would also bring attention to him or his lost work.

Delaney didn't start the engine. He had to face facts. He wasn't a cop, had no rights to pass judgement and it would be likely Martinet could quickly revert to zombie status and prefer being taken back to Summertree than face jail. The more he thought about it, the less likely Martinet would be at the airport risking all those CCTV cameras and face recognition. He was still in Berg City. He was sure of it. Worse, Asha was now in danger. She'd left her phone number at Denny's. The old man would greet the waitresses like old friends, and they'd tease him about this young woman who was looking for him. He wouldn't like that.

He headed back inside.

Asha was surprised to see him as Rufus jumped up to greet him as if he'd been gone hours.

"You made a copy of that memory stick?" Delaney asked.

"Yeah. Of course."

Delaney briefly wondered if they should wipe any evidence of it off his computer but decided it was best to hang on to the information.

"Get dressed. You've got to take everything back, put it back exactly as you found it."

Asha frowned. "I was intending to ..."

"We have to do it now, Ash. Before he gains access to his apartment again. I mean, we're going now. He's still in this city and he'll have back-up systems in place. Your phone number is out there. People know I'm looking for him. We're in danger."

Asha looked skeptical.

"He's just an old man ..." she began.

"He's an eighty-year-old Terminator, Ash. He's skilled in killing and covering his tracks. I'm not kidding. Unless he's talked to his son, which I very much doubt, he won't know if we are friend or foe. All he'll know is we're hunting for him, and he won't like that. Shoes, coat, memory stick, your bag. And ditch the post-it notes too. We're out of here."

Asha finally kicked into gear. Delaney wasn't kidding.

Delaney drove with determination on the wet road, he glanced briefly at Asha. "You think I'm overreacting don't you."

Asha stared out of the window at the apartment blocks and casually counted illuminated Christmas trees in windows. Maybe it was too early but there weren't as many as usual.

"I don't know what I'm thinking. This was supposed to be a simple trace thing. Find the writer, bank the money. Now it's a horror show. I don't know if the son is evil or if the father is a serial killer or if both things are true."

Delaney paused at stop lights on red. "Do I go left here?"

"No. Next turning and third street on the right. It's a dead end. How do we know if Martinet's not waiting there, hiding across the street or...? Shit, we still don't know what he looks like, that photo you sent was useless."

"If he's at the apartment building, we'll face that when and if it happens. He doesn't know we know about his history. We'll smile and make a fuss about locating him and how happy his son will be he's found."

Asha wasn't convinced that was going to work but held her tongue.

"All you have to do is put the photos and memory stick back where you found them."

Asha sighed. "What I don't get is who are we most afraid of here? The old man or the people who threatened Wolfie? And if they threatened him, were they protecting the old man Martinet? If so, why?"

"That's what we need to know. Right now, it doesn't quite make sense but..."

Asha pointed out the apartment block. "Next one over."

Delaney swung into a nearby parking slot.

"No, next building, Delaney."

"I know. If anyone's watching the place, no need to tell them what we're driving. We can walk."

Asha understood. He was right. She wasn't thinking defensively. She touched his arm as he killed the ignition. "What's our play here? I mean how do we get protection? People will laugh at us if we tell them we're afraid of an old man with dementia."

Delaney squeezed her hand. "It's kinda ridiculous, I know, but you have to give the guy credit. He's laid the ground well. He can use diminished responsibility as his get out of jail card."

"We're the only people who can prove he's a killer..." Asha began but Delaney cut her off.

"And even that is circumstantial. A good defense lawyer would make a meal out of it."

Asha shook her head. "Once, maybe twice, but to be present in so many cases of arson or murder. That would be pushing it."

Delaney turned to stroke Rufus who thought he was going outside. "You're guarding the car, dog. We'll do a walk after, ok?"

"Why do you think Martinet stored all those photos," Asha asked. "Why wouldn't he destroy them and all traces of his handiwork?"

Delaney shrugged. "Insurance? He killed to order. Paid to make everything look like an accident. It takes skill. I'm betting there's something else you haven't yet found on that stick. Names, numbers, money. Perhaps he saw it as his protection from them."

Asha wasn't convinced. "But if he has to use it, he'd be exposing himself to prosecution."

Delaney smiled. "Something like that would never get as far as prosecution. He'd be killed and so would the people who hired him. Scorched earth. Mutually Assured Destruction. You take me down; I take you down with me."

"You think anyone but us knows about that memory stick and the darkroom?"

"Martinet might have left specific orders with a lawyer to locate it if he meets an untimely death."

"But he'd gain nothing. He'd be dead."

"Revenge after death. Just knowing it would happen would give him comfort."

"You have devious thought processes, Delaney. I'm super anxious."

"Relax. I'm here with you. Nothing will happen."

They exited the vehicle leaving Rufus on guard behind. Delaney was looking up at the building, impressed.

"They built it in the French Beau Arts style. Love the ornate windows."

"Wait till you see inside. It's huge." Asha said as she took his arm.

"You should have seen my apartment in Paris." Delaney said.

"Big as these? They have to be two thousand square feet at least."

"Tiny and freezing. I thought it would be clever to live in an 18th Century building but turned out that was just the year they installed the heating."

Asha laughed. "You never talk about your life there or about your wife."

Delaney squeezed her arm. "It's, ... well, you don't talk about your ex-wife with your new partner, especially a deceased ex-wife."

Asha leaned into him. "She was French. I bet she could cook fantastic meals."

Delaney laughed. "Cook? Not Denise. Although she could make a decent omelet. Beyond that, if I wasn't cooking, she'd live on baguettes and jam. She'd often work fifteen hours a day. We ate out a lot. Lunch is a big thing in Paris.

Everything stops for lunch. She was a little bit like you actually. Obsessing over every little detail."

"Is that wrong?"

"Far from it, it's one of the many reasons I love you. And by the way, you still haven't told me what you want for Christmas. And don't say world peace."

"I'm vacillating."

"Ah."

She smiled. "As long as we wake up on Christmas Day together and we have some actual food in the house, I'll be happy."

"Hmmm, about that. Remind me to talk about Christmas Day later."

Asha looked at him askance. "Please tell me we're not working."

"It's a surprise."

"I think I've had enough surprises, Delaney."

They had arrived at the apartment block steps. A Maytag repairman was leaving the premises, shouting 'Happy Holidays' to the gray-haired woman in the lobby dressing a fir tree. They caught the door and entered the lobby.

Delaney stared at the wood paneling and the magnificent wooden staircase with genuine awe. "Wow, this is impressive."

"Love that highly polished brass mailbox," Asha pointed out.

"I just like the empty space. This was built to impress." He nodded towards the women dressing the tree. "Good morning. That's a fine tree you've got there."

She stood back to admire it. "Douglas fir. The committee always insists on the best. I have to get help to reach the top. My son will be here later. Won't let me use the ladder."

"Sensible," Asha remarked.

The woman suddenly remembered something. "Oh, you'll have to walk up. The elevators out. I've called but they can't make it till Christmas Eve."

"Statistical inevitability," Delaney remarked. "Elevators and washing machines always fail at the exact time you can't get anyone to fix them."

"Bad luck if you live on the top floor," Asha remarked.

The woman laughed. "Oh, they won't mind. Top two floors are mostly snowbirds. They won't be back until March at the earliest."

"Can't blame them," Delaney said as he headed to the stairs. He paused a moment and turned back to the woman.

"You haven't seen Mr Martinet around? Apartment thirty-nine?"

"Oh, no. But he must be coming back soon. The repairman just left."

"Repairman?" Delaney asked. He had a sudden flash as he recalled the Maytag man leaving as they entered. He experienced an instant sinking feeling.

"His washing machine must have broken down. Anyway, it's fixed now. Be nice to see him again. Such a nice gentleman."

Delaney hastened his steps up the wide staircase, Asha just ahead of him now.

She glanced back at him. "This isn't good, right? He walked right past us."

"You think he had the key code?" Delaney asked.

Asha was thinking about that as she slipped her gloves on. Six-digit code. There was probably a code breaker you could use.

They were both out of breath as they reached Martinet's floor. They walked towards the large oak front door. It was obvious immediately the Maytag man didn't have a code breaker. He'd jimmied the door, damaging the woodwork, splinters littered the corridor.

Asha pushed on the door, and it creaked open to reveal a total mess.

"He had all the time in the world," Delaney remarked as he walked in, impressed at the size of the place. Martinet had done himself proud. The long rosewood table was intact, but the chairs were strewn all over the room. The sofa had been slashed open and anything that could be damaged, was thoroughly wrecked.

"It must have been impressive last time you came," Delaney remarked. "He lived well."

Asha surveyed the room with sadness. It was almost sacrilege to spoil such a beautiful space. She moved further in, treading carefully over broken glass. He'd even slashed the huge photograph on the wall. It was total vandalism. Didn't seem to have any purpose. The huge, long bookcase was empty, books and photographs all dumped on the floor. There was no method here, just destruction.

"Do I still put it back?" Asha asked without turning around.

Delaney frowned. "I'm not so sure now."

"What if they come back? What if that's exactly what they're looking for?"

"He had plenty of time to find it," Delaney replied. "I don't think they'll come back."

Asha moved towards Martinet's bedroom, disappointed to see his suits and sweaters trampled on. The man knew he was looking for something small but clearly had no idea where it was. The bathroom was basically untouched except for footprints on the toilet seat when he'd inspected the ceiling high cistern. Delaney came for a look-see and shook his head at the wanton damage. The duvet had been slashed, the feathers all over the room.

"Incredible bathroom. I think it's bigger than my whole house."

"I know. It's beautiful. Is the kitchen still intact?"

"Mostly. The floor is covered in rice from the cupboards, but nothing broken. The washing machine is practically brand new so that's kind of ironic. I'll check the other bathroom."

Asha stared at the wreckage in the main bedroom, the safe door left wide open and emptied of any contents. She could hear Delaney was on the phone in the next room. She wondered who he was calling. The police? She doubted it.

Delaney was righting the chairs when she returned.

"All ok?" he asked.

She shook her head. "They opened the safe. Whatever was in there has gone. Who were you talking to?"

"Nicolas, our lawyer. I've arranged a meeting?"

"We need a lawyer?" She looked puzzled.

"We need counsel. Oh yeah, I called Brin Martinet, his P.A. Sheena answered."

"He has a P.A.? Of course, he does," Asha remarked, rolling her eyes.

"He's very sick. I told her about the break in and she'll arrange to have the door fixed. I also told her that his father is in good health and looking for him."

"That's mean. I'm not sure I would be so happy to get that message if I've just arranged to have him incarcerated in a dementia clinic."

Delaney raised his eyebrows. "Yeah, be interesting to be that fly on the wall when he hears the message."

"What now?" Asha asked.

Delaney was looking around Martinet's bathroom. "What's missing from this apartment?"

Asha shrugged "A dog?"

Delaney laughed. "Maybe. Show me the darkroom. I can't see any door."

Asha smiled, turning back to the main bathroom. "It's a very tight fit. You'd never see it if you weren't looking."

She discovered the dressing gown was left on the floor. She suspected they had known all about the darkroom. She moved the coat hook to one side, pulled the door open and was strangely disappointed to discover everything inside the space had been trashed.

Delaney pulled the light cord, and the red light came on. Boxes of photographs had been emptied onto the floor, it would be a mammoth task to sort them all back into time and date. It was if they knew they were looking for a memory stick."

"You still think they won't come back?" Asha asked.

Delaney shrugged. "Perhaps Martinet will come back first. Either way, this isn't our remit. We close up and walk away. We really don't want anyone coming after us. No point in putting your stuff back now. Just in case they come back to search again."

"Martinet will notice."

Delaney nodded. "Yeah, but now he won't be blaming us. It's evidence, Ash. Not that I would have any confidence that it would be investigated. No one in government would want this blowing up on their watch."

He pulled the cord again and closed up the room, making sure the coat hook was back in place.

Asha ran her fingers along the marble tiles. "I keep thinking this whole apartment is like something from a Hollywood movie around 1935. You kind of expect Fred Astaire to come out tapping from the other bathroom."

Delaney laughed. "I'm impressed you've even heard of Fred Astaire."

"You kidding? I took a minor in Hollywood musicals. I wish I'd done a major in it. It turned out to be the toughest course, but I loved it."

"So, what is your favorite musical?"

"Hmmm, that's so hard. American in Paris, On The Town, The Band Wagon, West Side Story, Spielberg's version, LA-LA Land, Sing. Impossible to decide."

"Sing? The kids' movie? You showed it to Maria, I remember her giggling for hours."

"It's brilliant. Piggy Power." She laughed just thinking about it. "I've seen it like five times."

Delaney smiled, happy to see her smiling again. "Come on, we need lunch at Harry's."

"We definitely do." They walked back through the debris in the living room. Asha picked up a framed photo of some smiling woman stood in front of the Eiffel Tower in Paris. She placed it on a side table. "I'm so sad he trashed this place. Why do it now? They had six months to do it whilst he was in Summertree."

"To be discussed over lunch."

Asha glanced back at him. "Will you ever take me to Paris?"

Delaney's face clouded over.

Asha put her hands up. "Sorry, insensitive of me. I was excited thinking about musicals. Ignore that, sorry."

Delaney shook his head and briefly kissed her.

"You're right. I will have to face that one day. Better to be with you looking at it with new eyes than my sad ones. We'll take Maria too."

Rufus was all agitated when they got back to the car. The moment Delaney opened the door the dog shot out and ran up the street.

"Shit. Stay with the car." He ran after Rufus; afraid he'd get tangled in traffic.

Asha got into the car and locked the doors, glancing around in case any windows had been smashed. Her heart was racing. Was Martinet watching them? Would the car explode?

Delaney ran across the street, narrowly missing a car. "Rufus? RUFUS!"

He stood on the opposite side of the street by a row of diagonally parked cars. He thought he's heard a bark. Rufus would only bark once or twice to get his attention. He began to worry about if they had a weapon, they'd be within their rights to defend themselves.

The singular bark sounded again. He dropped to his knees looking under the vehicles. He saw movement, scrabbled up and ran towards it.

Rufus had pinned a young guy to the ground and wasn't about to let him up. He held his hands up to his face to protect himself – clearly scared to death.

"Get this fucking dog off me."

Delaney stared down at a young man in a dark suit, lying on his back on the wet road, shiny shoes, fresh haircut, FBI rookie written all over him.

"Leave," Delaney commanded. "Good job, dog. Leave him now."

Rufus reluctantly complied backing off with a threatening growl.

"This dog's trained to protect my vehicle. Clearly you were attempting to interfere with it. This your vehicle?" He glanced at an anonymous black Chrysler sedan. He looked for an ID but couldn't see anything on display. A felony unless you were Government of course.

"I'm guessing FBI. Not private, shoes too clean for that."

The man got up, cursing his damp suit jacket and scuffed shoes. Delaney noticed he had a gun in his holster. Rufus got lucky he hadn't been able to use it.

"Why are you interested in the Beatie Building?" The guy asked with a southern drawl.

"Beatie?" Delaney asked, puzzled.

"The apartment building. I saw you go in."

"I didn't know it had a name. It's a very stylish 19th Century building."

The man seemed peeved. "You went from your vehicle to the Beatie building, so I'm assuming you had business there."

Delaney smiled and patted Rufus on his flanks to calm him down.

"Ok, we're getting somewhere. You're out here watching the building. I'm guessing you're waiting for Arnold Martinet to turn up."

Delaney noticed the guy's eyes dilate as he registered recognition. "You happen to notice a Maytag guy leave the building as we arrived?"

The guy tried not to blink.

"'Cause if you did, I hope you took his registration. He just trashed Apartment Thirty-Nine. Don't worry. I already let someone know. She'll get the door fixed."

Now the guy was confused. Delaney showed him his ID. "Delaney - City Investigations. Hired to find Arnold Martinet since he disappeared from Summertree. That enough for your report?"

The guy was annoyed now, realizing Delaney was mocking him. "The Maytag guy?" he asked.

"Stocky build, around forty, no facial hair. It's the small details to watch out for. Don't they teach that stuff anymore?" Delaney sighed. "I'm going now. For the record we haven't found the old guy. I have no idea why you're interested in him, but obviously you have competitors. I suggest you find him before they do. Have a good day."

Delaney walked away, Rufus close at his side. Neither of them looked back.

"You sure it was FBI?" Asha asked as they drove away.

Delaney nodded. "He didn't deny it. The trouble is, now they know my name."

"And then they'll find your name is associated with Wolfie's death. Not to mention the shooting at the airport two years ago."

"For which I was exonerated and commended for an award for saving lives."

Asha brushed his hair with her fingers. "I never did get you that new t-shirt for Christmas."

Delaney glanced at her briefly and smiled. "Well, guess what, it's Christmas. There's still time."

Asha was stroking Rufus. "You did good Rufie. Well done."

Rufus wagged his tail. He knew that.

"Rufus was lucky. The guy was carrying. He could have shot him."

"Poor boy. Thank God he didn't get the chance. I don't get it. If they're watching the building for Martinet..."

"They are."

"Then who is the Maytag guy, who is he working for?"

"I suspect his ex-employee or representative of."

Asha shrugged. It was hard to make sense of this. "The FBI must be watching for a reason. If they had evidence he killed all those people they would have grabbed him or shot him years ago."

Delaney began to look for parking again. "We're missing a very important piece of information, Ash. It wasn't the FBI that scared Wolfie, it was the other team. Assume Martinet worked for them. Maybe he manipulated his son to put him in Summertree for his own protection."

"That I get. I don't get why the FBI are interested, or why now."

Delaney found a parking spot one block from Harry's. "Remind me to check this vehicle for trackers when I get home."

Asha nodded. "Shit, they're going to follow us now aren't they. Jeez, how many people must they have to follow every day. How many people work for them do you think?"

"That is why their budget is in the billions." He turned to Asha as he switched off the engine. "This all was triggered by Wolfie asking questions. We need to review everything."

Asha closed her eyes a moment. "Actually, I was thinking it was a good time to forget all this. No one is going to pay us anyway."

Delaney understood and placed his hand over hers. "I know. That's why I want to see Nicolas. Get some legal advice. Like it or not, we know far too much for our own safety."

Rufus wanted to get out. Delaney turned around and rubbed the dog's ears.

"Don't worry Rufie, you're coming in with us. It's Harry's. I may have to get you a deputy badge for your collar."

He got out and let the dog loose who ran for some bushes to relieve himself.

Asha climbed out of the car and shut the door. She looked across the roof at Delaney. "I can't tell if I'm ravenous or about to be violently sick. I'm all churned up."

Delaney walked around the vehicle and wrapped his arms around her. "We'll be fine. We're the good guys, remember?"

They walked slowly towards Harry's as Rufus trotted ahead, happy to be included at last.

CHAPTER FIFTEEN

Puffer

"I had my first two exams," Maria yelled down the phone.

"How did you do?"

"Ugh, I dunno, probably ok. The tough ones are still to come. Bunty has to certify that I'm alone in the room whilst I'm taking the exam, can you believe that? They're watching me on zoom."

"For multiple choice?"

"It's not multiple choice. You have to do calculations and then explain your calculations. It's like medieval torture, Delaney."

Delaney was surprised. "Yikes, I don't think I could do that anymore."

"I know, right. Two more exams tomorrow."

"Sorry M. This is all about sheep and goats remember?"

She swore. "Enough with sheep and goats. I just want school to be over forever."

"Good luck with that. You've got four years of college to get through after that. It's the system, M, designed to keep kids miserable for a very long time so they turn into crappy dull adults."

He thought he heard her growl down the phone.

"How's Rufie?"

"He's a hero. Chased down someone who tried to break into my car today."

"That's my dog. I miss him so much."

"He misses you – keeps going down to your room to look for you."

"Of course, he does. You should have left him with me."

"How's the snow?"

"Stopped, but Mr B says it will return Saturday."

"Hmm, well enjoy the respite. I'm shopping for food right now."

"Don't forget Rufus this time. He likes the chicken flavored biscuits."

"I won't. We'll call you on the weekend. Good luck with the exams."

"Delaney?" He detected a hesitancy.

"Do you miss me?"

"Hmmm, that's a tough one, M. I'll have to think about it." He smiled. "Of course, we miss you. Asha and I are having to talk to each other for the first time. Can you believe it, we may even have to resort to having sex."

"Ewww, gross, good night, Delaney."

Delaney laughed as she disconnected. He pushed the shopping trolley along the aisle trying to remember what he was looking for.... Ah yes, rice, basmati rice.

Asha was at home with Rufus busy with her virtual pinboard. Just as Delaney had suggested she'd gone back to the beginning. She stared at the photograph of the shooting team at the Olympics. Zolloff, Martinet, Kinnerson and Calhoun. Same names as the Nocton Scimitars at college. They'd be very tight friends. Kinnerson and Calhoun had done well so it stood to reason they looked after Martinet too. What was it that Wolfie told Delaney? 'It started at school'. What started? They'd both assumed shooting, but what if it was something else?

She chewed on some stale nuts she'd found in a drawer and searched Google again, looking for any event from the time they'd enrolled at college going forwards.

Although the local paper had been digitized, it wasn't indexed. But she could progress by date. She tracked all kinds of student mayhem, drinking stunts gone wrong, rape charges, auto accidents, many sporting achievements, including more mentions of The Nocton Scimitars as time progressed, sadly nothing to get excited about.

She was about to give up that line of enquiry when she noticed that Henry Hall, a women's sophomore residence, had been destroyed by fire in 1963. Arson suspected. No one had died but she wondered, was this the first time Martinet had burned a building. Had he been spurned and taken revenge? Or was it a test?

She found Martinet up on a misdemeanor the following year. All the Nocton Scimitars were packed into the vehicle. It seemed the VW Beetle had left the road in icy conditions. His driving license was suspended for a year.

So, it painted a picture of an out-of-control boy who was incidentally a good shot. One of the boys, a drinker or was it weed? But was this significant? Not really. How many times had she been in a vehicle with a bunch of college kids off their heads with booze or pills? Too many times till Zuki took her in hand and stopped her self-destructing. All because she'd wanted to be popular even though she hated herself for it. Martinet was a typical male that's all, destined to be an Olympic winner and philanthropist. Somewhere in the middle of that he'd also trained to be an assassin.

She got up to make coffee, unsatisfied with what she'd found so far. Rufus was suddenly alert and scratching to go out. It had to be Delaney, she opened the door, and the dog ran out barking. Asha blinked. He never barked at Delaney. She slammed the door shut and locked it. Someone was on the grounds. How the hell had they got in? The gate was locked. They had to have climbed over the wall.

She dashed to her phone to call Delaney as Rufus barked again from the back. She dropped the phone. The back door wasn't locked. She ran for it as security lights flicked on in the back. She locked the door, caught a fleeting glimpse of Rufus dashing past, ears back.

Asha's heart was beating fast. She grabbed the baseball bat Delaney kept by the fridge and it gave her a brief sense of control.

"Shit." She didn't like to leave Rufus out there on his own. What if he got shot? This was twice in one day. What the hell was going on?

Her phone was ringing. She raced back to the table, but it stopped ringing. Unknown caller. Suddenly she had a terrible thought that Martinet had got her number from the waitress at Denny's. What was he going to do? Burn the house down, he was good at that. Delaney didn't keep a gun in the house. He was always telling her that people get shot with their own guns all the time. She stood there, shaking, unable to decide what to do. Where was Delaney? He should be back already.

Rufus barked again, then howled like he'd hurt. Her heart missed a beat. She desperately wanted to go out there to help him but hesitated, feeling desperately guilty for not going outside.

The gate doorbell sounded. She saw it open. Delaney was there, carrying grocery packages probably needing help. She ran to the front door, unlocked it, and shouted. "Intruder, back yard. Rufus might be hurt."

Delaney almost dropped the groceries and ran around to the back of the house, yelling to her to 'stay inside and lock the door'. Asha ignored him and forced herself to go pick up the groceries and bring them back into the house.

Delaney picked up a spade, the closest thing he had to a weapon out here. Security lights had flooded the backyard, but he couldn't see the dog.

"Rufus?"

Rufus answered with one bark. He was at the far end of the yard by the workshop. Delaney ran towards him, doing his best to avoid the holes the dog insisted upon digging out there.

"What have you got big boy? Show me?"

The dog was shaking, still angry his quarry had got away. Delaney pulled him close and hugged him for a moment to try and calm him down. "You did real good, Rufus. Good boy. Calm down now, they've gone. What have you got to show me?"

Delaney retrieved a shoe, suede, hardly suitable for being out here in the damp. He moved forward to the fence and three quarters of a puffer jacket lay there, one of the arms ripped off. He could see how someone had forced loose a panel and squeezed through. He couldn't see any blood in this light but hoped Rufus had got a good bite in.

He could hear the neighbor's dog barking but that cockerpoo wasn't going to give whoever it was any trouble. There was no point in chasing, they'd be long gone before he could squeeze through the fence.

He gave the shoe back to Rufus as they walked back to the house, Delaney's own heart pounding. Twice in one day now. Rufus was lucky he wasn't injured or dead. He wondered if the intruder was Martinet. He doubted it but then again ....

Back in the house Asha had retrieved the groceries and was packing everything away. She immediately broke off to give Rufus a hug, then pulled her hands away: they were covered in blood.

"He's bleeding, Delaney."

Delaney joined her and examined the wound. "Nasty scratch, there's brambles back there. It's not a knife wound. I'll wash it with antiseptic. Keep hold of him, Ash."

"Poor baby. Poor fearless Rufie. What did you get, huh?"

She prized the shoe from his jaws which he was reluctant to give up. She examined it and the remains of the deep orange jacket. She looked for the label and frowned.

Delaney returned with cotton wool and antiseptic.

"I'll clean it, but hold him, it will sting a little."

"He'll lick it off anyway."

"I know but I just want to make sure it's not a rusty nail or something."

Asha was looking at the puffer jacket. "It's Zara. Last season."

Delaney glanced up at her as he wiped the blood away from the dog's coat.

"Zara?"

"The jacket. It's a woman's medium size. Not sure about the shoe though, could be a man or woman. Size nine. Not appropriate for this weather."

"Woman?"

"You expecting an ex to drop by Delaney?"

Delaney looked confused. "So, it wasn't Martinet. Makes sense, she would have to have been slim to get through the gap in the fence."

Asha shook her head. "I was much more scared than I thought I'd be. Sorry. I didn't go out to save Rufus."

"He wouldn't appreciate it anyway. This is his domain. His job to defend it. Which he did pretty darn well. I'm not going to put antiseptic on, it's not deep and you're right, he'll only lick it off." He gave Rufus another hug and offered him a pumpkin treat, which he snatched from his fingers and dashed away to eat in the corner. Delaney smiled. "He's ok."

"You hug that dog the same way you hug me?" Asha told him, standing up.

Delaney laughed. "Is that wrong?"

"No, but I can see in your eyes how much you love him."

Delaney shrugged. "I do love him. I love you too. I'll try to think of a new way to hug you."

Asha shook her head. "No, don't change anything. I think it's good you love him. I mean, I love him too, but I feel really bad I didn't help him."

Delaney took her hand, pulled her towards him and kissed her warmly on the lips. Then broke away and squeezed her shoulders. "You were scared. You did the exact right thing, Ash. You put the dog out and locked the door." He closed his eyes and let his head rest against her brow for a moment. A whole host of worries coursing through his mind. He sighed and opened his eyes again.

"Now we need to think about our intruder. Pasta ok with you? I'll cook, you open the wine."

Asha was reluctant to let go. "I'll definitely open the wine. My hands are still shaking. I think I've spooked myself with reading up on Martinet."

"Did you search the pockets?"

Asha realized she hadn't yet. "No. I'll do it now." She watched Delaney walk over to the kitchen area and felt an urge to clarify things. "I didn't mean anything mean about you and Rufus. I think I'm sometimes a bit jealous and that's just so stupid. He loves you without question."

Delaney gazed back at her. "I love you without question, Ash. Never going to stop loving you. Even when you snore."

Her mouth opened in protest. "I do not snore."

Delaney grinned and took out some wine bottles from the grocery bag. "Hmm, must have been Rufus snoring."

Asha narrowed her eyes. "Definitely the dog. I have never snored."

She went back to examining the intruder's jacket realizing he'd distracted her deliberately. Sometimes it was probably best not to get between a man and his dog.

"I've got an AirTag."

Delaney looked across the room but couldn't make it out. "AirTag?"

"It's to track your iPhone. Or, some say, track someone's else iPhone."

"Well at least it's not in your pocket." Delaney remarked.

"Nor is her phone."

"So, is it tracking her phone or yours?" Delaney asked.

"God knows." Asha dug around for more and pulled out a receipt for coffee and one bagel and crème cheese. "Fuck, she was at Harry's. She was there watching us, Delaney. I guess your FBI guy passed it on. There has to be a tracker on your car. They couldn't have known we were heading there otherwise."

Delaney was pensive. "I searched but they're pretty sneaky and small these days. I'll take it to O'Reilly's tomorrow. If it's there, he'll find it."

"What about a microphone? Maybe they were trying to bug you too."

"I'm not sure he got inside but they'll check that too."

"Why are we the target?"

"Maybe they think we might find Martinet before them."

Asha discovered a diazepam tablet. "Whoever this is she suffers from depression. I'm not convinced this is FBI, Delaney. A Zara puffer, diazepam, even the clunky suede shoe, this is something else. You don't think Maria's mother is back, do you? You never described her, but she might know about the loose panels in the back fence."

Delaney thought about. "I hadn't considered that. She moved to Florida two years ago, gave up Maria. No way am I letting her get her back. Maria is a completely different person now. Her mother drove her to attempt suicide so there's no chance she walks back in and tries to make a claim."

Asha brought the jacket and shoes to the garbage bin and stuffed them in. "Who would have thought you would prefer the FBI to Maria's mother. Doesn't explain her being at Harry's though." She wondered what to do with the AirTag. Fry it in the microwave to be sure it died? She didn't want to wreck the microwave though.

"It's not Maria's mother. Doesn't fit at all." He handed Asha the corkscrew. "I need that drink now. Toss that AirTag over the cliff outside, Ash. It might confuse them for a moment."

Asha nodded. "I'll do it now. Did M call you?"

Delaney nodded. "Two exams today, more tomorrow. She sounds stressed. I think she's worried we don't miss her."

Asha rolled her eyes. "It's weird, I thought I'd enjoy having you to myself, but I do miss her being here."

"Let's enjoy it whilst it lasts." Delaney said, looking for two clean glasses.

Asha left to dispose of the AirTag taking Rufus with her for safety.

Asha woke up in the middle of the night. She could see it clearly now.

"Rusty red puffer, dorky shoes. She was sitting by the rest room doors pretending to read a book."

Delaney stirred, still half asleep. "What?"

"The woman in the Zara coat. Brown hair, glasses, reading, sitting on her own. She was watching us. I can see her."

Delaney put a hand out to her and stroked her arm.

"Well done, but you need to sleep, Ash."

Asha turned to look at him in the darkness, relieved she had finally resolved what had been nagging her for hours.

"Remember how you said Wolfie thought he was being watched all the time?"

"It was true."

"It's creepy."

"I agree." He leaned in and kissed her. "Sleep babe. We're seeing Nicolas Goodman tomorrow early."

Asha tried to settle back down but found it hard not to see the woman in the corner watching them. Why had she entered the property? What had she intended to do? Delaney nuzzled her but his heart wasn't in it and fell back to sleep.

Rufus stirred on the floor and yawned loudly, annoyed to have been woken.

CHAPTER SIXTEEN

Best Advice Available

They met at the grungy coffee shop just below The Goodman Practice on Yates and 6th. Asha wasn't impressed with the level of sanitation but kept it to herself and toyed with her coffee as Delaney and Nicolas Goodman caught up. She thought the lawyer had lost a lot of weight since they'd last seen him. Some guys look better for it, but it looked as if he'd been freeze dried or something and his skin was all lined like a prune.

"First she said I had to go on a diet, then when I lost a twenty pounds, she insisted I had to get a treadmill."

"These aren't good signs, Nicolas." Delaney remarked.

"Tell me about it. She was doing like six miles a day on the treadmill herself and spending hours in the gym. The kids were complaining she was never around."

Asha understood immediately what had happened. Poor guy had slimmed down for nothing. "She left you for the fitness instructor, right?"

Nicolas winced. "That was my punchline."

"I knew it the moment she asked you to go on a diet." Asha told him. "You should have asked for a divorce right then."

Nicolas shrugged and sighed. "I'm not good at reading the signs."

"And now she gets the house you built?" Delaney asked.

Nicolas shook his head. "She signed a prenup. She was worth a lot more than me when we married. Her lawyer insisted."

"But you'll be stung for child support," Delaney suggested.

"The kids are staying with me. She'll try for support, but she has a good job in marketing and it's a case of desertion. No one will look at her sympathetically. I hope."

"Good luck with that," Delaney remarked. "Whose looking after the kids?"

"My cousin Tonya. She's already moved in and won't let them give her any shit."

Asha sipped her coffee and thought she saw a roach crawl under the pastries display. She shuddered.

"Did you get a chance to look at the stuff I sent you?" Delaney asked. "Asha made the connections, I wouldn't have seen them, for sure."

Nicolas finished off his coffee and checked his Rolex.

"You're here for advice, right?"

"Yes." Delaney answered. "Of course."

"How many people know what you know?"

"Just Asha and me. Martinet obviously, the people who hired him and now you."

Nicolas looked around the coffee shop to make sure he wasn't being overhead. "Take a vacation, guys. I'm serious. Walk away. You already told me the FBI know you're looking for Martinet. That makes you people 'persons of interest'. You never want to be on that list. Plus, your name will come up with the dead writer in Cold Rock."

"Do we assume the FBI are protecting Martinet? Is that what you're saying?" Asha asked.

Nicolas puts his hands up in protest. "We have no idea what they know or what their interest is in Martinet. There's no way of knowing short of going up high enough to find out. And you really don't want to be going there. You haven't found him yet, correct?"

"I'm ninety percent sure he's still in Berg City."

"And burning down art galleries, you say."

"I surmise it's him. He would be the only one with a reason to do it."

Nicolas wagged a finger. "Not true. Could have been the FBI or whoever wanted those photos gone. I had an invite to the opening, but I was in meltdown with my lovely wife that week."

"I keep trying to think what's Martinet's play here. He's been hiding in plain sight in the care home, but that's busted. He doesn't know that we know about his other 'career'."

Nicolas shook his head. "You don't know what he knows. You can't assume anything. What about his son? You think he arranged to have his father put away because he knew about his past or what?"

Delaney signed. "We don't really know that either. Not for sure. It's weird he hired the worst biographer in the world to write his father's story."

Nicolas turned his attention to Asha. "You've been researching Martinet's past, right?"

Asha nodded her head. "I thought it would be all about shooting, but his specialty turns out to be arson."

"Which is broad spectrum stuff. More anonymous than a bullet, easier to distance yourself from. Although they say arsonists have a signature tell, so the FBI would know about that, if they were looking."

"We had an intruder last night," Asha mentioned. "She'd been watching us at lunch at Harry's, not that we knew that at the time."

"Harry's?"

"Best place for brunch in the city, Nicolas." Delaney told him.

"And you kept this secret from me?"

"Might conflict with your diet, best fresh bagels in the city," Asha told him with a smile.

"Yeah, well the diet is off. I can tell you that." He stared at Delaney and Asha a moment considering his next words.

"My advice stands. Walk away. There's no percentage in this for you. No money. No point in telling the FBI what you know because then you both become security risks. The fallout if this became public would be very ugly indeed. Frankly I don't think you would survive. I have already purged it from my laptop."

Delaney glanced at Asha, she shrugged. "What happens if they don't leave us alone?"

Nicolas stood up. "Disappear. I mean it. This is all going to blow up somewhere. Either someone will get to Martinet first and kill him or he'll make a mistake. It's ugly, believe me, no one will want this stuff to go public. It undermines faith in government. The son is sick with pneumonia you said. Is that real?"

Delaney nodded. "Caught it on the plane back from Italy."

"Hmm and why was he in Italy?"

"Some crypto award thing he handed out." Delaney answered.

"I haven't had time to corroborate that yet," Asha told them.

Nicolas wagged his finger again. "Don't check. Disappear. Come back when it's over. You wanted my advice, consider it given."

He offered them a brief smile and left them staring at each other.

"It's not the worst advice," Delaney said after a moment.

Asha wrinkled her nose without offering comment. "I have to pick up Maria's Christmas gifts. You need to get the trackers off your car. We can't disappear unless you do."

Delaney frowned. "Stay in touch. Pack for both of us when you get home."

"We're definitely walking away from this?" Asha asked.

Delaney stroked her face. "We'll see who follows us, I guess. Six days till Christmas."

"Where are we going? Back to the farm?"

Delaney smiled. "It's a surprise. Don't ask."

"Ugh, I hate surprises."

"You won't hate this. Besides it's best you don't know stuff in case they torture you for information."

Asha eyes widened, then she laughed. "Jeez thanks for that, Delaney."

"Go. I'll see you back in four hours tops."

Asha stood up and headed out the door, glancing back only briefly to smile at him. Delaney watched her leave, keeping an eye on the others in the coffee shop in case they were about to follow her.

O'Reilly was old fashioned but kept well abreast of current electronics in his little workshop on an Eastside industrial park. A go to place if you wanted to be discreet. Delaney returned from walking Rufus in the nearby park and was happy to see the Range Rover was ready to go.

"Someone thinks you're important enough to track not once but twice." O'Reilly said wiping grease off his hands.

He showed Delaney the devices. "Micro Cat 6 tracker which sends a GPS signal. It's still active." He revealed another, slightly larger tracker. "This is older, given the amount of encrusted mud on it. It's lost its charge. Your car had one previous owner, right?"

Delaney was distracted by a new tattoo on O'Reilly's arm. It looked raw.

"Yeah, the owner lost his license. I got a good deal."

"It may have been installed when new by the first owner. I'm surprised your insurer didn't insist you install one too. Range Rovers are in demand, as they say."

"I think they did mention it. It struck me as expensive to keep a monthly contract and besides, I thought people were only stealing EVs now."

"They are, but they'll take one of these too. If I were you, I'd install an old-fashioned door lock with a key. Nothing electronic. It's the only way to stop them now. I can do it. Some people worry about it devaluing the vehicle but believe me, a real deadlock baffles the new generation of thieves." He held up a slim piece of plastic for Delaney to see. "I found this in the footwell of the rear seat. Someone must have slipped it through the window. You keep the window open a crack for the dog I see."

Delaney nodded. "That a voice recorder?" He was looking at a slim piece of electronics no more than two inches long and perhaps a quarter inch thick.

"Bluetooth. Someone has to be close by to monitor a conversation, but these things will pick up whatever you're saying very clearly. It's state of the art. Voice activated, battery lasts 50 hours and it's got stand-by usage of six months."

Delaney now knew exactly how they were waiting for them at Harry's.

"FBI uses these? I have a dedicated following if you get my drift."

"Maybe. But these things are available to anyone online. Cost almost nothing. Surveillance has been democratized, Delaney."

"Depressing. How much do I owe you?'

"$395. Two hours work. I can give you discount of twenty percent on fitting a deadlock if you return within the month."

Delaney winced. This gig was costing him way more than he'd ever bring in.

"Deadlock sounds a good idea. I'll take that up with you in January, ok?" He had a sudden thought. "Can I plant this tracker on another vehicle?"

O'Reilly frowned. "You can, but I didn't hear that, ok? It's magnetic, best be clever where you put it."

Delaney took the live tracker off him. He definitely had to offload it so he could get out of Berg City unobserved.

He paid his bill with reluctance.

"We've got a monthly check-up deal," O'Reilly told him. "We can look over your car once a month to keep it clean. I'd advise it in your profession."

"Remind me in January when I've paid all my bills." Delaney told him. "Have a good holiday."

O'Reilly shrugged. "Yeah, life's a bitch. I do my taxes Christmas Day. The wife goes to her mother. It's the only time I get any peace."

He drove away from the business park a poorer man, thinking about taxes. He'd have to face that very soon himself.

He had one other place to go before they could leave. He checked on Rufus who was staring out of the window. "Won't be long now, Rufus. Hang in there."

He checked the time. Shouldn't take him more than twenty minutes to get to the hospital. Time to check if Brin Martinet wasn't faking it.

CHAPTER SEVENTEEN

Cutting Edge

"It's restricted. No visitors, not even family." The woman on the front desk informed him. "If he's in there it's serious."

Delaney could see she meant it. "But he is in there, right?"

She gave him a dismissive look. "He's in there. He's isolated."

"Can I get a message to him?"

The nurse shook her head. "We don't take messages. He won't be reading them. He's on oxygen."

"He's very anxious about his father. He wanted to know the moment I had information."

The woman's lips curled. "If his father comes here, we won't let him in either. No visitors period."

He'd already looked around the visitor section outside the ward and found no anxious P.A. looking out for Brin Martinet's interests. Delaney accepted the woman wasn't in the mood to be cooperative. The few nursing staff he could see were all staring at computer screens studiously ignoring the conversation at the front desk. He shrugged and gave up. He exited the ward and headed back towards the elevator.

He didn't have long to wait. The doors opened and he stepped inside closely followed by a man in a white coat, incongruously clutching a black beanie in his hands. Delaney pressed the button for the ground floor. The other passenger leaned forward to press a button but turned half-way and abruptly produced a knife which he pressed against Delaney's neck. Caught off guard Delaney did nothing but register the man in the white coat was too old to be working in a hospital.

"What do you want with Brin Martinet?"   He growled.

Delaney turned his head and stared into the pale blue eyes of a killer. He took a few seconds to adjust and think things through. The knife was pressed hard against his neck.

"You're a hard man to find Mr Martinet."

Martinet didn't seem surprised he knew who he was. "Why are you looking for me?"

"Your son hired me to find you. He's worried. You left the care home. You should be happy the son cares so much about a man who is supposed to have chronic dementia."

Martinet didn't seem to care about his answer.

"As you can see my dementia is greatly exaggerated."

Delaney abruptly pushed violently against the man's arm. He twisted away, forcing the man against the elevator wall, ramming a fist into his gut as he slammed the knife hand against metal sides. The old man doubled up in pain as Delaney stomped on the knife, swiftly swooping down to grab it.

"You don't need the knife, Mr Martinet. I've found you. Mission accomplished. I'd mention it to your son but as you probably already know, they won't let anyone see him."

Delaney closed the blade and watched the old man gasp as he tried to regain his breath.

"Have you been home today?" Delaney asked calmly. He could feel the elevator slowing.

Martinet clutched his stomach and stared at him with contempt. "The key code's been changed. Know anything about that?" He tried to stand up straight but was still out of breath and in pain.

"You son changed it. You should know that someone broke into the apartment and turned it over. You shouldn't have any trouble getting through the door now."

Martinet barely registered this. "You went in?"

Delaney nodded. The doors opened and he walked out of the elevator. Martinet followed but very slowly. It almost made Delaney sorry for slugging him. Almost.

"I could take you there," Delaney offered.

Martinet leaned up against a wall as people went by their own business. He was weighing up the proposition. "They're watching the building." He rasped.

Delaney nodded. "FBI seem very interested. Unfortunately, they are watching me now, but they didn't notice the Maytag guy who went in and trashed your place."

"Maytag?" Martinet looked confused.

"A disguise. Seems you have two parties searching for you, aside from myself. Was it you who burned the art gallery? It's pity, I was promised one of those photographs. Nice little thing you have going with contrast there I think."

Martinet stared at him as if he was crazy. Delaney felt a lot safer out here in the corridor with people around.

"If you need to talk this over, we could get a coffee," Delaney suggested. "I'm guessing it must be confusing for you right now."

Martinet was looking beyond Delaney at the security guards taking an interest in them.

Delaney pondered his options. Walk to the hospital coffee shop and hope for safety in numbers or head out of the hospital and hope Martinet wasn't going to attack him. The guy looked old and frail but remained lethal, even without a knife.

Martinet grabbed his arm. "Coffee."

Delaney offered the guy a tight smile. "I warn you: the coffee here isn't great."

"It's coffee," Martinet replied, staying close to Delaney, possibly a little unsure on his legs.

Delaney paid for two Americanos as Martinet walked unsteadily to a free table. He did momentarily contemplate leaving but vaguely felt sorry for the old guy. He looked lost.

"Sugar and cream over there," the counter girl told him.

Delaney grabbed some sugar and plastic containers filled with 'whitener' and took everything over to the table. Martinet didn't say thanks.

"Why did my son hire you?" Martinet asked. "Why you?"

Delaney took a closer look at Arnold Martinet. He looked pretty alert for an eighty-year-old but definitely underweight and his fingers looked like he had osteoarthritis. Martinet reached for his coffee mug and wrapped his fingers around it to reduce the pain in his fingers.

"He hired me to find the guy who was supposed to be writing your biography. He took the money and ran. You son didn't appreciate being stiffed."

Martinet shook his head, barely keeping a lid on his anger. "I didn't ask for any stupid biography. Who the hell needs one of those?"

"Nevertheless, your son figured you deserved one, what with you being a legend in the charity business."

Martinet didn't respond to that. Delaney could see he was trying to make calculations.

"Unfortunately," Delaney continued, "the writer was murdered. He didn't get around to writing much about you and claimed he was being watched and threatened by person unknown to stop work."

"Person unknown?" Martinet asked, curious at last.

Delaney was watching a young woman and a tall older man arguing outside the café window. It looked heated. He looked embarrassed. She wore knee length suede boots which she stamped on the snow repeatedly.

"I thought the writer meant the FBI, but unfortunately, I didn't think he was credible. My mistake. He was killed shortly after we had a little chat. Why did you burn the art gallery? Those were pretty impressive photographs."

Martinet frowned. "I didn't burn any damn gallery. I don't know what the fuck you are talking about."

"Forty black and white images of colonial houses, lonely places, Americana. The kind of photos that look good on a study wall."

"My photographs? These were my private photos?" Martinet seemed genuinely shocked.

"All forty. You are, after all, a well-known photographer."

"Who authorized this?" Martinet was angry again.

"Your son. He's very proud of you. Wanted the city to share in his celebration of your professional life."

Martinet closed his eyes. His left leg was jittery. Delaney stared at his swollen fingers. Surprised he could even hold a knife with them.

"Why now? Why did he do it now?" Martinet mumbled.

Delaney sipped his coffee. It was worse than he remembered. "You were in Summertree. As far as he was concerned you were lost to dementia. You should be proud he wanted to respect your name and achievements."

Martinet was staring at the rowing couple outside the window. She was in tears now, refusing the man's lame attempts to soothe her.

"I should congratulate you on your quick recovery," Delaney remarked, hoping it sounded almost genuine.

"Recovery?" Martinet asked.

"Dementia. I guess you went into sudden remission or something."

Martinet glared at him. Clearly it wasn't something he was going to debate.

"What are you going to do? Your son has a severe case of pneumonia. Neither of us can communicate with him. You sure I can't take you home? It's a mess but it can be tidied."

Martinet continued watching the couple arguing outside. He commented. "Married doctor, girl, probably a nurse, thought he'd leave his wife. They never leave."

Delaney tended to agree. "At least he looks guilty." The young woman reached up and slapped the guy. One could see he momentarily thought about hitting her back but just in time remembered where he was, who he was. "What are you afraid of?" Delaney asked.

Martinet drank his coffee. "I don't know why people are watching my apartment. I feel I've lost control."

Delaney nodded. "Did you enter Summertree voluntarily?"

Martinet nodded. "My son must have thought it best. I remember I had several bad episodes when I wasn't able to remember where or who I was. I guess it got worse." He smiled suddenly. "Turns out it was a large tumor. They removed it in early November." He turned his head to reveal a raw vivid scar.

Delaney was impressed. "That's a lot of stitches. Did your son know about this?"

Martinet shrugged. "I haven't seen him in months."

Delaney was puzzled. The son had definitely remarked about visiting his father.

"Well, you're a lucky man, second chances are rare I think."

Martinet replaced his hat. He didn't seem so impressed. "But why are people watching my apartment. Why are they watching you? Why did they murder the writer?"

Delaney wondered if Martinet was testing him or had simply forgotten his other life.

"Do you have friends you can stay with?" He asked.

Martinet slowly nodded. "Yeah. Do you know where my son lives now? I went to his old house."

"St Paul's. The old Catholic college. The East Wing."

Martinet seemed surprised. "I remember he bought it, but it's a wreck."

"You'd be surprised what a few million dollars can do to a building in need of repair. You'd have to get someone to let you in. Lots of security."

Martinet waved his hand. Delaney suspected he wasn't bothered by lots of security.

"Mr Martinet, consider yourself found. I can bow out now. I don't know what to recommend about the FBI or the other people, but if I was to surrender, I think the government would be the safer choice. Assuming you have something to surrender for of course."

Martinet gave him a look that plainly said he wasn't about to do that.

Delaney left his coffee and stood up. "You should probably let the care home know you have discharged yourself. Otherwise, they will keep charging whether you're there or not."

Martinet looked surprised. "Yeah, you're right. That's exactly what they'll do." Martinet stood up, steadying himself with the table. "Look, I'm sorry about earlier. I didn't know what the situation was. I was confused. I couldn't get to my son."

Delaney watched the arguing couple finally part, the young woman still angry. The man was wearing scrubs under his jacket. Martinet had been right. "Any ideas on why anyone would hate your photographs so much they'd burn down the gallery? I'm sorry but all the negatives will have burned too."

Martinet shook his head. "I just know it wasn't me. Don't even know any art galleries in this city."

Delaney wasn't entirely convinced by this remark.

"Any place I can drop you?"

"Denny's on Fifth. I'm hungry."

Delaney reached home thirty minutes later. A very pensive Asha was packing in the bedroom.

"You're kidding, Delaney? A knife?"

Delaney pulled the knife out of his pocket. "This knife."

Asha stared at it like it was a live snake. "What did you do?"

"For a second, I turned to ice. Then I figured I'd better do something before he could slice me up."

Asha sat on the bedroom floor. All afternoon she'd sensed something had happened but not imagined this.

"Then I dropped him off at Denny's. A waitress greeted him like a long-lost buddy. If she calls you remember to say thank you, say you're relieved."

"I'm definitely changing my number."

"He seemed a little confused," Delaney remarked. "He can't speak to his son, knows his apartment is being watched. Oh yeah, it really was a miracle cure. He had a tumor, not dementia. I checked online; it can present the same way."

"A tumor? So, he has his memory back?"

Delaney shrugged. "Maybe, or he has a great excuse not to remember anything. The scarring is genuine. Funny how Brin Martinet didn't mention it though. He must have seen the bills. Something very odd about their relationship."

Asha grabbed Rufus who'd just wandered into the room and hugged him. "Shit Delaney, I honestly don't know how you remained calm."

"I wasn't calm, I just knew I had to act. He's old, his reflexes are poor. A younger guy wouldn't have given me the chance. The funny thing is he denied burning down the gallery."

Asha was surprised. "He did? You believed him?"

"Maybe. I know his M.O. is arson but he seemed genuinely ignorant of the gallery or that it was his photos on display. In general, humans don't like to burn down their own stuff."

"But he knew about Wolfie."

"He knew about the biography, but we didn't discuss it much."

"So, what now?"

"We stick to plan A. We disappear. He's well and truly found. Send an invoice to his son, tell him we left him in Denny's, and he tried to see his son in hospital. Can't do much more than that. His P.A. will pick it up. She seems to run his life."

Asha looked up at him. "Aren't you curious as to how it all plays out?"

Delaney resumed packing his case. "Not as curious as I am to see Maria grow up or spending the rest of my life with you with my neck still attached to my head. Nicolas was right, we're the meat in the sandwich. We just don't know what kind of sandwich it is."

"Don't forget your toothbrush and razor." Asha told him. She got up off the floor and came over to hug Delaney. He kissed her, brushing the hair from her face. "We know too much for our own good, Ash. Safety first."

She pulled away from him a moment wrinkling her nose. "You really did work in insurance, didn't you."

Delaney laughed and leaned back in to kiss her again. "It's all about percentages."

Asha spread her fingers over his back trying to expel the image of a knife pressed against his neck. They stayed that way a while, reluctant to let each other go.

The lock was broken, the heavy front door splintered, Delaney hadn't lied to him. He entered cautiously; his heart sank when he saw the extent of the damage. This wasn't the work of the FBI; he was sure of it. But it didn't look like his own people either. Leave no trace was their motto. Not this vandalism. Perhaps someone trying to make it look like an amateur. Was that what this was? He barely glanced at the slashed photographs and upholstery. He went straight to his bedroom and stood there frozen to the spot. His clothes had been tossed all over the place. He stared at the chaos in his closet and the emptied safe. He tried to remember what was in there, he hadn't used it in years. Some Treasury Bonds maybe, some cash... he suddenly remembered the dark room. *Please let them not to have found that.*

He opened up the door, pulled the light cord and stared at the boxes of negatives spilled out across the floor, his anger rising. They had no right to do this. It would be one hell of a job to resort them into years. There was no method here. Just wanton destruction. He searched for the memory stick he'd left in a green folder. Couldn't find it. Why take it now? No one knew about this room. Except Brin. He was sure of it. No one. It had always been his vanity to keep a record of everything, but he'd told himself that he was a photographer. It was entirely normal to keep the negatives. It was Brin who'd suggested he needed a digital back-up. He'd often worried that this day might come.

They'd want him dead, and all traces of his existence gone with it. This had to be Kinnerson or Calhoun's work, or both. Could they open the memory stick? He swore. Of course, they could. Then he saw writing above his desk and his heart sank. He'd left his fucking passwords on the wall. He recalled how hard to it had been to remember anything a year ago. He'd had to write everything down. Of course, it was just raw negatives. On their own they wouldn't be a threat: unless you knew the context.

They'd been happy to let him have this cover story and his charity work. Never said a word about it, but he'd instinctively known the moment he'd heard about that biography being written that trouble was coming. They'd be frightened he might say something, settle scores. No matter that he had never betrayed them. Never. But he put himself in their shoes, they couldn't be sure, after all, what might a guy with dementia say and not even remember he'd said it? They'd want him gone and soon.

He didn't bother picking anything up. He'd have to think about where to store the rest of his negatives when he returned. Nothing he could do about it now. He had to deal with the immediate problem. They'd be looking for him everywhere. He was under no illusion of a reprieve; he was marked for termination. Someone would have been hired. Someone more discreet than whoever had trashed his apartment. They could come at him at any moment.

He felt nauseous. He'd been pushing his body hard since he'd got out. Needed sleep, needed a lot of things. He needed a moment to think. A hot shower always helped him think. He stripped off and turned the shower on, unimpressed by how old and thin he looked now. Later he picked up a change of clothes and shoes. It felt good to be in dry warm clothes, even if they felt a tad loose.

He grabbed a favorite hat to hide the head scars and his spare pair of prescription glasses, relieved to be able to see things in focus again.

He pushed the bed to one side, lifted a floorboard and brought out a small box. He withdrew his standby ID cards and cash. He reckoned he was ahead of them by about a day at the most.

At five pm, a plan of action firmly in mind, he silently slipped out of his home and left by the service stairs as usual.

CHAPTER EIGHTEEN

The Star

"I think we need protection," Asha remarked as they drove out of the city.

Delaney agreed. "What do you have in mind?"

"You could call your friend at The Star."

"And let him know what exactly?"

Asha stared out of the windshield at the darkening sky hoping the threatened snow wouldn't get dumped on them.

Delaney checked his mirror to see if they were being followed. The coast road was surprisingly empty. His dash pinged informing him there was risk of ice and snow.

Asha was thinking. "We have to find a way to get the truth about Martinet Senior to the right people."

Delaney wasn't so sure. "And who exactly are the right people? If we confess to the FBI all that we know do you think they'll say thank you or lock us up? We could approach the *New York Times* or a media organization that could afford the counter lawsuits that might follow the revelations. We could put it out there online but then risk it being just another conspiracy theory. I'm all for Martinet getting some justice but remember the Maytag man. Who is he working for? By now they know I'm involved somehow. I don't know if there's anyone I'd trust with the information right now."

Asha wondered if the mainstream media would believe them. They could draw completely different conclusions to the arson attacks. "Where are we going?" She turned her head as they rounded a bend. "Hey, wasn't that where you went off the road?"

Delaney glanced at the gleaming new crash barriers they'd erected at the cliff edge.

"It remains a mystery to me how Rufus got out alive but thank god he did."

Asha looked over her seat to where Rufus slept in the back. "I still have nightmares about that day. It was a miracle either of you survived."

Delaney reached out momentarily and squeezed her leg. "Yeah, but you remember more about it than me. I have a memory of plunging down the cliff but almost nothing after that until you rescued me. That and briefly waking up to discover someone was sewing up my head whilst a kid was holding me down. That I definitely remember."

Asha shook her head recalling that day. Finding Delaney lying on a makeshift bed with a bloody tea towel wrapped around his head had been a shock. "I wonder what happened to that woman and her husband. All that pain he endured for nothing. No one got paid."

Delaney shrugged. "She left him. I gave her a deposit for a month's rent on an apartment downtown. It was the least I could do."

Asha stared at him astonished. "You did? When? You never said a word about it."

Delaney smiled. "I might have bled to death if she hadn't sewn me up. She approached me when you were visiting your father about eighteen months ago. She was desperate. It was the right thing to do."

"I guess. Impressed you kept it secret. Wow Delaney, you're a sly one. I'm going to have to keep my eyes on you. You know what they say about couples who keep secrets from each other."

"No, but I guess you're going to tell me."

Asha rubbed his arm. "No, just teasing. I'm glad you helped her."

"Maria was with me. She said it was all about karma." He slowed as they came up behind a truck struggling up a steep hill. "You're right about secrets though. Just so you know, I require at least two weeks' notice if you ever intend to have an affair so I can mentally adjust."

Asha protested. "Not going to have an affair. Ever. I saw what it did to my parents. Made them into monsters. My mother in particular. Two weeks' notice? Does anyone ever do that?"

"Don't know. I don't ever want to be in that situation."

"Talking of secrets, Delaney, where are we going? This is the road to Oyster Point."

Delaney briefly glanced at her. "Don't spoil the surprise."

Asha smiled. She knew exactly what he was planning. "We're going to see Zuki?"

Delaney shrugged. "I said don't spoil the surprise."

Asha was suddenly all smiles. "Does she know? We're hiding out there? I haven't got her a Christmas present. My god, I haven't seen her for at least three months."

"She's been away."

"And you know this and not me? She's my best friend."

"I bought a book for her. It's in the back. It's from both of us."

"A book? Zuki reads books? Since when?"

"Thought she'd like something on the world's best boutique hotels."

Asha was astonished. "She might throw it at you. Don't be upset if she doesn't say thank you."

"I thought she was enjoying helping to run the hotel."

"I think if she could run the hotel without guests, she would like it more."

Delaney smiled. "Yeah, I guess hospitality doesn't come naturally to her. She called three weeks ago and made me swear I'd get you there for Christmas and make sure it's a surprise."

"I can't believe you kept that secret." She gazed at him then smiled. "But yes, it's a nice surprise. No wonder you didn't make a fuss when Maria chose to stay with Bunty."

"Added bonus. I figured you and Zuki needed to catch up."

Asha felt happy but sadness too that she and Zuki were separated by the distance. She felt doubly guilty that she hadn't called her in a month. Had they drifted apart so much?

Delaney's phone rang. He saw it was Jonas from *The Star*. He pressed answer as he slowed and pulled off the road for a moment.

"Delaney?"

"Jonas. What terrible thing did I do now that you should be calling?"

They heard Jonas chuckle a moment. "Your name flashed up in connection with a certain murdered writer in Cold Rock."

"Did it mention if I was a suspect?"

"No. I wasn't going to bother with it but then I saw your name and I just knew there's a story there for us. Wherever you go there's always a trail of bodies."

"Just one, so far, Jonas, well maybe two, to be exact. The report mention anything about a crazy female ornithologist called Yeaver? She abducted said writer, gagged, then bound him, then ploughed his motorhome at speed into solid rock on a snowy road."

Jonas swore. "No, the report wasn't quite so graphic. You're listed as the person who found the motorhome on the road to Porcupine Ridge."

"Correct. And many witnesses will state I was one of the last to see the writer alive the night before. Luckily for me two others drank whiskey with him after I left."

"And you were there for any particular reason? We're not off the record here, Delaney. I can't keep you out of the story this time."

Delaney glanced at Asha thinking fast about how this could be turned to their advantage.

"I was hired by Brin Martinet to find the writer Wolfie Sigurdsson."

"Bitboy? Now the story gets interesting. He's sick in hospital, pneumonia I hear."

"Bitboy paid the writer $10,000 upfront to write a biography about his father. He wanted the world to know what a great guy he was and felt sorry that his father was stuck in Summertree with Dementia."

"Is he a great guy?" Jonas asked. "I know he's given away a lot of money."

"Ex-Olympian, Jonas. Bronze medalist. Don't forget that. There haven't been many in Berg City."

"Ok, I get it. Heartstrings stuff, philanthropist struck down with dementia. But why are you involved? You don't know anything about writing biographies."

"Sigurdsson disappeared with the money, Jonas. Enter super-sleuth Delaney to track writer down and find out why he thought he could get away with it."

Jonas laughed at the super-sleuth remark. "That's why we never pay advances."

"I heard you never pay, period."

Jonas bridled. "180 days is standard, unless they have lawyers on call."

"Which is why writers never have any money, Jonas. Anyway, to add a twist to the lemon, I found the writer but then Martinet Senior disappears."

"We published something about him disappearing two days ago. We couldn't find a photo of him in the library. I might have gotten a little too angry about that."

"Seems he just walked on out of the care home. Summertree might get sued about that. However, Martinet Senior no longer has dementia."

"They cured him? That would be big news."

"Misdiagnosis by his doctor, who's probably quaking in his boots awaiting a lawsuit. He had a brain tumor. It can present the same way as dementia I'm told. They operated and he's fully recovered. That would make a great story in your health and lifestyle section if you can find him."

"Didn't you find him?"

"First, I need to mention that the dead writer claimed he was being watched by the FBI or A. N. Other."

Jonas groaned. "Please not a conspiracy story. You can't verify anything."

"I can only verify that he was murdered (asphyxiated actually) the day after he told me he'd sent the manuscript off to publishers in New York. Told me that it was full of explosive stuff, and he'd make the big time with it. He'd also told people who frequent the Lobster Pot bar and restaurant he was going to make a killing."

"So, you're saying he found out something sinister about Martinet Senior."

"I am saying that. He was very confident that it would go off like a bomb in New York (not literally)."

"Arnold Martinet is one of the most respected people in Berg City. Shit, that exhibition of his photographs got burned out before we got around to publishing the review. It's scheduled for this weekend's magazine. Is that a coincidence?"

"Someone didn't want those photos seen, I guess. If you took photographs of the exhibition, those are the only ones left, Jonas."

"I knew I was right to call you."

"Find the old man. He's scared to go home because he thinks his apartment is being watched. I can confirm that it was vandalized recently. You might find him in Denny's on Fifth. Look for a guy with a permanent beanie on his head."

"What's in the book, Delaney? That explosive biography. What's in it?"

Delaney smiled turning to wink at Asha. "Wolfie hinted at the truth behind the grassy knoll Jonas, but he might have been pulling my wire."

Jonas laughed. "Fuck, that would be something. How old was Martinet back in '63."

"About twenty and already a crack shot and medal winner. Nocton Scimitars, look them up."

"It gets better. And your role now?"

"We're over and out, Jonas. I found the writer; I found the father. I'm out of the picture, we're on our way to the Bahamas for Christmas."

"They'll let you in?"

"Ha-ha. I really don't know more than this."

"Delaney you always know more that you're telling me."

"Track down that manuscript. Talk to Martinet Senior or call the FBI. I'm in the wind."

"I'll just follow the trail of bodies, Delaney."

"Merry Christmas, Jonas."

"Here's hoping you don't get what you deserve, Delaney."

"As long as it isn't socks. Bye."

Asha looked at him with bemusement as he rejoined the road. "Explosive manuscript in New York?"

Delaney glanced at her and smiled. "Just messing with them. Send the FBI off in a different direction. They'll go ape-shit and maybe, just maybe, they'll forget about us."

"In your dreams. They're hard to shake off."

"But think of the great Christmas they'll have in the Bahamas looking for us."

Asha laughed. "You are way more devious than I give you credit for."

"Merely trying to keep us safe."

"How long have you known Jonas?"

"We used to compete against each other in the junior races. He was a great sailor but lacked the killer instinct, didn't take risks."

"And you did?"

Delaney shrugged. "I was a different person then. Needed to keep proving myself."

"You think I'll change when I'm forty?"

"We're all changing day by day, Ash. Little decisions, big ones, everyone evolves."

"Martinet Senior isn't going to like what you've just done to him."

"No, but a little media attention will cause a reaction. If he's smart, he'll disappear to his Florida home."

"You think he'll get away with what's he's done?"

"The explosive manuscript will blow up in his face. Now everyone will want to know his secrets and start digging. And then there will the other side trying to keep a lid on it."

"Including us, it seems."

"We're keeping our cards close to our chest, Ash. Let's see what happens after Jonas publishes. For now, I'd rather no one knows what we know."

"I really hope he mentions the grassy knoll." Asha said, unable to hide a smile.

Delaney grinned. "He won't be able to resist."

CHAPTER NINETEEN

ZUKI

Zuki greeted Asha with a scream of joy and whisked her off to the other side of the hotel before Delaney had even got the cases out of the car. Rufus disappeared too, scampering down the steps to the beach.

"Thanks for the help, guys." Delaney muttered to himself. He dragged everything inside whilst the girl on the front desk found him a key.

"You're a day early but the room is ready for you. You only want the one room? I thought there was..."

"Kid's gone to grandparents. We're temporarily free."

The girl smiled as if she cared about this and told him how to get to his room. "Sorry we don't have anyone to help with the bags. The elevator's working again. Will you be eating in the restaurant tonight?"

"I hope so."

"Karaoke at nine. We have a lot of Korean guests tonight."

Delaney's heart sank. "We'll be out of there by nine for sure."

He took the bags upstairs and dumped them in a decent sized room with a separate seating nook and balcony. He dug out the dog's bowl and filled it with water. He wondered about the sound proofing – karaoke could be painful.

He needed to stretch his legs on the beach and check on Rufus. He glanced out of the windows and appreciated they had a great view of the ocean. He hadn't checked the room rate and wasn't sure if they were guests or paying guests, but he'd face that when it came to it. He figured he had a lot to think about and this was a perfect place to do it.

Asha was staring at Zuki thinking she looked so well and happy. Zuki was explaining about surfboarding and the 'community' that lived for the waves. "I hate the cold but love the adrenaline. I was out there at least three times a week in summer."

"You're looking so fit, and your skin is glowing."

"You're looking thin and stressed. Are you still swimming?" Zuki asked.

"Twice a week. Maria is faster than me now. I never hear the end of it."

"But you didn't bring her?"

"She's staying with Bunty for Christmas. She loves it there."

Zuki winced. "Watch out Ash, she's going to steal that place from under your nose. Bet she has Bunty wrapped around her fingers."

Asha had to admit that was true. "Wait till Mr B gets to see her having one of her tantrums."

"I thought she'd got passed that."

Asha shrugged. "She's almost fifteen. Everything is fine as long as she gets her own way."

Zuki smiled. "God, fifteen Ash. I dread to think about how badly I behaved."

Asha laughed. "Me too. Have you found anyone up here? I kind of expect there's a trail of broken hearts out there on the waves."

Zuki tilted her head and looked away for a moment. "I thought there might be someone but ..."

"But?"

"It didn't work out. I'm too demanding apparently."

"You demanding?" Asha mocked. "I'm shocked."

"Everyone says they love an independent woman until they actually meet one. But hey, so much has happened in the last month I have to tell you everything."

Asha threw a stone towards a rock pool, briefly catching sight of Rufus running hell for leather towards Delaney walking on the far side of the beach.

"Are you happy here?" Asha asked. "I think I would be."

Zuki stood up and stretched her arms, the last of the day's sunlight illuminating her face. Asha still felt jealous of her exquisite beauty. She still looked five years younger than she was and probably always would.

"Grandma is selling The Marine."

Asha looked shocked. "Noooo! I thought this was your forever home. What now?"

Zuki grinned. "Turns out I am not very good at hospitality. Shit I'd turn away at least half the morons who check in here if I could. Guests are incredibly demanding, dishonest, filthy, and stupid. I had never quite appreciated this until I got to sit at the front desk or be the housekeeper. My grandmother is a saint for putting up with what happens in the rooms. The honeymoon suite is the worst. It's gross what people do to each other."

"Didn't she send you on a hospitality course last year?"

"She did. It didn't make it any easier. They have smiling classes; can you believe it? I had to practice smiling at obnoxious people on Zoom. It felt like indoctrination. No matter what shit people tell you, you have to keep smiling. I think I got a D, might have been an F."

Asha felt for her. Zuki was not the kind of person who'd smile if she didn't want to.

"Anyway, just when I thought I was going to kill the next guest who complained about the food, the beds, the carpets, the elevator, or the fact that the lighthouse flashes at night or that the ocean was the wrong temperature – Grandma got an offer she couldn't refuse. Ten million."

"Wow, I can see she'd be tempted. She has to want to retire."

"She felt so guilty accepting the offer because she thought I'd want to take it over."

Asha nodded. She'd hoped for that herself.

"Anyway, I encouraged her to take the offer and she's setting up a trust fund for me and paying for me to do my MS in Artificial Intelligence – at Columbia. I'm finally going to be doing what I always wanted, Ash."

"Jeez, New York. Congratulations, I think. Full time?"

"It's two years but I've already lined up a part-time role at a think tank that needs algorithm analysis. I'm working for them already. Zoom calls with geeks who can barely articulate a sentence is like sheer craziness. I love it. They don't even notice when I'm being sarcastic."

"You'll miss the surfing." Asha said watching kids in the wetsuits catching the last waves before the light faded.

Zuki leaned forward and hugged Asha. "Yeah, but not the cold. I hear there are waves at Rockaway. I've got a line on an apartment one block from the beach. Will you come and visit me?"

"When will all this happen?"

"The new people take over on January the 2nd. So, I intend to have a great Christmas with you and the family, and I guess Delaney too. You still love him?"

Asha nodded. "Of course. I'm very committed."

"And he's treating you right?"

"Always. Although I worry. We don't make much money and there's always someone who wants to kill him or me or both. We're hiding out right now."

Zuki stared at her with surprise. "Seriously?"

Asha nodded. "You think the investigation will just be a simple search and find job and bang, someone is killed, and people are following you. It's interesting but sometimes scary. We bought an old boathouse down by the harbor to convert into our offices. But I'm strongly hinting at turning it into a coffee shop. I think we'd make more money, and it would be a lot safer."

Zuki stroked her arm. "But you'd be dealing with the assholes who want six different kind of alternate milks, ten kinds of coffee blends, and they'll block the toilets. People *love* blocking toilets. We have a plumber on speed dial. I never knew how much I hated people until I started to run a hotel. Believe me, a coffee shop isn't as easy as you think. Besides AI is going to replace baristas. No one stands a chance against the march of the machine."

Asha laughed. "Add doom music to taste. I need to walk Zukes, been in the car for hours. You coming? You haven't said hello to Delaney yet."

Zuki checked her Apple watch. "I'm on duty. See you for dinner at seven. You can still eat fish, right? Delivered fresh every day here."

Asha hugged Zuki back. "I'm very happy for you, Zukes. We're trying to be strict veggie, but we can still eat fish, especially if Maria isn't policing us."

Zuki kissed her and dashed away up the steps towards the hotel. Asha watched her go feeling oddly sad that Zuki was finally getting to do what she always wanted to do. She walked down the steps to the beach, the wind in her hair, wondering if running a coffee shop could be as bad as Zuki said it was.

Rufus brought Delaney a stick to throw and he tossed it along the beach. The dog bounded after it, seemingly oblivious to the bitter cold wind.

His phone rang. He didn't recognize the number but answered anyway.

"Mr Delaney? Sheriff Enzo, Bridgetown. I'm leading the Cold Rock investigation."

"Good evening, Sheriff."

"This is a follow up call; I believe you spoke with a deputy in Porcupine Ridge before."

"Yes sir, I did. How can I help you."

"You were first on the scene that morning, correct?"

"Yes."

"You reported that the driver of the vehicle was dead at the wheel."

"Correct. I managed to scrape some snow away from a window and saw the white hair, but the whole area was filled with exhaust fumes. The engine must have been running for a while. I had to back off."

"So, you didn't see the second occupant of the vehicle?"

"No sir, but I've since learned that Sigurdsson was in there."

"You knew this person?"

"Only briefly Sheriff. I was hired to find him to retrieve a manuscript he was supposed to have written."

"And did you?"

"No. Sigurdsson claimed to have sent it off to a publisher in New York. He also wiped his laptop after that, which I verified."

"I can place you at the campsite until 10.15pm. Witnesses saw you leave with a dog. In what state was Sigurdsson when you left?"

"Not good. He'd drunk the better half of a bottle of whisky. I made him drink some coffee, but he puked it all up. He was definitely alive when I left."

"Yeah, he received two more visitors that night. Can you confirm where you went after the campsite?"

"The Lobster Pot. I spent the night there. They should verify that."

Delaney could hear the Sheriff going through his notes. "Yeah, that's confirmed. Do you have any ideas as to why the assailant Yeaver would have bound and gagged Sigurdsson and stolen his Motorhome? It puzzled us she would abandon her own much newer vehicle for his."

"Sigurdsson claimed that he was being watched. I dismissed this as paranoia I'm afraid. I even walked by the assailant on the way to my vehicle. It simply didn't occur to me that she was the one watching him."

"This book Sigurdsson was writing. What was it about?"

Rufus returned and dropped his stick at his feet. Delaney threw it again.

"A biography of Arnold Martinet, the photographer and philanthropist. I imagine it would be the dullest book ever written, Sheriff."

"And this Arnold Martinet is listed as missing I understand."

"Not anymore. He voluntarily checked out of Summertree nursing home. I located him at a Berg City Denny's on 5th Avenue. I imagine he's now at home in his apartment."

"You actually saw him?" Delaney could hear the doubt in the Sheriff's voice.

"Yes sir. Spoke with him very briefly. He was looking for his son who is currently in hospital with pneumonia."

"You seem very well informed, Mr Delaney."

"I was hired to do a job and that job is now completed."

"And you have no prior knowledge of the woman, Yeaver who abducted Sigurdsson."

"None. If I was to speculate, it might have been a lovers' tiff gone wrong or a dispute about money, but I don't think we shall ever know."

"Ms Yeaver was an ex-offender. An embezzler."

"Interesting. So perhaps she knew Sigurdsson had been paid $10 grand in cash. Several people in the Lobster Pot were surprised when I mentioned he had money. Robbery might well have been the motive. A shake-down gone wrong."

The Sheriff paused again. "We found a large sum of cash hidden in the Motorhome."

"You have your motive, Sheriff. All the people wintering in Cold Rock are broke. Maybe they thought they could frighten Sigurdsson into revealing where it was."

"Makes sense, little else does. Thank you for your cooperation. I may need to call you again."

"Happy to assist, Sheriff."

"Erm, before I go. That manuscript? Any ideas about which publisher he might have sent it to?"

Rufus returned and Delaney threw the stick again.

"My guess it will be sitting in someone's spam folder for two years before they delete it. Sigurdsson wasn't exactly a popular author."

"Thank you."

Delaney pocketed his phone and smiled as Asha was walking towards him along the beach. Rufus dashed towards her with his stick.

"Don't let him shake," Delaney warned her. He shook.

Asha knelt down and rubbed Rufus's head. "It's way too cold for him. Let's get inside, Delaney. I think I need a hot shower, a drink, and a hug."

Delaney hugged her and kissed her, frowning when he noticed her eyes were wet.

"What's happened?"

"Zuki's going to New York to study for her masters. She's so happy about it but I dunno, it made me feel so sad. She's drifting away from me so fast. Stupid tears. Sorry."

Delaney kissed her again and wrapped his arms around her. "You'll always be best friends, Ash. Believe me. You two are connected. There'll be times when she needs you again and you'll need her. Plus, you'll have excuses to visit New York and I'll be all sad instead of you." He grinned.

Rufus dropped the stick on his shoes to remind them he was still there.

Asha looked up into Delaney's eyes a moment, then gave him a sly smile. "I think you owe me some bedtime, Mr Delaney. I'm in serious need of some affection."

Delaney nuzzled her then grabbed her hand. "Let's go. Rufus? Leave it. We're going in."

Asha rolled off Delaney and savored the moment, wiping sweat from his chest. She was smiling again. They stared at each other without words. Delaney kissed the tip of her nose and grinned. Neither one of them wanted to break the silence. Asha glanced down at Rufus snoring on the floor, his legs twitching. She felt reinvigorated and could barely stop smiling.

"That felt different," she said softly, licking sweat from his neck.

Delaney studied her brown eyes, aware that he absolutely loved this woman. "I know, felt so intense."

Asha closed her eyes as his fingers traced her warm body. "I felt like I'd gone to someplace else. Sort of out of body thing."

"I know I watched you go. It was beautiful."

Delaney's watch pinged and he groaned. "Shit, we have ten minutes to get down to the bar."

Asha turned away and quickly headed to the bathroom. "I get to shower first."

Delaney watched her turn the water on standing on her toes. He never tired of looking at her beautifully toned body.

"I think there must be something in the air here. Maybe that's why so many couples come here to cheat on their partners."

Asha glanced back at him. "You would think about that."

"Blame Zuki for that piece of information."

Asha stepped into the shower. "Zuki asked if we were going to have kids."

Delaney was surprised. It wasn't a topic Asha usually brought up. "What did you say?"

"Same as ever. We've got Rufus and Maria. I reminded her that we both took an oath not to have kids when we were eighteen. A solemn oath."

Delaney got out of bed and pulled the duvet back to air it. "You still feel that way?"

Asha was shampooing her hair. "Will you kill me if I said yes. I still don't want kids."

Delaney joined her in the shower as she rinsed her hair. He kissed her as steaming hot water coursed over their bodies. "I think I'm too selfish to want to share you with anyone else." He said, backing off and soaping down.

Asha smiled at him, wrinkling her nose. "I reserve the right to change my mind of course. But I want us to stay intense, stay like this. I actually love you Delaney. I don't want it to change."

"Me neither. Turn around, I'll wash your back."

"Zuki's bringing her grandfather over for dinner. She wants you to meet him."

"Doesn't he have Alzheimer's or something?"

"Yes, but he's sweet, lives in the past mostly. She's very proud of her grandparents. And it's you who helped her find them. She's never going to forget that."

Asha left the shower before him. Delaney called after her.

"There's an early Christmas present for you on top of my case."

Asha was surprised and quickly looked around the room for his case. A small box lay there wrapped in festive paper with a skating penguins design. "Love the wrapping paper. Remind me again about the penguins in the manger story."

Delaney laughed as he turned off the shower.

Asha removed the wrapping and took out a bottle of Guerlain Shalimar and smiled. This is why she loved him. A casual remark made weeks before about scent and he'd remembered. She dabbed some on her neck and breasts sparingly. The scent quickly filled the room.

"Shalimar?" Zuki asked when they met and hugged in the bar. "You get a raise?"

"Early Christmas present," Asha confessed.

"You look different. Happy? What happened to that frazzled girl who got out of the car earlier."

Asha kissed Zuki. "It's so good to see you, Zukes. I miss you every day."

"Likewise. I've missed talking to you. The number of times I've wanted to call and just scream about all my problems."

"Why didn't you?"

"Because I know you'll listen and give good advice and I'll completely ignore it and then get upset I didn't listen to you."

Asha took her hand and squeezed it. "Won't you miss all this?"

"I'll miss the ocean, the weather, and my grandparents but I'm not leaving forever. They'll still be here when I can't stand Manhattan anymore."

Zuki's grandparents arrived. Andrea Lowe leading her smartly dressed husband who make his way carefully to a seat against the wall. His white hair was even whiter, but he was still a handsome man. Mr Lowe looked at Zuki with surprise. "Esme, you're here."

"It's Zuki," Andrea pointed out to him. "Your granddaughter."

A vague look of recognition was registered but Zuki already knew that in his eyes, she'd always be her mother, Esme.

Delaney returned from the bar having selected a bottle of wine for dinner. He pointed to all the photographs on the walls – every celebrity that had ever stayed at the hotel, with or without their legal partners.

"Dean Martin was here? Is that Ted Kennedy?"

All the photos were signed, some with messages about how much they loved The Marine.

Andrea smiled. My husband took all the photographs. There's Norman Mailer with Anita someone, I can't recall. All the main acts who stayed here for Jazz Week. That's Darius and Catherine. And this is Stephen. He came here twice."

"Sondheim?" Delaney asked.

"All the celebrities came here, Mr Delaney. We're very discreet about who they come with."

Zuki took her grandmother by the arm. "They all have to come down next week. The new owners are going to rip everything out and make it ultra-modern. They want a younger crowd."

"What will you do with the photos?" Delaney asked.

Andrea shrugged. "No one remembers these people anymore. They're all history."

"You could sell them on eBay," Asha suggested. "I bet someone will pay for a photo of..." she glanced at the wall. "I actually don't know who that is."

"Lauren Bacall," Mr Lowe told them. "She was promoting her book."

Delaney was impressed. "Asha's right. Someone will pay. Don't throw them out Mrs Lowe. Nostalgia is big business."

Zuki was less impressed. "Who was this, Grandpa?"

He stood up to look more carefully. "He was Governor of New York. I can't remember the name. He came here with his mistress. A lovely Puerto Rican dancer. I remember that."

Delaney smiled. It was good to see the old man was engaged.

"And this man Eli ran the Jazz Week. Lovely man. But it died with him. No one was prepared to put in the work to get people here and put up with all their nonsense," Andrea Lowe remarked. "I'm afraid no one will remember him after we're gone. Or us. Mr Lowe's father was the first African American hotel owner here and now he's the last."

"I'm surprised you didn't get bought out earlier, Mrs Lowe. This is an amazing location on the bay."

"Mr Lowe senior was adamant that it should never be sold. He was ex-GI. Won medals in Korea. This place has grown so much since even I came to live here. It needs new investment. It's hard running a hotel, as Zuki found out."

"It was like jumping off a cliff," Zuki remarked. "My grandmother is a saint for putting up with it all."

Delaney was about to suggest they go in to eat when he noticed another photo on the wall. He reacted with surprise. Four familiar faces wearing sporting clothes and proudly holding up their rifles.

"Is that...?" Asha began staring with surprise.

"The Nocton Scimitars," Delaney answered. "1973."

"Olympic shooters," Mr Lowe recalled. "My father still ran this place then and he invited them to the annual Skeet weekend." He pointed to one of the group. "This one came every year after that."

Andrea smiled. "My husband took over the running of the hotel from his father in 1981. He remembers all the guests up until about 2010."

"Arnold Martinet liked to fish," Mr Lowe declared pointing at the photo. "We'd go out looking for Tuna or Swordfish."

Delaney was confused. "You pointed to this man, right?"

Mr Lowe frowned. "No. The second one in the sweatshirt is Mr Martinet. He was always very nice to me."

Delaney glanced at Asha with raised eyebrows. Mr Lowe had definitely pointed to Gus Zolloff. "Remember how Mr B said Martinet was short and tubby the first time he met him and then tall and thin the second?"

Asha nodded. "So, who died? I remember Zolloff died in 1975."

Delaney smiled at Mr Lowe. "Mr Martinet was tall and thin, yes? When you knew him."

"Yes, very fit man. Did exercises on the terrace every morning. Everyone liked him."

Asha knew Delaney wanted to discuss this, but she didn't want to spoil the evening.

"We can discuss this later, Delaney."

Zuki finally figured it out. "This is your client?"

"His son is our client. I was supposed to look for his father who went missing from the care facility." Delaney told her.

"Care facility? You guys lead such exciting lives," Zuki mocked.

"Can I take this photo, Mrs Lowe? And are there any more of Mr Martinet?" Zolloff had filled out some since the early days, but this was definitely the same man who'd attacked him in the hospital elevator.

Mr Lowe was pleased he was showing interest in his photos. "There's two more. Give me a moment."

Mrs Lowe looked on anxiously as Mr Lowe slowly paced up and down the walls looking at all the faces he recalled with clarity. "I haven't seen him so animated in a while."

"All the more reason to hang on to the photos, Mrs Lowe. They're his memories after all."

She nodded, trying to think where she'd put them all.

Asha was at Mr Lowe's side. "I think this is one. 1991. Look it's him holding up a Blue Marlin."

Delaney was impressed Asha knew the name of the fish. She turned to him with a smile. "Dad goes game fishing. He used to drag me with him."

Mr Lowe handed her the photograph with another. "Mr Martinet is still alive?"

Asha nodded. "He's old now but still very much alive."

"Please tell him Mr Lowe sends his regards."

"I will. I most certainly will." Asha reassured him.

"Let's go eat." Mrs Lowe suggested. "By chance we have fresh swordfish on the menu if you like."

Zuki clutched Asha's spare hand and led her towards the dining room. "I get how you two work now. I saw that spark of electricity between you when he saw the photo."

Asha leaned her head onto Zuki. "We click. Remind me to tell you the real story about Mr Martinet after supper. I can't believe he was a regular customer here, but it makes sense, this is a great place to go fishing."

"Very generous man," Mr Lowe was saying as he followed them towards the dining room. "He saved a life once. Saw someone was drowning and swam out to them in a very rough sea."

Mrs Lowe took her husband's arm and smiled at him. "It's nice to have you back, Mr Lowe."

CHAPTER TWENTY

Zolloff

Zuki was scouring the web for anything on Gus Zolloff. Asha lay on Zuki's bed staring out the window at the full moon rising.

She'd just spent an hour catching Zuki up on the Martinet case. The more Asha talked, the more absurd the whole escapade seemed.

"You're right, someone has scrubbed the web of photos of either of them. I can't believe people didn't notice the body switch. It's not as if they vaguely looked alike. They had no resemblance."

"I know. But that's what happened." Asha told her. "Remember how upset you were when boys used to confuse us?"

"I was?"

"Very. Your grandfather is African American, my father is Indian. It shouldn't be confusing at all but ..."

"But we're both mixed." Zuki said.

"Blended, my dad would tell me."

"Yeah, I remember. Jeez we put up with a lot of shit. Wouldn't happen now I guess." Zuki said. "Only it does. I know it does."

Zuki stared at some links on her screen. "You said Zolloff had no living relatives. What about Martinet? His family must have noticed the change. How many hitmen get to live to eighty I wonder. Must be unusual."

"Let alone become a philanthropist and semi-famous photographer. You sort of have to admire his chutzpah."

"How many people did he kill?" Zuki asked.

"I think I lost count at thirty. I couldn't look at it anymore. The moon is huge tonight." Asha remarked. "The sky is so clear here. I think it's so sad they're going to rip everything out. This place is so old school. It's cute. I hate large anonymous hotels."

"They might even demolish it. It's the location they wanted, and we've got gardens either side. It a huge lot." Zuki was searching digitized newspapers in New York State, looking for anything that would bring up Gus Zolloff's name. "You said he studied at Cornell?"

"One of the colleges there. It was great to see your grandfather come alive at dinner. He told me a story about what people used to get up to in Jazz Week. It sounded very raunchy."

"I suspect my grandfather got up to a lot of naughty things himself back then. He was a cool dude and very good looking. My grandmother is almost twenty years younger than him."

Asha smiled. "Almost the same between Delaney and me."

"Well don't forget to ditch him before he gets dementia, babe."

Asha pulled a face. "Don't be mean about him. It might be me who gets to go crazy, Zukes. I'd expect him to look after me."

"Really?"

"Yeah. I love him. I love the way he looks at me. He's very caring."

Zuki shrugged. "Ok. I guess my grandparents are happy so go for it."

Asha wondered what time it was and whether she should go back to Delaney's room. He'd taken Rufus for his night walk about an hour ago. It was too cold to stay out so long.

"Grandpa Lowe made a real effort tonight," Zuki remarked. "Even if he can never remember my name."

"Well, you do look exactly like your mother. One of the Korean women asked me if you were a TV star."

Zuki laughed. "TV star? Not Hollywood? I'm gutted Ash."

"I could see you in a TV series. The lone cop versus the corrupt machine or, maybe the boss of major fashion magazine making everyone miserable."

Zuki nodded. "Yeah, that's my role, for sure. Get to work bitches, bring me the best evil gossip or you're fired." She turned to glance at Asha and grinned. "It's good to see you, Ash. Promise you'll come and see me in New York?"

"Of course. There's talk of them building a fast train to connect with Boston and maybe all the way to Manhattan."

"In your dreams, Ash. This isn't Europe or China. No one invests in trains."

"They should. By law. It's the only way to save the planet."

"Not going anywhere at all will save the planet. I don't see that catching on either."

She turned back to her screen and did a double-take. "Ah ha. Gus Zolloff is mentioned at last."

Asha sat up on the bed. "What you got?"

"Olympic shooter meets untimely death in tragic auto accident. Rear seat passenger Arnold Martinet survives with minor injuries. It is believed Zolloff swerved to avoid a deer and collided with a tree. The Olympic Bronze winner was returning from the funeral of his father Borysko Zolloff. The last surviving Zolloff. Arnold Martinet is quoted as saying 'America lost a great patriot and one of the best riflemen in the world. He will be missed by all his friends.'"

Asha frowned. "That's it?"

"No photos. Small notice in the Rochester Gazette. I nearly got wiped out by a deer once. They come out of nowhere, no idea of road sense."

"Shit, I remember. You were shaken up for days. But I still don't get why Zolloff and Martinet swapped names."

Zuki forwarded the link to Asha's email and shut down her laptop. "I'm exhausted. I'm back on duty at seven tomorrow. I guess Zolloff must have had a good reason to swap. He must have calculated that giving up his identity to become his best friend was worth it."

Asha stood up. "Maybe he had a good reason to be dead. Walk away from debts maybe?" She tilted her head from side to side until the bones clicked.

"Or he was being pressured by Russians to give up information. He was from the Ukraine which was still part of Russia back then."

"Makes sense to me. Becoming Martinet, he escapes being Zolloff. Who also didn't seem to have any living relatives. What are the chances of that?"

"High for his generation I guess," Zuki remarked. "Wars, people didn't live so long as they do now."

"It's weird," Asha declared. "What about his employers? They must have seen a difference in him."

"Or didn't know. Suppose they never met. He's an assassin. They'd want to keep a distance from him."

Asha nodded. "Delaney said he was likely to get his instructions via a dead drop someplace or a cut out. They would have to keep a distance from him and as long as he does the job they don't care. The money would have been wired to an account in the Caymans or Panama. Zolloff just took it all over. Started this new life in a new place, no one was the wiser."

"You're missing something. No idea what, but something." Zuki said.

"I should go," Asha said. "You were going to tell me about Mikel."

Zuki rolled her eyes. "It's a stupid story, Ash."

"But you were in love with him."

Zuki shrugged. "Thought I was. Mikel came to stay at the hotel. Booked a month. Paid up front. It was one of those explosions, y'know. I saw him and wanted him, and it seemed he couldn't get enough of me. I really thought he was 'the one' but was dreading him leaving and knew I couldn't walk away from Grandma. She came to rely on me a lot by then. I was acting a bit crazy – never had so much consistent good sex in years. Mikel was funny, smart, fantastic in bed and then quite by accident I discovered he was hiding out from some drug dealers he'd scammed."

Ash winced. She knew how much Zuki hated the drug scene and all the shit that went with it.

"I was waiting for him on the beach to go sailboarding and suddenly had a very bad feeling. He didn't show. He didn't call. A week went by when suddenly some cops showed up. They'd found him in his Ferrari with his head blown off. They came to see me because I'd called him like fifty times that week."

Ash came forward and hugged her. Zuki laid her head on her shoulder.

"You know I'd never go with someone who deals in drugs. I never suspected anything because he lived so clean. He had me completely fooled. I completely lost my sense of judgement. Grandma Lowe had warned me he was too good to be true. He didn't have a job for god's sake or even want one. I should have realized he was doing something illegal. He'd bullshitted me that he'd made some money selling NFTs and he was into crypto. I believed everything he said."

"Sorry, that's tough. You always did go in head first."

Zuki shook her head. "That was you, remember. I was always the skeptic."

"And now you're going to start a new life again in New York. You'll be a trust fund baby."

Zuki protested. "I know. I'm going to be exactly the kind of person I hate. If I start to show signs of grandeur or arrogance, take me out back and shoot me."

Asha shook her head. "I'll assume you're acting entirely normal."

Zuki stuck her tongue out. "You know what I mean."

"I'm sorry about the guy. You must have been devastated."

Zuki shrugged. "Disappointed, depressed, felt stupid. Then Grandma sat me down and told me to think about the month I was happy and so much easier to live with."

Asha laughed. "Yeah, you were always like that when you met someone you liked."

"Why can't I be like that when I'm on my own?"

Asha kissed her. "Because we're all like that. I'm in a nice safe bubble with Delaney, except when Maria has a strop or Rufus throws up in the kitchen. I feel secure. The sex is good and he's affectionate. I always craved that. Someone who'd remember to hug me when I'm down. But never bring me down."

"Sweet and sour, Grandpa Lowe says. Life is all sweet and sour."

"True."

"What are you going to do about Martinet or Zolloff?" Zuki asked.

Asha let her go and glanced out of the window at the moon again. "Delaney set a false trail to get people interested in investigating him. When enough people are convinced that he should be investigated we have a shitload of evidence to show them."

"Why not hand it over now?"

Asha shook her head. "It might disappear. There's a lot of people in Washington who wouldn't want people to know what actually went down."

"Which makes you guys very vulnerable."

"And you know nothing, Zukes. Don't even think about it."

Zuki nodded. "For the record, I'm not totally against you opening up a coffee shop. It's got to be a whole lot safer than this job."

Asha wrinkled her nose. "I don't know, at least we don't have to unblock toilets."

"Yet." Zuki told her, then laughed. "Come on, I have to get some sleep. You need to get back to your boyfriend. I only hope he brought Delaney back with him."

Asha pouted, then laughed. "Rufus is pretty amazing. I adore him."

"Asha is a dog person now. Who would have thought it."

Asha blew her a kiss and left Zuki to head to her bathroom.

CHAPTER TWENTY-ONE

Headcase

Delaney wasn't in the bedroom. Nor was Rufus. Asha's instincts kicked in. She grabbed her coat and ran down the stairs to the ground floor. There were only a few well-oiled Koreans left in the bar singing karaoke. The bartender told her hadn't seen Delaney or a dog.

Asha seriously doubted he was still walking on the beach. It was freezing out there.

She headed down there anyway, growing seriously worried. She shouted out Delaney's name but crashing waves from the rising tide drowned out her voice. She ran out onto the beach, heart in mouth. Something bad must have happened. Where was Rufus?

"Rufus?" She screamed. Nothing.

She dug out her phone and called Zuki.

"I'm sorry Zukes if you're asleep but Delaney's missing."

"I'm not asleep. Missing? Didn't he go walk the dog?"

"That was two hours ago. It's totally freezing out here. I'm on the beach, the tides coming in. I just know something's wrong."

"I'll be there asap."

The full moon gave her enough light to search from one end of the beach to the other. She pulled up her hoodie and shivered as she ran to the waterline, praying all the time that Delaney wasn't in the water or ...

She saw a flashlight moving fast down the hotel steps.

"Zukes?"

Zuki appeared wearing a snow jacket over her pj's. "Any sign of him?"

"No."

"Any reason you should be worried, Ash? Something you haven't told me?"

"Delaney removed the trackers from his car before we came. No one can possibly know we're here."

"Zolloff might know. The guy's a fucking serial killer, Ash."

Asha doubted it. She glimpsed movement near the jetty. Rufus struggling.

"Rufus?" They ran towards him, but he didn't move. A wave barreled in and swamped the dog, but he still didn't move as he desperately tried to stay afloat. Asha got there first and discovered a terrified Rufus was tied up to a metal stanchion.

"I'll get the dog free, keep looking for Delaney." Asha shouted as a freezing wave swamped her. She struggled with the rope as Rufus strained – anxious to be free.

"Why didn't you bark, Rufus? Where's Delaney? My god, you'll freeze to death in this ocean."

Zuki was up on the jetty, aiming her flashlight over the water, dreading finding him floating out there.

Rufus suddenly coughed up something and Asha snatched it up before it washed away. She stared at what looked a lot like someone's finger.

"Jeez, you do this? Who? Where?" She got the rope free at last and Rufus bounded away up towards the hotel. Asha could only follow, wrapping the finger in a tissue in case it was Delaney's, but she couldn't believe he'd bite his master.

"Zukes, follow Rufus. Hotel gardens."

"On it. Rufus?" She sprinted towards the trees.

Asha waded out of the water, she'd cut her hand on the rope and shivered. She was soaked right through. She began to run towards the hotel.

"Rufus?" Zuki shouted again. She couldn't see him but heard him bark once. She headed to the gardens on the south side of the hotel. "Delaney? Where are you?"

Rufus was waiting for her at the top of the steps and ran off again to show her where to go. Zuki followed, careful not to trip on any tree roots, calling back to Asha to follow her.

"Delaney?" She yelled. "Where are you?"

Zuki found him slumped by the base of a fir tree. She turned her flashlight back towards Asha. "Over here. He's here."

Scared Delaney was already dead she rolled him over and saw he'd been struck on the head. Asha arrived, knelt down and cradled Delaney's head. "Is he breathing, Zukes?"

"He's bleeding." Zuki said, shining the light on his wound. "It's swelling."

"He's freezing. We need to get him inside. Where's his coat?"

Asha began to vigorously rub him to warm him up. Zuki did likewise to his legs.

"We need to carry him, he can't stay here, the ground is frozen," Zuki said.

Delaney stirred as Rufus whined close by, ever anxious for Delaney.

"Can you speak?" Asha asked. Rufus came in close and licked Delaney's face.

"Back off, Rufus. Sit boy. You did good, real good." Zuki told him.

Asha gave Rufus a brief hug to calm him down as Delaney tried to sit up, clutching his sore head. He groaned, unable to open his eyes at that moment.

"What happened, Delaney? Speak to me. Do you need an ambulance? Should I be calling the cops? Can you stand?"

Delaney forced his eyes open and tried to focus. "There's three of you."

"One of us is a dog," Asha told him. "That's one nasty lump on your forehead."

"She hit me with a metal pole I think."

"She?"

"She dragged Rufus away."

Asha glanced at Zuki. She hadn't expected the assailant to be female.

"Whoever it was tried to drown Rufus. Tied him up by the jetty so the tide would swamp him. Shit, I feel so guilty for not looking for you earlier."

"You think you can walk, Delaney?" Zuki asked

Delaney grabbed her arm and tried to haul himself up. "Yeah. Get me inside, I'm freezing. Where's my coat?"

"She took your coat?"

"She's crazy. Get me inside. Ow." He clutched his thigh, felt a lump there and eventually pulled out his car keys. "Digging in. She must have thought the coat had my keys in it."

Zuki got him standing. "You are one lucky guy, Delaney. Come on. Let's go"

Asha took the other side and he put his arms around both their shoulders.

"World's going around. Sorry guys. I'm not quite..."

"It's OK. Concentrate on one foot in front of the other." Zuki told him.

"She just showed up on the beach and attacked me. No fucking warning."

"She, she, she? Who is she?" Asha asked.

"The bitch who tried to get into our house, remember?"

"The Zara coat girl? The one who stalked us at Harry's?"

Delaney leaned heavily on them both as they walked towards the hotel. "She kept asking what did I know, what did I know? Where is he?"

Rufus led the way, constantly looking back at them to make sure they were following.

"I don't get it. How did she know we were here? Didn't you get the tracker removed?" Asha was asking.

Delaney had no answer for that. He concentrated on staying upright. "She's not FBI."

"I figured that. She has to be bleeding badly."

"Bleeding?"

"Rufus bit her pinkie off."

Delaney looked at Rufus with pride. "Good dog. Should have taken her whole fucking hand off."

"She'll need medical attention. We need to call the Sheriff's office. She must still be around."

"Just get me inside. I need some ice."

They helped him up the steps. Asha was confused and angry. Who the hell was this woman and what did she want?

"He'll need medical attention," Zuki was saying. "He's been concussed, Ash. The Medical Centre won't open until 7am tomorrow."

"I don't need a doctor. I need to lie down, get some ice on my head."

"You will see a doctor tomorrow," Asha told him firmly. "You might have had a bleed."

Delaney didn't argue as they led him along the uneven path towards the hotel front entrance.

Delaney lay on a lounge sofa, pressing ice to his forehead as Zuki called the Sheriff's office. Asha returned with some blankets which she tucked in around him. She wrapped one around Rufus as well. He whined and shivered, and she had to hug him to warm him up.

"Sheriff? Zuki at The Marine. We've had an incident." She paused a moment. "Yes Frank, I know it's late, but this is urgent. Someone attacked one of our guests, tried to drown his dog and the attacker is out there injured – she'll be needing medical attention. The guest is alive but wounded. The woman who attacked him lost a finger in the attack."

Zuki looked over at Delaney. "He's sending the deputy."

The Sheriff came back on the phone. Zuki listened a moment.

"Frank, I know it's a full moon and you're busy with the crazies, but I have the finger in the fridge here. It's definitely a woman's finger. I've got that fingerprint app on my iPhone. I can send it to you as an image. If we're lucky she's in the database. No Frank, I'll send it to your personal email, you open it up just like photos of your dog that I know you like taking." She smiled at his reply. "Sending now, Frank. I'll fill you in on the backstory later."

Zuki disconnected and sent him the fingerprint she'd already taken. Then looked up and smiled at Asha.

"You have a fingerprint app?" Asha asked.

"We had a spate of robberies a few months ago. I tracked down the thief. One of the summer workers in the harbor. Got lucky he had a criminal record."

"You're amazing, Zuki," Delaney said. "But we probably shouldn't hold out much hope that my assailant has a criminal record."

"Frank hates full moons, especially the Cold Moon. All kinds of strange things happen around here."

"Sheriff drinks here?" Asha asked.

"Sheriff is dating the Chef, Cheryl. I keep telling him to marry her but he's not in a hurry. He's been divorced twice already."

Rufus lay his head on Delaney's chest. He rubbed his head. "I'm sorry you had to go through that, Rufus. You must have been terrified."

"Tied with a nylon rope to a support pillar. He would have drowned for sure if he didn't freeze first," Asha told him. "He kept that finger in his mouth all the time. Like he knew it would be important."

Delaney hugged his dog even closer. "I just can't work out who she is or how the hell she found us."

"You sure you removed the trackers on your vehicle?" Zuki asked. "Asha told me about them."

"There is no way she could have put a new tracker on my car. Unless she followed me to the hospital. That was the only stop I made before we left town."

He removed Rufus's leather collar. "This needs to dry." He examined it more closely then exhaled. "Shit, she's relentless this woman." He tossed the collar to Asha.

She examined it and her eyes widened. A tiny tracker was dangling next to his ID tag. That's why she'd broken into the grounds of Delaney's house. She must have known they'd release the dog. "I can't believe it."

Zuki examined it as well. "She's fucking smart. Brave too. Rufus must have resisted."

"I heard him yelp but he seemed ok when he returned, apart from some scratches." Asha remembered.

"Can't have a big range. She'd have to be close to keep tracking you." Zuki said. "You didn't see anyone sleeping in their car or ..."

Delaney shook his head. "I looked for cars I didn't recognize near our house at the time, but who the fuck is she?"

"Either way, she's going to find it hard to stop the bleeding," Zuki declared. "If she wanted answers, why did she knock you out? Why try to drown Rufus? It isn't going to make you any more cooperative."

"Is that deputy coming soon? I really need to get some sleep. My head is killing me."

"You'll definitely need to get a doctor to see it," Zuki said. "The swelling hasn't gone down yet."

"I'll be fine. Can you find me a couple of painkillers, Ash."

"Really? You hate painkillers."

"It's the pain is right behind my eyes."

Zuki came close and shone her phone flashlight into his eyes. "I can't see any bleeding but that doesn't mean you aren't bleeding internally. Like I said, we should get you to the medical center first thing. This is a very bad town to have a heart attack or accident in after eight pm. And guess when most heart attacks happen."

"I can guess," Delaney replied. He was frowning as he lay back on the sofa. "She has to be close by somewhere. Is there a late-night pharmacy? She'll need medical attention. She wouldn't be able to drive far."

"No. Nothing's open late. There's a number you can call for emergencies and you might get lucky, and someone turn up but that's more for when we're in season when the population triples. In winter it's like a ghost town. I kind of like it quiet."

Asha returned with some painkillers. "I saw a vehicle arriving. Might be the deputy."

Zuki nodded and went to look.

"The bartender says you should definitely get medical attention if you were unconscious. I've got two Advil's here. But I don't want you taking more until you've seen a doctor in the morning, Delaney."

He took the pills from her. "Yes nurse."

Zuki returned with the deputy. Asha stared at him with surprise. "Arran?"

Zuki struck her head. "Shit I totally forgot to mention you were the deputy, Arran."

Arran smiled at Asha. "Good to see you, Asha. You look great."

Asha turned to Delaney. "We were in the same year at college. Except, something happened to him in our final year."

Arran shrugged. "I broke my leg playing football. Then I caught measles in hospital. Never been so sick in all my life. How I graduated that year I have no idea."

"But you were going towards a business career. I remember you wanted to be a millionaire by twenty-five. My god Arran, you're taller than ever."

Arran smiled. "I'm just happy I made it to twenty-five, Ash. Covid changed everything. I wanted to get away from people and cities and they were desperately short of people in the Sheriff's department. I used to surf here, remember. No more cities for me."

Asha didn't remember but was happy to see him again.

Zuki affectionally punched the deputy's arm. "Arran is way overqualified for the Sheriff's office, but I reckon will make Sheriff the moment Frank retires." She pointed to

Delaney. "This is Delaney. Frank mention I sent a finger-print to him?"

"No. Frank's in bed with a cold. You won't get much use out of him right now."

Delaney glanced up at the deputy. "I don't suppose anyone has reported a finger missing?"

Arran laughed. "No. No reports. There was a car accident out by the Supermart, and a teen gone missing but I'm hoping she will return before we have to organize a search party. Not much else so far but it's nearly midnight and a full moon, so I expect to be busy later." He took out his notebook. "Ok, let me have it from the top."

"I'm thinking you've had a lot of head injuries. Did you play football?" The Doctor remarked. "When did you get these stitches?"

Delaney sat on the hard chair. He felt nauseous. Desperately needed a coffee. It had been tough getting up early. The Doctor was East Indian. Delaney wondered why he practiced medicine in such a small quiet fishing town.

"Two and half years ago. Crashed off a cliff. Forced off the road actually."

"And you're a private investigator?"

"Yeah, I guess."

"The assailant hit you with an iron bar. You're incredibly lucky it was only a glancing blow. Could have smashed your skull."

"It was metal stake in the ground. She must have grabbed it. I remember I heard a sound and turned."

"That movement may have saved you. People watch TV and see people being struck on the head all the time and watch them get up with no problem – but in reality, someone hitting you that hard, you're lucky you didn't bleed out, or freeze to death. You were investigating this individual?"

Delaney shook his head, immediately regretting it. "No. We're here on vacation. Completely random attack. She tried to drown my dog too. The deputy sheriff intimated it was something to do with the full moon last night."

The Doctor laughed. "That moon gets blamed for so many things. I have to say there has not been much werewolf activity since I got here."

He shone a bright light into the corner of Delaney's eyes. "Look up. Look down, to the left...now the right. No visible signs of bleeding. Your blood pressure is good, not great but acceptable, and your vision seems ok. You still have a headache?"

"Nausea. But I haven't eaten. My partner got me down here before breakfast."

"Hmmm, well if the nausea persists, or your vision alters, or you feel dizzy again, you call me. The x-ray is clear. I can see multiple historic scarring, but I think you were remarkably lucky, Mr Delaney. Do you know how long you were unconscious?"

"I can't say but at least twenty, twenty-five minutes. She stole my coat. Can't believe how cold I was when I came to."

"Might be the cold weather helped. Your body would have gone into shock. You should have a CT scan, but the nearest facility is in Berg City."

Delaney nodded. "If I get headaches, I'll definitely check in on that. I live in Berg City."

The Doctor went back to his desk. "No driving, and no alcohol for 48 hours. Promise me that, Mr Delaney."

"I will."

The Doctor smiled. "You might want to reconsider your career. I'm never met a private investigator before but judging by your x-ray, I'd say this is a high-risk profession."

Delaney stood up, gripping the chair to keep him steady. "It is, Doc. Do me a favor. If anyone reports in with a missing pinkie, will you report it to the Sheriff's office?"

"Pinkie?"

Delaney waggled his pinkie. "My dog bit hers off when she tied him to the jetty as the tide was coming in. Rufus doesn't take kindly to drowning."

The doctor looked most concerned. "It was a very high tide last night. The whole jetty would be underwater. Your dog was quite right, I think."

"Yeah. He must have been terrified."

The doctor thought about it. "It would be hard to staunch the blood from a lost finger. The assailant would need to seek medical attention."

"I'm hoping that's exactly what she will do." Delaney replied.

"They'll sort out payment at reception. I'll send it through now. You are staying at The Marine?"

"Yes."

"I am eating Christmas Day lunch there with my wife. I hope I will see you in one piece."

"Me too, doc."

Asha was walking towards the medical center with hot coffees in her hand as he emerged. She smiled and handed him the paper cup. He showed her the bill.

"$550. We are a long way out of pocket on this investigation, Ash."

"You're alive, Delaney. Even if you do look a bit pale."

Delaney bent over and kissed her. "I have to eat. Is Rufus ok?"

Asha smiled. "The chef treated him to fresh liver for breakfast. He's very happy."

Delaney shivered. "It's going to snow. Let's get back to the hotel."

"What did the doctor say?"

"I'll probably live. Not sure, but probably."

Asha wrinkled her nose. "You'd better. I have plans."

"This still involve a coffee shop?"

"It might," she grinned. "Although Zuke's trying her best to put me off."

"Actually, I'm suddenly beginning to warm to the idea," Delaney told her. "Doc wants me to have a CT scan. I said I would if the headaches get worse. Has to be done in Berg City anyway."

"You want to go home?" He could hear the disappointment in her voice.

"No. We're staying. We only go if I... y'know, get headaches."

Asha frowned. "I'll take you now if we have to. You had a major blow on your head. Your forehead is still swollen."

"The only thing I want to do is eat breakfast." He sipped his coffee and felt better for it as it went down. They began the walk back to the hotel.

"Two things," Asha began. "Arran found your coat down by the harbor. She must have ditched it when she went to her vehicle. It's fine."

"Second thing?"

"The Sheriff put the fingerprint on the system and got a hit. Emily Brookshire."

Delaney was nonplussed. "Brookshire?"

"She's an EFL teacher working in Berg City."

"With a criminal record?" Delaney asked.

"She used to work for Bunn and Deke – personal security. They all have to be fingerprinted."

"She's a bodyguard?"

"Was. Left them during Covid. She was an anti-vaxxer back in '21. Deep rabbit hole stuff. She's got a social media presence, lots of photos of her at protests. Might explain how come she hit you so hard and is pretty focused about tracking you."

"Ok, so why the fuck is she attacking me?"

"I'll explain over breakfast. By the way Maria called. I didn't mention you had been injured. Told her you had a cold. She's gone out riding with Mr B and all her exams are done. So, she's happy."

"As long as someone is happy," Delaney said.

Asha took his arm and leaned in on him. "I haven't quite got over last night yet. It really shook me up."

Delaney put an arm around her and squeezed. "I'm so lucky you and Zuki found me in time. Freezing to death wasn't on my Christmas list. We need to get something special for Zuki, but I have no idea what."

"She doesn't want anything. She's happy we're here for her. You think she'll be happy in New York?"

"For a while. She's so stunning, I can't believe she hasn't found someone to love her yet."

Asha shook her head. "Best not to bring that up. I'll explain later."

Delaney smiled. "Ok. What about Arran? What were the chances you knew the deputy sheriff in this little harbor town."

"I was so shocked, but it makes sense. He loves his job. How many people can you say that about."

"Ah yes, what happened to the Great Resignation, hey? Are they all happy they changed chairs when the music stopped?"

"Sounds like a cue for a musical," Asha laughed. "I'm so hungry. I hope they're still serving. It's nearly ten am."

"They'd better, otherwise we'll have to move to another hotel."

"Zuki would kill me."

Delaney was looking forward to lying down when the Deputy called.

"Shouldn't you be asleep?" Delaney asked him.

"Might say the same to you. A local woman dropped by the pharmacy this morning seeking advice on what to do if you chopped your finger off."

"Local woman?"

"I'm heading there now. Mrs Hargreaves is about seventy so it's not your assailant but could be she's acting for someone else. I am informed she doesn't have any fingers missing."

"Can I come with you?"

"If I find the assailant there, I'll bring her in. We take animal cruelty seriously here. There's CCTV on the jetty and it shows her tying the dog up. Didn't see it bite her but I'm not arresting your dog if that worries you."

Delaney smiled to himself. "If it's her, I really want a conversation, Arran. With you present. She put a tracker on the dog collar."

"That's kinda weird."

"Promise me you'll call me if it's her?"

"I will. Get some sleep Mr Delaney, your head has to be pretty sore."

Asha was working in the hotel back office to give Delaney some time to sleep. Zuki was making last minute orders for Christmas deliveries.

"We have to dress the tree," Zuki informed her. "You'll help?"

Asha smiled. "God when was the last time we dressed a tree together? Must be about ten years ago."

"You were recovering from chicken pox, and I was desperate to get an Xbox One. We were up in the mountains with your grandmother, remember?"

Asha was shaking her head, smiling. "You got the Xbox and shut yourself in your room for about a week and we had to beg you to eat."

Zuki laughed. "I was such a geek back then. Can't even remember what games I played."

"Assassin's Creed. I'm pretty sure. You were obsessed."

Zuki smiled. "Shit yeah. You were out riding most days. How is the wonderful Mr B?"

"Still wonderful. Maria adores him. It's going to be hard to get her back from there."

Zuki glanced at her. "You took on a lot when you moved in with Delaney. You don't regret it?"

Asha shook her head. "I was always so insecure before. I mean, I couldn't stick with anyone, and he just makes me feel safe. Maria has really calmed down and studies hard. She's very hormonal and sometimes it's true I just want to slap her, but we're close. Other days she really reinforces my determination never to have kids though."

Zuki reached out a hand to her. "You are a saint, girl. But our pact still stands. No kids. I might get a dog one day though. I can see how Rufus looks at you. He can't decide who he loves the most I'm guessing."

"His tummy first," Asha replied. "Delaney, Maria and then me. That's the pecking order in our house. I've learned to accept it."

Zuki smiled. "You're still number one with me."

Asha grinned, then suddenly frowned as her eyes caught a name on her screen.

"Jeeze, Zukes. How did I miss this? Look here. Brookshire. Henry Brookshire and his wife are on Martinet's list of victims." She opened up another window. "House fire in 2009. Emily Brookshire was the only survivor. Her father was the finance director for a major defense contractor in Rochester, New York."

Zuki got up from her seat to stare at Asha's screen. "Are all his victims like this? Defense contractors?"

"Many or auditors or anyone who could threaten the scams they were pulling on the US Army. Martinet would make the problems go away or at least scare everyone into silence."

"Each time arson? Didn't anyone pick up on the co-incidence?"

Asha shrugged. "He's pretty careful about how he sets the fires. I've seen the stats Zukes. About 350,000 houses burn every year. Over two and half thousand people die every year in these fires with another eleven thousand injuries. His arson attacks will look incredibly natural. That's his skill."

"But how the hell did his daughter connect to Delaney and you?"

Asha shrugged. "That's what I want to know. Why not attack Martinet's son? How does she know Martinet senior is responsible?"

"You need to ask her when did she know? Has she been looking for him all this time? If she thinks it's arson, why hasn't she been to see the police about it?" Zuki asked.

"Because she wouldn't have any evidence. She's a survivor but how old was she in in 2009?" Asha checked her notes. "Fifteen in 2009. She's almost thirty now."

"And wants revenge." Zuki pointed out. "She must think you guys know where Martinet is."

"I'd feel sorry for her if she hadn't tried to drown Rufus and kill Delaney," Asha said quietly.

"Come on. We have that tree to dress." Zuki told her. "Then I have to make sure all the staff are still coming in to work on Christmas Day. Dealing with people is a nightmare, Ash. It's never going to be one of my key skills."

Asha got up from the desk and hugged her. "You're doing great. You'll miss it when you're in New York."

Zuki doubted it but enjoyed the hug.

CHAPTER TWENTY-TWO

Jailbird

"So let me get this straight, you want to sue the owner of the dog you tried to drown. What do you think your chances of success are?" The Sheriff asked his prisoner.

"The animal is out of control; it bit my fucking finger off." Brookshire complained.

The Sheriff shook his head, amazed at her gall. "We have CCTV of you tying up the dog against its will. You think a dog doesn't know the tide's coming in? We can charge you with abduction of an animal with intent to drown, assault with a lethal weapon and fleeing the scene of a crime. You're spending the next few Christmases in jail, lady."

The prisoner gave him a look of pity. "Yeah right. I need a shit and a shower."

"Maybe you should have thought about that before you attacked someone. The shit can is right there. Don't forget to wash your hands. You're lucky, the old jail only had a bucket."

He sighed, blew his nose, and went back to his desk to find some pills to help with his sinuses. He wanted to go back to bed. Didn't need this hassle. He wasn't sure what to do with the woman. He'd been hoping for quiet holiday season.

His deputy Arran returned with two coffees and handed the Sheriff one.

"I found the metal pole she struck Mr Delaney with. There's blood and fingerprints. Jackie's dusting it now."

The Sheriff nodded and inhaled the steam from the coffee cup to clear his airways.

"How is he?"

"Doc Raj says he needs a CT scan back in Berg City. He's coming in shortly."

"He the angry type? I mean, he wants to talk to her but I dunno..."

"They've discovered she's connected to the investigation they're working on. She's a possible victim. Doesn't mean he'll forgive her, but I said he could talk to her if I'm present."

The Sheriff frowned. "Hmm, well if you can get him to drop the charges against her it will make our lives a lot easier. She wants to sue him for her loss of a finger."

Arran laughed. "Yeah? She know Judge Jensen is an animal rights fanatic?"

The Sheriff briefly smiled. "I guess not."

Arran stirred sugar into his coffee. "Go home Sheriff. You look beat."

"I hate having a cold. I swear I caught it from those kids I gave a talk to."

Arran nodded. "Yeah, they come fully loaded with germs. Go home. My mother would recommend chicken soup to fix your cold."

"It work?"

Arran shrugged. "It can't hurt. You know, feed a cold, starve a fever."

"You can't pull another night shift, kid. Close up at eight. If anything happens, I'll take the call."

Arran smiled. "Thanks. Last night was kind of crazy."

"You'll need to feed our guest. She tells me she's vegetarian."

Arran rolled his eyes. "Bacon sandwiches then."

The Sheriff laughed, then remembered. "Zuki said she'd send something over for her. I'm outta here." He ambled towards the door looking for his car keys.

Arran sat down at his disk and started on his paperwork.

Asha brought Delaney over thirty minutes later. She handed over cake and a meal for the prisoner. "Zuki says you go crazy for carrot cake."

Arran smiled. "Darn, my best kept secret blown." He took the prisoner's meal and put it in the fridge. He looked at the label. "Thai curry? That vegetarian?"

"Yeah. I was wondering if you're setting up a five-star hotel in competition to The Marine?"

"It seems so. You want me to bring her out or you speak to her in the cell?"

Delaney fingered his bandage. "Inside, as long you're covering her with a taser or something. She's pretty lethal."

"Sheriff doesn't like tasers, but I'm armed and prepared to use it, if that's what's worrying you."

"I should bring in the dog. He's collecting fingers."

Asha saw the worry in his pale blue eyes. "He's joking, Arran. Rufus is in the car."

Arran stood up to fetch the key. "Keep a safe distance, she's hostile."

"I think I got that message earlier," Delaney told him.

The prisoner sat hunched in the corner of the cell with a blanket wrapped around her. She didn't look so dangerous any more. Asha noticed her tattoos and a scar on her neck. She was used to trouble she figured.

"Where's my lawyer?" Brookshire demanded to know as Arran unlocked the door.

"You didn't request one, remember?" Arran told her. "And anyway, he'd have to come from Berg City."

She stared at Delaney and Asha with malice. "Why the fuck are they here?"

Delaney was trying to assess this angry young woman, unsure of how to approach her. Her hand was bandaged, it had to be sore. She seemed the type to get herself into an awkward situation quickly and not know how to back down.

"I'm hungry. You said there'd be food," she accused the deputy.

"Room service is slow around here," he told her. "Get used to it."

"You probably already know my name is Delaney and this is Asha," Delaney began. "We're here for an informal discussion."

Brookshire laughed showing two broken teeth. "Get the fuck out. Informal? I'm going to sue you for everything you've got." She waved her bandaged hand at them.

Delaney glanced at Asha. "Go ahead sue. But then the Sheriff will be charging you with attempted homicide not to mention abduction of an animal with intent to kill."

"It doesn't look good for you, Brookshire." Arran added. "We don't take kindly to animal cruelty here."

Emily Brookshire stared at them with all the hatred she could muster. "You came to gloat? Or what? Why are you here?"

Delaney looked at Asha's notes. "Your father was Henry Brookshire, finance director for a defense contractor in Rochester, New York. Yes, or no?"

Emily stared at him, confusion showing on her face. She said nothing, merely stared with hostility at Asha.

"Your parents died in a house fire on March 16th, 2009. You would have been around fifteen. You survived the fire somehow."

Brookshire looked angry again. "What? You think I set the fucking fire now. Is that what this is?"

Asha responded quickly. "We think you know who did."

"She speaks." Brookshire sneered.

"She can also guess your weight," Delaney told her. "I don't know why you decided to stalk Asha and myself, Emily, but what we're interested in is how you found out about us and why you think you know something no one else does."

"I don't have to tell you anything."

"You do if you want them to drop the charges," Arran told her.

"What about my charges? I lost a fucking finger."

"You attacked Mr Delaney and tried to drown his dog, Brookshire. You have a criminal record for stalking and an outstanding traffic violation payment. No one is going to be interested in your charges. Ever."

Brookshire gave him the finger. "Why would they drop the charges? It's some kind of scam."

"Ask them yourself. I hope they don't. You need to be put away." Arran told her.

Delaney leaned up against the wall, still dizzy from the blow to his head.

"I want to know how long you've been looking for the people who burned your home? I want to know how you made the connection. Even the FBI haven't made that connection, as far as we know."

Brookshire shrugged. "I never thought about it. Never once suspected someone set the fire. I just know I had a crappy life handed to me. Eight foster homes. Each one shittier than the last. I haven't been looking till now."

Asha put her hand up to Delaney's shoulder and squeezed. She wanted to say something. "You happen to go to a photographic exhibition in Berg City lately?"

She saw a flicker of recognition in Brookshire's eyes confirming her hunch.

"You think I go to exhibitions?" Brookshire said, mocking her.

"No, I don't think you're the type to enjoy art, but I do think you happened to wander into this one and suddenly make a connection."

"What type am I then?" Brookshire asked, her mouth tightening with hatred.

"Someone who wandered into a gallery by mistake," Asha told her.

Brookshire shook her head. "You think you're so much better than me."

"I know I'm better than you," Asha told her. "I'm not sitting in jail suspected of attempted homicide. But I also know you went into that gallery."

Brookshire hands repeatedly clenched and un-clenched; she was ready for a fight.

"It was raining, that's all. It's a free country they say. I can go where I like."

"So, you went in, and you saw the photograph of your house, the one you grew up in. It was right there on the wall, and you couldn't figure out why," Asha told her.

Brookshire was unable to say anything, squeezing her eyes shut. Asha glanced at Delaney as she pressed on. "You're the one who burned the gallery."

"You don't know shit." Brookshire answered. "It was my fucking house. I didn't know why it was hanging there, or how but I knew I had to get answers. That weird guy at the gallery tried to give me the runaround. Tried to pretend it couldn't possibly be my house. Told me the photographer was in a dementia home, but I knew that wasn't true."

"How?" Delaney asked.

"Because you were looking for him. It was in The Star."

Delaney frowned; he'd forgotten about that.

"I use newspapers for class. I teach aliens English. I have qualifications. I'm not some stupid bitch, whatever you think. There was a photograph of you in The Star. I knew if I followed you, it would lead me to him."

Delaney silently cursed Jonas. He'd told him he couldn't keep his name out of the paper.

"I was hired to find the guy who was supposed to be writing Martinet's biography. He was murdered."

Brookshire frowned. She hadn't expected that.

"Those photographs on the wall of the gallery. They were all targets, Emily." Asha told her. "It wasn't art, it was evidence. Unfortunately, you burned it all."

Brookshire looked away frowning as she tried to process that piece of information.

"If I were you Emily, I wouldn't admit to burning the gallery," Delaney told her. "You have enough problems right now."

She glanced at Delaney puzzled at his warning, but noticed the deputy was taking notes.

"Did you never suspect your parents' death wasn't an accident?" Asha asked.

Brookshire shook her head. "They said there was insurance money. But I never saw any of it. I was still only fourteen back then. I got passed around by the county. The foster homes were like prisons. I wasn't exactly the most likeable kid; angry my folks had been taken from me." She covered her face with her hands a moment thinking about that night. Her voice softened a little as she focused on that day.

"I walked into that gallery and when I saw my home on the wall I kinda lost my shit. I couldn't believe this guy I didn't know, never heard of, took a photo of my home. The guy at the gallery showed me about twenty other photos of the house, back, side, front. Every fucking angle. Even my swing. I flipped out. I'd blanked it all for years and now it all flooded back. I mean, what are the chances of your childhood home that burned down being on a gallery wall? Huh? Wouldn't you flip out?"

Delaney nodded. "I would. So, you wanted to find Martinet. I get that. But why attack me or try to drown my dog? That makes no sense at all."

Brookshire looked down at her feet, one toe sticking out of a hole in her leggings. "I thought you were hiding him." She shrugged. "I don't know. I kinda lost it. I hadn't eaten. I was cold. I hate dogs ..."

Delaney glanced at Asha as she signaled to wrap it up and left the room. Delaney thought hard about it for a moment.

"If I drop the charges you need to promise to go back to Berg City. You have a job there?"

"Holidays break. I got to be back January the second."

"I don't want you hunting for Martinet. For your information, he's old but sane and he'd kill you with no hesitation. You understand? He's a killer. The FBI are looking for him. I don't want you to get in the way. I don't want you near his son either. Martinet will find justice, Emily. We've got a long play going. You will be an important witness. You understand? Do nothing that will diminish that. Make sure the deputy here knows where you live, phone numbers if you move on. Can you do that?"

Brookshire looked at Arran to confirm that this was legit, then Delaney.

"No charges?"

"None. However, you will need to sign an agreement not to bring any against me and the dog. If you are interested, I left your finger in Doc Raj's fridge at the medical center. It might be too late to save it but perhaps for aesthetic reason he could sew it back on. Maybe."

"The dog ate it." Brookshire protested.

"The dog spat it out. He doesn't particularly care for fingers."

"Doc Raj? How will I pay for that?"

"You don't have medical?" Arran asked her.

"My plan probably doesn't cover it," she replied.

"Then act nice, appeal to his good nature, if you know how to do that," Arran told her.

Brookshire snorted as if that was way too hard for her.

"You decide," Delaney told her. "For the record, another inch to the left you'd be definitely looking at a homicide charge."

Delaney signaled to Arran that he was done and left him to it.

"I'll heat up your supper," Arran told her. "Thai curry."

Brookshire said nothing. She had a lot to think about.

"We'll do the paperwork later. You got anywhere to stay?"

Brookshire sighed. "Yeah, if she hasn't thrown my stuff out."

"She hasn't. I'll call Doc Raj – maybe I can soften him up for you."

"There's no soap in here," Brookshire remembered to add as Arran locked the door.

Asha was waiting for Delaney in the parking lot. Rufus earnestly sniffing the nearby trees.

"What do you think?" She asked.

"You're right. She's a victim. Get me back to the hotel, I'm still a bit dizzy."

Asha looked concerned. "Promise me you'll rest."

Delaney smiled. "Definitely. You think I'm wrong for letting her go?"

Asha shrugged. "I probably wouldn't be so forgiving but I admire you for it, Delaney. This is why I love you. Arran might pass on the information about burning the gallery."

"Might be hard to prove and then they would question him as to why he let her go."

Delaney climbed into the car as Rufus came bounding over tail wagging.

"I hope she doesn't disappear," Delaney told her. "She must have had a shitty life, Ash. You have to wonder how many others are like her after Martinet's been to call."

"Always the same, people forget about the victims."

CHAPTER TWENTY-THREE

A Dose of Reality

Delaney was sleeping. Asha was looking at an on-line forum about the perils of setting up independent coffee shops when Delaney's phone rang, she didn't recognize the number. She picked it up.

"City Investigations. Asha speaking."

"Brin Martinet." He coughed for a few seconds. "Sorry, having trouble getting my voice back."

Asha wondered if she should wake Delaney but decided against it. "Hi, glad to hear you're alive."

"I'm not so convinced of that yet," he replied.

"Are you still at the hospital? Delaney tried to see you, but they were pretty strict about visitors."

"Still are. I'm vulnerable to reinfection apparently. Another week I think before I'll get home. Any news about my father?"

"Delaney found him. He sent you a message."

"Oh, I haven't seen any messages. My P.A. is trying to keep me in a stress-free bubble, took my iPhone away. How is my father and where is he?"

"Delaney said he was in good shape and completely lucid. He left him in Denny's. He's afraid to go to his apartment, it was ransacked. We informed your P.A.; we also told your father your new address. He was upset he didn't know you've moved."

"I guess I never told him. It happened after he went into Summertree. You said he was lucid? Really? How lucid? I mean that's not how he was six months ago."

Asha wondered what Delaney would say to him. "When did you last see him Mr Martinet?"

Brin Martinet hesitated. "I can't remember. Sorry."

"Did you know about his tumor operation?"

"Tumor?"

"Brain tumor. Apparently, it has the effect of presenting itself as dementia. I'm surprised you didn't know. There had to be heavy medical bills."

There was another pause. Asha wondered who was with him.

"My P.A. deals with all that. I guess she forgot or something."

"It's a pretty big deal. He recovered all his memories after the operation. That's why he walked out of there."

"You're sure about this?"

"Absolutely. You need to speak to Summertree about it. They wouldn't have performed the operation without someone authorizing it. Delaney suggested that he stays in your home for a while."

"If he can get in. There's tight security."

"He might have gone to his home in Florida. You know about that?"

"Yes, he always winters there. That would make sense. I'll call him there. I can't believe he's cured. That's fantastic news."

It sounded genuine. "Did your P.A. tell you about the gallery burning down?" Asha asked, wondering just who this P.A. was who had such autonomy.

"What did you say?"

"The gallery with all your father's photos. It burned down."

"You have to be kidding me."

"Afraid not, Mr Martinet. Total loss. The police say it was arson."

"Why don't I know about any of this? The nurses tell me some journalist from The Star has being trying to see me about my father's biography. NBC news have left messages too, and others. What the fuck's going on? Something about a New York publisher? Secrets about my father. It's a piece of crap. I read what he wrote, it's worthless. Why is anyone interested at all?"

Asha could hear he was getting upset. "Delaney thinks the writer bigged himself up bragging to people in Cold Rock that he was going to get a publishing deal with the book. It's just a rumor. I agree with you, it's worthless as it's written."

"I don't like it. It's sinister. My father has no secrets. He's a good man."

Asha wondered if Brin Martinet could really be this ignorant about his father's life. Had he never suspected anything about him?

"You should know that the FBI have been staking out his home. We ran into them."

"What the fuck? Because of what that lunatic writer said in a bar?"

"It might be connected. You should also know that Delaney was attacked by a woman who has been stalking us. She thought we were hiding your father somewhere. He was nearly killed."

"Seriously? She was looking for my father? Why?"

"It's connected to the photos in the gallery. She was there. Albion met her apparently, he would be able to tell you more. Delaney was struck with an iron bar. It's a bit random. For the record we're considering the tracing closed. We found your father. He also tried to see you in hospital but met with the same brick wall. However, he's well and able to look after himself. I'm sorry it's not as conclusive as you'd like."

"You're sure he's able to fend for himself?"

"Absolutely. He has friends. He contacted his ex-accountant who believes he's gone to Florida."

"What about the FBI? I don't find that credible at all. Why?"

"I'm pretty sure they know where you are if they want to talk to you, Mr Martinet."

He fell silent a moment. Asha wished she could see what he was thinking.

"Send your account in. If I need you again, will you people be available?"

"Yes, Delaney bounces back pretty quickly."

"I'm sorry he was attacked."

"So is he. Enjoy your Christmas in hospital, Mr Martinet and if I were you, find a more communicative P.A."

Asha disconnected. She wondered if it was possible he could be so indifferent to his father he didn't know about the tumor. He'd told Delaney he was a regular visitor to the care facility. That had to be a lie. But then why all the fuss over creating a biography and staging the gallery exhibition? It made little sense.

Rufus looked at her and stretched his legs. "Ok, I know. You need a walk."

She grabbed her coat and scarf, wrapping it twice around her neck. Rufus bounded towards the door, full of anticipation. He obviously held no fear of going back out there, but Asha wasn't able to forget what had happened to Delaney so easily. She grabbed the baseball bat Zuki had given her and felt a lot safer for it.

The snow was falling again, and the wind chill was brutal. He pulled his hoodie tight around his head and zipped up the goose down anorak he'd bought at the thrift store. Snow crunched underfoot as he made his way along the country lane towards the main road. He checked his watch; the bus would be due in ten minutes if it was sticking to the timetable. He liked busses, they were so anonymous, every single passenger kept themselves to themselves, either too poor or too old to use anything else. No one ever asked your name, you simply dropped cash into the box, and it would whisk you away. No one would remember anything about any passenger who got on or off, still less describe someone wearing a grey anorak or snow-covered boots.

Another passenger was waiting at the stop, stamping her freezing feet in the cold. Somebody's cleaner he guessed. Certainly not anyone who lived in the multi-million-dollar mansions in the gated communities around here.

The CDTA bus was eight minutes late. Both of them waiting were covered in snow by the time the brakes hissed, and the doors slid open. He let the woman get on first, helping her with her heavy bag full of cleaning materials. Seemed strange to him that the house owners didn't supply the bleach and polish. Always wanting to chisel the little people.

He dropped $1.50 into the fare box. Didn't take up the senior citizen half-price offer in case the driver asked for ID. The driver didn't even look at him. He was running late on a tight schedule and the snow wasn't helping any.

He found a seat in the half empty bus took out his sanitizer bottle and discreetly sprayed the seat and the surroundings as was his custom. You never knew who'd been sitting there before you and he'd seen some pretty disgusting leavings over the years on public transportation. He checked his cheap watch, another purchase from the thrift store. He'd allowed for the bus being delayed by the snow. He sat down and peered out of the window. The snow was thickening. The weatherman had said the temperature would fall to arctic conditions by nightfall. He'd overnight in Manhattan at a warm bar he knew, then catch the morning Acela train to Baltimore. He could take a train all the way to Florida but thirty-six hours on a train was more than he could endure. Besides he had business in Baltimore to attend to.

He checked his notes. In the old days he could keep it all in his head but now he had to have notes. Bennett would return from the golf club at four. Even though no golf could be played in this weather, he still went to the office every day and returned at four. Bennett was not the type of man to retire to his Lazy Boy, he was chairman of the Westbury Golf and Country Club now. Respected and still influential after his long stint in the Pentagon. He was also a man of routine. He'd been observing him for two whole days – no easy task standing there in the snow, invisible to all intents and purposes. Bennett had no security and the guards at the gates to the complex were bored out of their minds. It hadn't taken long to find gaps in the fences, just follow the foxes. They always find a way.

He checked his watch again. The express bus to Manhattan would leave in thirty-seven minutes. He'd just have enough time to grab a happy meal and take a piss. Always eat something, that's what his mentor had told him all those years ago. A hungry man makes foolish mistakes. The moment Bennett would turn on the gas hob he'd understand that this was no time to go back on a deal.

CHAPTER TWENTY-FOUR

Events

Delaney called Maria after breakfast on Christmas Eve. She sounded sleepy, annoyed to be woken.

"Just checking you're still alive, M."

"Barely. My back's killing me. I must have shifted a ton of snow yesterday. Mr B is like a robot. He just keeps on shoveling."

"I told you the countryside is hard work."

"You weren't kidding Delaney. When are you coming back?"

"You missing us?"

"Nah."

Delaney smiled. "So, we can leave you there till Easter maybe, when the snow stops?"

He heard her shriek. "Easter! Are you out of your mind? It snows till Easter?"

"Summers are nice, I hear."

"I'm going back to school January 2nd, Delaney. You'd better come and get me."

"Well, I'll have to think about it. Asha's got you gifts but you'll have to wait for those."

"I haven't found your gift yet, but I will." She trilled.

"Hmm, Asha and I were talking about an extra gift. There might be a trip to Paris in the summer; if you're up for it. Rufus would stay at the farm before you ask."

"Paris, France?"

"Not Texas, that's for sure. We'll have get you a passport."

"Seriously? We can go to Paris?"

"That's the plan. Asha wants to see all the sights. You might want to enroll in some French lessons."

He heard her groan. Delaney smiled to himself. "France is better appreciated if you can ask for stuff in French. I'll get you some books to help you along."

"How's Rufus?"

"He's waiting for his morning walk. I've been a bit under the weather but I'm going out there with him today."

Delaney heard shouting.

"Bunty's calling me for breakfast. I'm going tobogganing with some kids from the next farm."

"Wear a helmet."

"Yeah right. Send my love to Asha and Rufie. Got to go."

"We'll call you tomorrow."

"Ok. Bye."

And she was gone. Maria was growing up so fast. The promise of Paris was made now. He'd have to stick to it.

Delaney was on the beach with a scarf wrapped around his head against the cold wind when he got a call from Jonas. He huddled behind a granite boulder to shelter from the wind. Rufus was playing with another dog, madly racing up and down the beach.

"It's Christmas Eve, Jonas, you don't have a paper to put out tomorrow. You should be tucked up in bed at this time."

"Ever hear of 24-hour news? Bastards got me running the digital paper as well now. Got to keep those subscribers scrolling along, Delaney."

"Sounds tough. Maybe time to switch careers?"

"Believe me I think about it every day, but who's going to hire a guy my age? I'm a dinosaur like you in this world."

"Forty-six isn't old. You can be anything you want with your skills."

"I was hoping for a big redundancy package but they're discovering this Gen Z crowd doesn't want to work 24-hour days. I lose staff faster than I can hire them."

"I'm out walking Rufus and it's like the Arctic out here, so what can I do for you?"

"Aren't you supposed to be in the Bahamas or some place?"

"I had an accident. Been laid up."

"Accident?"

"Mugged, ok. Not for The Star's consumption, Jonas."

"But related to the case you're working on?"

"I'll tell you later."

"I know you're holding out on me, Delaney."

"I can't tell you everything, especially over the phone, but when I get back, I will sit you down and blow your mind."

"Fairy dust doesn't get into print, Delaney. I've got nothing. You get me all interested in this Martinet guy. The gallery burns down with all his photographs, he goes missing and there's rumors of his explosive biography and it's all evaporated. There's no story, Delaney. He's a saint. No one has turned up anything interesting about him. Not even a traffic ticket."

Delaney thought about it. "I can't give names, but have the police found out who burned the gallery down?"

"Fire department say it was an accident. There's no active investigation."

"Suppose I told you someone walked into the gallery – recognized one of the photographs on the wall as her childhood home and claims that Martinet burned her house down turning her into an orphan."

"She got any proof of that?"

"She was a child, Jonas. Her parents were murdered, what more proof would you need? It's a possible reason the gallery got burned down - sadly with all the incriminating photos on the walls. It might have been the person who did it, or it might be someone who didn't want any of those photos to be seen. Asha says they're evidence, not art. Think on that."

"I'm not running a philosophy course, Delaney. I have a newspaper to run. We need facts."

"As if. It's a fact-free world these days, Jonas. Print and be damned right?"

"Who's your source?"

"The person who slapped my head with an iron bar was the one who went into the gallery. She's not a little orphan anymore. She's on a mission to find Martinet. Got some mistaken impression that I was hiding him." Delaney saw Asha running towards him and waving her arms. "Hold that thought, Jonas. Asha's running towards me. Might be a late breaking story here."

"I'll hold. But it better be interesting, Delaney."

Asha arrived at his boulder and had to catch her breath first. Rufus bounded over to join them, and Delaney made a fuss of him.

"Another arson attack. It has to be Martinet. It just has to be."

"Explain, Ash. I've got Jonas from The Star on the phone." He gave the phone to Asha.

"Jonas? Asha here. You checked the breaking news lately?"

"Not this hour. What am I looking for?"

"House fire, gated community, death of a Chairman of a Golf Club near Albany and ex-senior officer at the Pentagon."

There was a pause. "I see it. Not major news but..."

"Colonel Bennet Kinnerson was a former Olympian shooter on the team with Arnold Martinet back in 1972. Martinet is a serial arsonist whom we believe worked for Kinnerson when he was at the Pentagon. All Martinet's victims suffered an arson attack of one kind or another. All appeared to be completely natural house fires or vehicle accidents. We think Kinnerson was his ultimate boss. Martinet was hired to erase problems for defense contractors and keep all the kick-backs secret. His cover story is all his wonderful charity work. Who would ever suspect that nice old man of being an assassin?"

"Nice story Asha. Any actual proof? We keep looking for the guy and the FBI don't comment of course, so we don't know if they are watching him for certain."

"That's the problem. We have the proof; but can't trust anyone in Government or the police to give it to. Martinet must have been in Albany yesterday. His apartment was broken into last week. We think something happened and Kinnerson or someone else, possibly Regie Calhoun of Blackwand - the only other survivor from the Olympic team - decided that Martinet was a liability."

Delaney took the phone from Asha. "This all started when Brin Martinet hired Wolfie Sigurdsson to write the biography of his father and organized the gallery showing of his photographs. Red flags began popping up all over when Wolfie started asking questions. Someone raised the alarm. I'm guessing hitmen don't normally get to retire in peace. The woman who saw the photograph of her family home in the gallery is collateral damage in my opinion."

Jonas was thinking. "Can I see this proof you have?"

"No way it's safe to send it to you. You have plans for Christmas?"

"Pizza with a sprig of holly on it, same as always."

"I'll send the address via WhatsApp. Drive safe Jonas, it's snowing, make sure you have snow tires. Tell no one where you're going. They have people watching and listening everywhere."

"You can't come to me?"

"No. Head injury, remember. You might want to call a friend of mine, the lawyer Nicolas Goodman, he has government connections. Scoops have consequences when it comes to national security. He told us to leave this stuff alone, but it won't leave us alone."

"I know him. Send the number. I'll call."

"You still driving that clunker?"

"It's practically still new, Delaney."

"It might die of shock on a long drive. Lunch is served till 2.30pm."

"Lunch?"

"Get going, Jonas." Delaney disconnected and made a face to Asha. "Well, now we're in trouble."

Asha leaned in and kissed him. "Send him the address of the Boatyard Inn."

"Isn't that closed for the winter?"

Asha nodded. "Just to be safe."

Delaney smiled. "Smart thinking, you're learning. Um, I'm thinking we should round up the wonderful Ms Brookshire."

"Really?"

"She wants justice. Jonas might give her that. Good emotional stuff. The papers like that. Y'know how it goes ... The Good Man Martinet ruined my life..."

Asha's eyes widened. "I'll go look for her. Go back inside Delaney, your face is turning blue. It's freezing out here."

CHAPTER TWENTY-FIVE

Brightside

He watched the bus pull away along Bellona Ave before he crossed over and walked back up aways towards the Brightside Road turnoff. Freezing rain blighted his vision. He was very glad of his anorak and fur-lined hoodie. He shouldered a canvas bag and made his way along the road, grateful there was little traffic in this neighborhood. Regie Calhoun had done well for himself, as you would expect for a billion-dollar defense contractor. Each mansion he passed was well hidden from the road by trees. Calhoun's place he knew would be huge. Five thousand square feet, or more. He'd never seen it of course. They'd had no direct contact in decades. That was the system. They'd kept him in regular work all this time until he'd abruptly had to retire. He hadn't known then that his shakes and memory loss was caused by a growing tumor. Never once had a health check in all that time. Sheer luck he'd fallen at Summertree and bumped his head so hard they were forced to arrange a CT scan.

They could have left the tumor, after all he was nearly eighty years old with advanced dementia. He was surprised they'd even considered an operation until the nurse told him afterwards it had cost close to a hundred grand. Nice little bump in their profits. They must have been sickened when he recovered his memory and walked on out of there. No more charging five thousand a week for keeping him starved and unwashed. He intended to reflect on whether to take revenge on them or send them a note of thanks. Perhaps no need to burn the place down. Never clever to leave too many bodies.

He knew Calhoun would know by now that Kinnerson was dead. He'd wonder if it was an accident but instinctively worry in the back of his head that their friend and former employee was out of the care facility. The odds on it being an accident were too slim given that Kinnerson had given the orders to terminate over thirty 'clients' the same way. The thing about arson is, never be in a rush. Never execute it the same way, never establish a trademark or a tell. Be innovative. Regie Calhoun would be waiting for him. There wouldn't be the element of surprise.

Martinet was a little confused the fence wasn't electrified. Didn't mean the ground wasn't booby-trapped. There would be cameras, ground triggers, armed guards. Calhoun could afford the best. Blackwand had a big operation in Baltimore, with thousands of employees. The man had shunned living in D.C. He knew he had a home in Annapolis too, but the maid there had helpfully told him that Mr Calhoun was in Baltimore for Christmas with his family when he'd called. Calhoun had grown careless. Never let anyone know exactly where you are at any time. Especially when you've decided to delete the one person who could give you trouble.

He made his way along the trees up the slope to take him behind the house. It was a huge mansion, as he'd expected. He counted seven SUVs and at least four armed men positioned in front of house. There would be more inside. The men looked cold and miserable. He kept well away from the fence; in case he triggered something. But eventually it curved back around, sweeping over to the other side of the property around the tennis courts and swimming pool. He glanced at his watch. The next bus wasn't due for an hour. He checked his escape route, a firebreak in the tree line where some powerlines were strung up high leading towards Lake Roland. He could make his way through the trees back to Bellona Ave. He hoped he had the stamina to do it. His legs weren't as reliable as they used to be.

He slipped on a pair of latex gloves, no need to make it easy for any investigation if something went wrong. He set up on a boulder that gave him a great view of the rear of the house. He unpacked the bag and extracted his rifle and scope, fitting them together with practiced ease. Calhoun would be expected a fire perhaps. After all that was his specialty. But their friendship was based on shooting, and this was as close as he could get to his target.

The rain eased up a little, but a mist was forming. He'd need to get this done at pace.

He stared down the scope and found Calhoun waving his arms around in the kitchen, no doubt giving orders to the security detail, thinking he'd be safest at the back of the house. He counted three men in the kitchen with him. Calhoun was drinking from a mug. He briefly glimpsed his wife, thirty years his junior. Nice inheritance for her if she hadn't been forced to sign a prenup, like his previous two wives.

He could take the shot now but so could the three security guys and he'd not get off the boulder in time. He waited. He had time.

Two of the security guys left the kitchen. He had to make a decision. Calhoun deserved to die, but he didn't like collateral damage. It was messy and unprofessional. But maybe he could wing him so he couldn't return fire. Hard to do at this range.

Calhoun walked to the kitchen window; he was pointing to something in the garden. Martinet followed his gaze. Two security men walking towards the tennis courts. This made escape more awkward. He really didn't have a beef with those guys, but he'd return fire if he had to.

He returned his gaze to Calhoun. He was on the phone now, gesticulating angrily. The other security man was leaving in a hurry. He took the shot. He didn't bother to check if he was down. The bullet had hit him square on the back of the head.

He was off the boulder, disassembling the rifle and scope in record time, stuffing them into the bag. He didn't bother looking back, just put as much distance between him and the fence as he could. He knew the security men in the garden would struggle to find a way through the fence. They'd have to run back down to the house and all the way down to the driveway to get around.

He kept moving. Disturbed a coyote who fled in fear. He could hear shouting, a scream, urgent commands being shouted out. There would be panic and confusion. He kept moving. Ran across the fire break and into the trees beyond. That was their chance to get him, but they moved too slow, and he was already deep into the trees the other side. His heart was beating fast, his blood pressure was up, he wasn't used to moving quickly. He couldn't run. Too easy to trip. He thought he heard the whirring of a drone overhead and they'd certainly be looking for someone moving at speed. He slowed his pace. Kept to the fir trees that gave him cover. Bellona Avenue wasn't far away. This would be the risky part. The bus wouldn't come for (he checked his watch) fifteen minutes. He skirted around another large property. Dogs on patrol. There was a chalky slope heading down to the avenue. He'd be exposed there. He heard shouting. Looked back but it was someone calling for the dogs. He watched them slope off. The whirring drone was close by. He stayed absolutely still, blending with the trunk of a nearby tree until he saw the drone veer left and head over the house.

He moved quickly, half sliding down the wet chalk, nearly falling as he jumped a small stream. He pushed his bag as far as it would go into a drain under the road. He regretted leaving evidence behind, but it would be hard to locate and easy to retrieve some other time, if there was another time. There was a risk if they used tracker dogs they'd find it, but he didn't want to be the fool standing at the bus top with a weapon in his bag if he got stopped. The rifle was one he'd stolen from the back of a hunter's vehicle at the gun club earlier. If they ever came looking for the owner, he'd be suspect number one for a while.

He took out a small leather cloth and dipped it into the stream to wipe the chalk and mud from his anorak and boots. Two minutes until the bus would arrive. He checked the sky for the drone deciding it was clear and strolled across the road walking the last one hundred yards to the bus stop.

It was on time. The bus slowed. As he climbed aboard, he saw security vehicles streaming out of Brightside Road heading north and south at speed.

"What's that about?" The driver asked him.

Martinet shrugged. "Donut time," he muttered. The driver laughed. Martinet dropped money into the box and shuffled towards a seat. He was the only one on the bus. The driver would probably remember some old guy in an anorak but nothing else.

Revelations

Asha called Delaney from the coffeeshop opposite the Boatyard Inn. The one barista was closing up as there didn't seem to be any business.

"It's freezing out here. Snow's still falling. No sign of Jonas yet, but get this, there's an out-of-town vehicle watching the Inn. Two men and a woman. I guess they're the only people around here who don't know the hotel's closed for the season. Has to be FBI as they're all wearing suits."

"So, whose phone got hacked?"

"Take your choice. I'm betting on Jonas. Jonas is the most vulnerable. Or us. But I thought we were on a secure call."

"What's our play, Delaney?"

"You think the pizza place is open?"

"You're thinking about food?"

"I'm thinking we could organize a delivery to the Inn and see what happens."

Asha smiled. "Devious."

"Meanwhile we do what the cowboys do."

"Cowboys?"

"Head them off at the pass, Ash. Can you take Rufus to the turnoff at the top of town? You can flag Jonas down maybe, bring him the back way to the hotel. I know it's a long walk and cold."

"I'll do it. Rufus hasn't had much of a walk yet."

"I'm going to order a pizza meanwhile."

"I've got a question."

"Shoot."

"Are the FBI here to stop Jonas discovering the truth? If so, why not grab you or me?"

Delaney didn't reply immediately. "I guess that's exactly why they are here. No one wants this stuff to get out into the public domain. Maybe they're waiting to see who his contact is."

"Which means they don't suspect us? I'm pretty sure they are looking at you."

"I don't honestly know. Did you find our witness?"

"She's willing. Didn't take much to persuade her. She's had her finger reattached – Doc Raj says there's a possibility one or two nerves might have survived. She's sleeping it off right now. I said we'd call when he's here."

"Someone should give that doctor a medal. Message me if anything happens."

"On my way. Don't stray far from the hotel. That head of yours needs time to heal babe. I mean it."

"I know. I won't." Delaney disconnected and looked up the number to call for a pizza. He looked around the bedroom for his coat and gloves wondering what his next move was once the pizza got delivered.

Zuki stopped him as he was leaving. "Where are your guests?"

"We're hoping still on their way. Maybe you could persuade the chef to put something aside we can heat up later?"

"She's not going home. She's got tonight's dinner to put together. We've got about fifty diners. It's the one time of the year the locals get together here. The hotel's last hurrah before we close after Christmas."

Delaney smiled. "If you need help, just ask us, Zuki."

She came forward and gave him a hug. "Thanks. I'm happy to see you walking again. How's the head? Your bruise is a spectacular purple now."

"Weirdly, I feel fine today. Vision's still a bit fuzzy. Got to go, got a little business to attend to."

Zuki watched him go with a worried expression. She didn't think she'd feel so fine with a bruise like that.

Delaney stepped out into the snow and followed an elderly couple up the main street carrying small gifts in their gloved hands. They were arguing about something as they headed towards their car. It reminded him that he had meant to organize some flowers for Zuki and her grandmother. He didn't think he'd seen a flower shop but then again hadn't been looking. Almost all the shops were closing up. No last-minute panic buying in this little harbor town.

The Boatyard Inn stood proud at the high end of Main Street overlooking the small marina. It looked neglected with faded timbers and signage, a relic from another age.

The Ford parked across from the Inn stood out like a sore thumb. A sedan, who the hell drove sedans anymore? Maybe the FBI hadn't got the memo.

He loitered outside a coffee shop; a young girl was busy putting up the shutters. He looked down the street and glimpsed a kid on a bike heading up towards the Inn trying to keep to the tire-compacted tracks in the snow. He checked the occupants of the Ford. All three were heads down looking at their phones. He watched with anticipation as the boy with his pizza warmer on his back reached the hotel and dismounted, shaking the snow off his jacket. The people in the Ford didn't noticed him until the boy walked up the three steps towards the hotel doors.

Suddenly there was activity and confusion in the car. They were trying to get out and the doors were locked. Someone was loudly cursing in the vehicle, confused about how to unlock. Delaney and the girl watched with increasing amusement as they tried to get out of their vehicle. The kid at the hotel door was knocking as the bell didn't seem to work. He was about to give up and turn back to his bike when the FBI agents finally got out of their vehicle and ran towards the kid, guns drawn, shouting at him to put his hands up.

The kid looked terrified thinking he was about to be robbed or murdered. These people in suits looked dangerous.

"Who's that pizza for, kid?" One of the men shouted.

The kid, who was no more than fifteen, just slipped the pizza box out of the warmer and meekly handed it over. He wouldn't be getting any tip and was thinking he'd be lucky to escape with his life.

The FBI agents examined the delivery slip, looking at each other in astonishment and then back at the kid who cowered behind his bike.

"Here let me help you. Those shutters look heavy." Delaney told the girl. She was puzzled anyone would help but happy to let him do the lifting. She hated this part of the job.

Delaney felt sorry for the boy. He hoped they wouldn't hurt him. But they couldn't really complain. He'd done his job, delivered the pizza to the FBI at the Boatyard Inn. They knew they'd been had and frantically looked around for someone to blame. There was no one else in the street except the people shutting up the coffee shop.

They questioned the kid but knew it was pointless. He was just the delivery boy. They let him go and he cautiously got back on his bike and set off back down the street. The girl hailed him, and he skidded to a stop in the snow, wiping tears from his eyes.

"Who are those people? What did they say to you, Charlie?"

The kid looked deathly pale. "Pizza was for the FBI. I thought it was a joke. I mean, the Inn's closed, right? I said it was prank call, but Luigi said the payment went through, I had to deliver it."

Delaney stepped forward and pressed ten bucks into his hands. "Bad luck kid. I guess the FBI don't tip. Go home, forget about it. Enjoy Christmas."

The kid looked down the money and brightened a little, glancing at the girl for confirmation that this was legit. She smiled at him and mussed his hair. "Go back Charlie. Smoothie on me next time you come in, ok?"

The kid smiled, his confidence returning and set off again. Delaney looked towards the Inn and saw the FBI people talking on their phones, eating slices of pizza. They were awaiting new orders, had no idea what to do.

The girl turned to Delaney. "Can you believe that? They really the FBI? What are they doing here? It's freaking Christmas Eve; they could have tipped the kid. You didn't have to do that."

"It's Christmas. Someone played a joke, no reason for the kid to lose out. Have a great one tomorrow," Delaney told her with a smile.

The girl shrugged. "At least it's a day off. Merry Christmas, Mister."

He set off back to the hotel hoping Asha had managed to intercept Jonas.

Asha trudged through the snow worried that she had no idea what Jonas looked like or what kind of vehicle he drove, or even if she could stop him before he drove into the arms of the FBI. Rufus was enjoying the snow, even though his coat was matted with the stuff, and he seemed to have grown a white beard.

She finally crested the slope to reach the town turn off. She didn't have to worry about spotting Jonas. He was already there. He'd missed the turn for Oyster Point and slammed into a snowdrift. A tall man with thinning hair was staring at his vehicle in despair. He wore only a thin coat and town shoes that would freeze his toes off if he wasn't careful. He hadn't thought this thing through at all.

"I'm guessing you're Jonas," Asha said as Rufus inspected his ancient VW Rabbit.

She was looking at his car: it was seriously old; the color had faded to a mottled green and it had little dents all over the sides. "Seems you've had one or two accidents on the way."

Jonas stared at her, snow melting on his spectacles. His nose was already bright red, and his hands looked frozen.

"I haven't left the city in twenty years. I had no idea Oyster Point was so far away."

"From the looks of it, I'm kinda surprised you got this far. Can you walk?"

"Walk?"

"Well, you can't drive. I'll call someone to arrange a tow. Might be a tough ask on Christmas Eve."

Jonas felt stupid. He went back to his car to retrieve his bag and fish out an old blanket which he wrapped around his shoulders.

"How old is this wreck?" Asha asked curious.

"1975, I think. It's only done ten thousand miles. Not really run in yet."

Asha laughed. "It's run out of road for sure."

"It's a collector's car they tell me."

Asha smiled. "In your dreams. Come on, we've got a ways to go. Leave the keys under the visor for the tow truck. Believe me, no one is going to steal this."

"You sure?" He followed her instructions anyway.

Asha called Rufus and they set off along the ridge to avoid Main Street. Jonas followed, struggling to keep upright in the snow.

"It wasn't snowing in Berg City." Jonas informed her.

"There's probably a weather app on your phone, Jonas. Delaney's waiting. Talking of phones, you might want to sweep your office when you get back. There are three FBI agents waiting for you outside the Boatyard Inn."

Jonas caught up with her, looking at her with surprise. "FBI?"

"Who did you tell?"

"No one. I couldn't get hold of the lawyer. Well, my deputy editor, of course. She needs to know where I am. Three agents you said?"

Asha nodded. "All waiting for you."

Rufus led the way down a slippery slope between the empty vacation homes. Just a few were occupied and draped with an excess of holiday lights.

"Where are we going?" Jonas asked.

"If I tell you I might have to kill you," Asha told him, then turned to smile. "Best you don't know in case the FBI wise up and grab you between here and there."

Jonas wasn't entirely sure she was joking and looked anxious.

"I'll call someone about getting a tow," she told him as she called Zuki. She answered on the fourth ring.

"Hey, finally. You ok? Haven't seen you since this morning." Zuki asked.

"Frozen but ok. Need help. Stranded vehicle up at the junction turn off. Our visitor ploughed into a snowdrift. It's a road hazard where it is."

"Now? It'll cost plenty."

"Yep. But he can afford it, he drives a '75 Rabbit."

"Seventy-five? Can't believe it even got here. I'll call Ziggy."

"Tell him to bring it to the hotel."

"I should tell him to take it to a museum. You hungry? Delaney's back. The Chef's offering goujons with roast potatoes. Better get here soon or I'll eat them all."

"On our way, Zukes. Ten minutes."

"Stay safe, Ash. Apparently, there's some very pissed off FBI agents in town."

Asha laughed and disconnected. Jonas slipped and fell. She pulled him up. "Come on, lunch is waiting." He dusted snow off his clothes and tried to regain his dignity.

"Tell me Jonas, you think news matters anymore?"

He picked up his bag and gingerly started walking again. "I wouldn't be here if it didn't."

"But you think people my age read mainstream news?"

"You want an honest answer?"

"Of course. Watch out for the steps, they're slippery. Take my arm."

He grabbed her arm and clung on. "No one reads the news. Our print run is one third of what it used to be since Covid and working from home, or general apathy. The online Star is gaining traction, but mostly it's the sport and celebrity pages that make the advertising money. No one has any idea how to attract people under twenty-five away from the conspiracy sites and Tik-Tok."

Asha kept a firm grip on him as they descended the slippery steps. "What we're going to show you Jonas is big news. If we can get it out. National news stuff. Might even rock the foundations of trust in government."

Jonas chuckled. "Be hard to find any foundations after what Trump did to trust. I'm here because I know Delaney comes up with the goods. If it goes national it can only raise our profile. We're on the edge of survival on a daily basis, Asha."

"This story will go national. I guarantee it. As long as they don't kill it first."

"You're pretty confident." Jonas told her.

"I guarantee no one wants this story out there, Jonas. You'd be taking a huge risk."

Jonas smiled. "It's all about gaining eyeballs, Asha. I hope what you've got will shake the world. That's what The Star lives for."

"Watch for black ice here. We're nearly there."

Emily Brookshire stared at her phone and the photographs of her childhood home with misty eyes. On the other side of the room Jonas was scrolling through each arson attack, making notes of every photo batch, the victims, and the dates. Asha was explaining how she'd made sense of each of them.

Delaney stood at the window watching the white-caps across the bay. Seagulls swooping around a lone small fishing vessel slowing coming into the harbor. The snow was abating but the wind was getting up again. Delaney turned towards Jonas.

"You say it's all circumstantial, but the statistical like-lihood that Martinet was a casual bystander taking photos at every single house or apartment building that burned down is impossible to wish away. He was there, he took photos. He burned those homes and killed those people. The fact that the fire departments classified each attack as 'accidental' is testimony to his skill in arson. Emily here is living proof of the consequences of his guilt. It's impossible to refute the evidence."

Jonas sighed. He was looking at this with his editor's hat on and instinctively knew what he could get away with before the lawyers waded in.

Asha pointed to a slim black notebook she'd taken from Martinet's apartment. "His notebook confirms it, Jonas. It's coded but look at the dates. He was very methodical. He lists payments one week after every fire. Each one listed as a 209/UBP. I don't know how much they paid him, but it had to be a lot. How else would he have been able to give it all away to charity later?"

Delaney suddenly recalled something. "A 209/UBP is a simple confirmation code you get when you've transferred money to a particular Swiss bank. Our office used to get those when I worked in Paris. You can be sure he'd quickly move it out of there to the Cayman's or Panama. Keeping money secret from the IRS and whistleblowers is a lot harder than it used to be, even in Switzerland."

Jonas scratched his head and stared at the ceiling. He knew this was a great story, but it was also an unexploded bomb. He had to think about the proprietors of The Star and how close they were to the State Governor and others in government.

"This is why the FBI are here, Jonas. We're pretty sure they didn't want you to see this," Asha told him.

Jonas turned his gaze to Asha, his head filled with mixed emotions. "And you claim he killed the man who hired him. Colonel Bennet Kinnerson, his former Olympic teammate. You have no actual proof he was in the Albany area. The wires said it was a gas leak."

"That's his specialty," Delaney pointed out.

Emily frowned. "That's what they said about my house fire. Propane fire. Made no sense. I don't even think we used propane. Mom cooked electric and it was summer."

"I think he'll be going after his last surviving teammate now, Regie Calhoun," Asha pointed out. "He knows he's been betrayed. Discovering that someone was writing his biography would have given his employers a shock. They must have thought they'd taken care of that, getting rid of Wolfie Sigurdsson. Perhaps they were happy to leave him be as he had dementia, but once they discovered he was out and recovered his memory he became a huge liability."

Jonas was still skeptical. "But we're talking about an eighty-year-old man, just out of a care facility. You really think he's still capable of this?"

"Yes," Delaney replied. "He has a very strong sense of survival and no empathy, a classic sociopath. I wouldn't be surprised if he also punishes his son for organizing that biography and photographic showing."

"Yeah, what about burning down the gallery? It would make sense he did that," Jonas declared. "Have to say that I wouldn't blame him. Must have been a real shock to discover his reconnoiter shots were on display for anyone to see."

Delaney glanced at Emily who declined to admit to anything at this moment.

"We're not conspiracy nuts, Jonas. The FBI would have closed it down and confiscated the photos if they'd made the connection. Someone who did make that connection burned the gallery. When I spoke with Martinet, he was completely unaware that it had burned and never knew about the show. He knew about the biography however, but he's innocent of kidnapping and killing the writer."

"This everything you've got?" Jonas asked. "This black book doesn't prove anything. I get that every 209 could be a payment confirmation but lawyers could easily explain that away. And good luck getting the Swiss to cooperate. They use numbers, not names."

Asha opened up another file. "Brin Martinet is a victim too."

"What?" Jonas exploded.

"See the baby in the pram in this photo. See the woman hanging up washing on the line? That's his real mother. The target was the father of the child. All the newspaper reports about the auto-fire never mention any child. Maybe it's a moment of contrition or simply he always wanted a son. Whatever the reason, he arranged for the kid to be raised by a woman he pretended was his sister. That's when he moved to Berg City."

Jonas stared at the screen. "Shit. Have you told Brin this?"

Delaney and Asha shook their heads. "We left this off the list for now," Delaney told him. "Didn't think it would be fair. It will be bad enough when he discovers his father is a mass murderer."

Jonas screwed up his face for a moment. "He might appreciate the distance from him genetically speaking. The kid made his own money. He's not contaminated by anything the father made."

Emily stood up. "You have to tell him. It won't ruin his life like it did mine. Jonas is right. No one would want to be the son of a serial arsonist."

Asha put out a hand to her arm. "You're right. And I'm sorry, none of this really helps you get any real justice Emily. We'll find a way to tell Brin when we get back to Berg City."

Jonas was studying Emily. "I want to record your testimony in a moment, Emily, but tell me, what do you want? What would made you happy? Compensation? Martinet is rich, I'm guessing he hasn't given away all his money."

Emily put up her hands, her eyes half closed. "I want him to suffer. He has to pay for his sins. I want him to hang in public, like they used to do."

Jonas winced. "No public hanging for a long time in this state. We don't even have the death penalty."

"Jail isn't enough," Emily told them. "He'll just fake dementia again and get special treatment."

Asha shook her head. "People, we're getting ahead of ourselves. The question is, will you print this, Jonas."

Jonas sat back his chair with a vexed expression. "I'd have to run it past the lawyers."

Delaney didn't like that answer. "They'll tie it up. It's bound to leak; the FBI will come in and seize everything. You need to keep the whole thing under wraps until you print. Swear everyone to secrecy. You're protected by the First Amendment. We still have freedom of the press whilst it lasts. Most of the people he killed worked for the government or military or private contractors. Their deaths enabled key individuals to make billions out of fraudulent contracts."

Jonas nodded. "Precisely, that's our angle here, Delaney. We investigate and name names of those who profited by eliminating certain people. It's all here. We just have to join it up better."

Emily wasn't so sure. "A lot of this shit happened so long ago. Will anyone even care. No one cared when my parents were killed."

Jonas turned to her. "Someone made money because of it. That's what will get people's attention, Emily. I'm genuinely sorry your life was wrecked. You've got every right to be angry, although I'm guessing Delaney wasn't too happy to get that bump on his head."

Delaney grunted. He didn't need reminding.

Asha stood up frowning. "We have to widen the net, show just how widespread the fraud was and demonstrate that this wasn't the act of one man. He was acting under orders."

"But the man who issued the orders is now dead," Emily complained.

"The man who made the most money is still alive," Delaney pointed out. "Regie Calhoun made billions and escaped all those audits precisely because he was able to eliminate key people."

"And he will have the best lawyers in the land," Jonas pointed out. "It will be a battle, believe me. It's a fantastic scoop. I get it. I don't want to lose it, but I can see the downside in lawsuits. Calhoun could bury us."

Asha's phone pinged. A news alert. She glanced at her screen. She had to read it twice unable to believe what she was seeing. She slid her phone over to Jonas.

"Calhoun was shot dead about three hours ago."

Delaney blinked. "No way? Shot? Not arson? They say anything about the shooter?"

Jonas's phone pinged with the same story. He opened up the link and read it aloud.

"Manhunt underway. Shot to the head. Right now, I'm not sure this helps us. Kind of takes the air out your tires re Martinet."

Asha wasn't so sure about that. "If it was Martinet, it makes perfect sense, Jonas. He's already eliminated Kinnerson. You forget he was an Olympic shooter. So was Calhoun. Taking him out with a rifle makes perfect sense to me."

"Martinet is still out there," Asha insisted. "I swear it was him. He's clearing the decks. Where did this happen?"

Delaney was reading the alert on his phone. "Baltimore. Martinet is following the route down to his hideaway in Florida, Jonas. I don't think he knows we know where he's going. He'll want to change ID and disappear fast."

"You don't know any of this for certain," Jonas pointed out. "He's probably sitting at home in Berg City decorating his tree. The two people who could prove he's an assassin beyond doubt are now dead. He's got the upper hand now, whether he did it or not."

Asha looked hard at Jonas. "You're backing out?"

"I'm going to take advice. I agree it's a huge coincidence that Calhoun and Kinnerson are suddenly dead but unless the cops turn up something fast, I think you would have a very hard time proving Martinet has anything to do with it. He's the master of coincidences it seems."

Delaney glanced at Asha. Both of them had a terrible sinking feeling. Jonas definitely had cold feet.

Asha looked at her phone again. "Zuki says your car is here. No damage. $250."

"$250?" Jonas was shocked.

"That has to be more than the car is worth," Asha commented.

"Are you going to take the information away with you?" Delaney asked.

Jonas thought about it. "I want to interview Emily here. Make me a copy. What's the weather doing? You think I can drive back tonight?"

Asha frowned. "Really? In that Rabbit?"

"The road will freeze in about an hour." Delaney told him. "Stay the night. Travel in daylight, Jonas. It's not worth the risk and you'll have a problem getting rescued if you get into trouble on Christmas Day."

Jonas wasn't sure and got up to look out the window. "How much is a room here?"

"It's free. Zuki already arranged it. There's a party tonight. Might do you good to have some fun."

Jonas rubbed his face. He couldn't remember how long it had been since he'd had any fun. He was more than nervous about this story. He knew they were disappointed with his reaction, but it was big. Bigger than anything he'd ever handled before.

"Let your deputy editor put together the next edition, Jonas. You need to think about all this." Delaney told him. "Talk to Emily. Join us in the bar after. You too Emily. I'm not holding grudges."

Emily was surprised at that but said nothing. She wasn't used to people not holding grudges. She'd spent a lifetime crafting hers.

They left Jonas to question Emily. Asha was feeling deflated. She'd thought that what she'd presented was incontrovertible evidence. Jonas had seemed underwhelmed; it undermined her confidence. Delaney squeezed her shoulder. He knew she was disappointed.

"He'll use it. He's been an editor for years, Ash. He has to balance all the angles. He has to take advice. I'm just worried it will leak before he can get into print."

Asha paused on the stairs looking up at Delaney with doubt in her brown eyes. "We've lost Kinnerson and Calhoun. The only people who could corroborate the evidence."

"They would have denied it and hidden behind divisions of lawyers anyway. Have faith. I just can't believe Martinet moved so quickly. We must have missed something. He needed to act fast for a reason."

"The Maytag man maybe," Asha said. "He knew it wasn't the FBI who trashed his apartment. He must have known they were coming for him."

Delaney agreed. "Maybe. I still say this all goes back to Wolfie. It all began when he started asking questions about Martinet around town."

Zuki came running out of the kitchen area. They could see panic in her eyes.

"Ash, I need you to take the front desk. Crisis in the kitchen. Can you do it? Please!"

Asha glanced at Delaney. "Do it, Ash. Zukes, anything I can do?"

"Keep the fires going in the bar and the dining room. Logs are out back. Chef fell. Doc Raj is coming and so is Grandma."

"Does that mean?" Asha began.

"You might be helping us cook tonight. We're fully booked for two sittings. The hotel is full, so we're not taking any reservations period. Anyone coming in for dinner must show ID. Names only tonight. Accept no bribes."

"People bribe to eat here?" Asha was skeptical.

"We're the only place open tonight. Even the pizza place closes early. Can you do it?"

Asha smiled. "Of course. Go, do whatever you have to do."

Zuki looked relieved and headed back to the kitchen as Asha ran towards the reception area. Some people had gathered there and looked pissed off already.

Delaney called after her. "Think of it as work experience for your coffee shop."

Asha screwed up her face. "Ha. Ha. Jeez, the phone's ringing already."

Delaney signaled to Rufus to follow him. "I'll go find the logs."

CHAPTER TWENTY-SEVEN

Savannah

He wearily climbed down from the Greyhound accepting that Savannah was as far as he was going to get on Christmas Eve. It was a chilly night but at least he'd left the rain and snow behind. He knew the old city well and where to go and not be faced with awkward questions. He wondered if Henry's was still open for supper but was resigned to Wendy's if they weren't. Savannah was not a friendly city to doss down in any doorway. He hoped there would be a room at the hotel on Bull Street with clean linen and a working shower. He'd hole up here for two days. It was too much of a risk to travel over the holidays. Hold-ups, fewer people, he'd be too visible should anyone start looking for him.

He knew that shooting Calhoun would make big news. It was never his plan to cause any media attention. That's why his fire 'accidents' were in demand. Never leave any doubts behind as the cause of a fire. Assassinating one of the richest men in America would bring a whole heap of trouble. They'd want to know why and start digging into all his enemies, and he'd made many over the years. Someone would remember his Olympic past and realize that Kinnerson had died just two days earlier. That would ring bells. The most superstitious would be saying 'death comes in threes', where's Martinet, will he be next? Then they'll be asking where is he? How did he get out of the nursing facility if he had dementia? He could see a whole pattern of enquiry. He ruled out anyone connecting him to the assassination. It would be so unlikely that an 80-year-old could achieve anything at all let alone take out the CEO of Blackwand in a house full of security personnel.

The Travelers Hotel looked worse for wear than he remembered, but at least it was open and had one room available. The night clerk behind the glass was irritated to be distracted from his basketball game on TV.

"Two nights. That'll be $175, cash only."

Martinet frowned. He remembered when it used to be $25 a night and he'd thought that expensive for a place that hadn't been refurbished since 1950.

"Is the shower working?"

The clerk shrugged. "No one has complained. There's no ice. It's busted."

He paid. Signed the register Leonard Singer and flashed Singer's stolen ID at the clerk. All old men looked alike to him. Didn't care as long as people signed something.

He wasn't worried about ice. He snatched up a sticky key and was about to head to the stairs when the clerk remembered something. "Take the coupon. 25% off breakfast next door."

Martinet took it. You had to save money where you could these days. He ignored the elevator. Seen enough people stranded in those things on holiday weekends to know better.

CHAPTER TWENTY-EIGHT

No Room at the Inn

Asha was making coffee for two guests when the woman came in. She didn't need to show her ID, this was one of the FBI agents. The black suit looked tight on her, like she was fighting bloating. Her cropped mousey hair did nothing for her.

"Hi, we're here on business and need a room. There's three of us." She flashed her FBI ID. Asha wondered if she was supposed to be impressed or intimidated. She handed over the coffees to the waiting guests. She shook her head sympathetically.

"I'm afraid we're absolutely full. No prior bookings, no room."

"What about dinner?" The woman called Sandrine enquired.

Asha winced, trying to be 'nice'. "Sorry. We're over-booked as it is, and the chef has just taken ill. We're in crisis mode here."

Sandrine looked very disappointed. "Is there no way?"

Asha tried to look as though she was considering it. "We just can't. Sorry. I appreciate you're doing government work and everything, but I can't exactly tell a guest to leave. There's an Airbnb on Cross Street." She looked for the number to call. "You want me to call them?"

"Cross Street?"

"Red house three blocks over. They called to say they had space if we had overspill."

"Give me the number. Thank you." Sandrine told her and seemed to mean it. Asha wrote it down. "The Pizza place is closing early if you want to eat. This is early bird country. Everyone goes to bed by ten."

Sandrine smiled. "Thank you for your help. Good to see you're busy."

"We are. No idea how we're going to feed everyone, I'm only good for making toast."

Sandrine attempted a nervous laugh and quickly headed out into the cold, shaking her head at the other agents waiting for her in their vehicle.

Asha remained still, trying to calm her beating heart. She wondered why the FBI were still there. Did they know Jonas was here? Then remembered his car had been towed to the overflow car park. It was there to be seen if they were looking. They must have put a tracker on it.

Delaney was in the bar with Jonas and Emily. She messaged him. Wasn't quite sure what the play was, but keeping Jonas out of view was important, keeping Emily safe too was an issue now.

Delaney answered seconds later. "*Has Jonas signed in?*"

Asha checked. She breathed a sigh of relief. She'd skipped that bit when she'd brought him to the hotel.

"*No.*"

"*Keep it that way.*"

"*Tracker on his car?*"

"*Will investigate.*"

Asha smiled at arriving guests wheeling a suitcase behind them.

"Welcome to The Marine. Do you have a reservation?"

CHAPTER TWENTY-NINE

Midnight Run

Asha was disappointed but understood. It was the only way. She hugged Delaney and found it hard to let go. Delaney nuzzled her head a moment, filled with regret. This was not what he'd planned at all. He'd wanted this Christmas to be special for her.

"Will you come back?" Asha asked.

Delaney pulled away. "I don't know. Take his Rabbit after Christmas and head to the farm. Ask Zuki if she wants to go too. I'll go directly there."

Asha frowned. "She needs help in packing up here. I said I'd help."

"You're a good friend. I'll get to the farm as soon as I'm done, Ash. I know it sucks but it's time to end this. I'll call Maria in the morning."

"I'll call too. Don't do anything rash, Delaney. It's late, please don't fall asleep at the wheel."

"Zuki's making me a flask of coffee. I'll go check on Jonas. With luck he'll sleep the whole way, otherwise I'm going to get one of his lectures on the ethics of modern journalism."

Asha pretended to be amused but felt anything but. She really didn't want him to go. Christmas was meant to be a special time for them and now she was not only losing him but having to work in the kitchen from seven in the morning.

Delaney hugged her close and kissed her. "I'm going." He glanced at Rufus sprawled on the bed out for the count. "Look after Rufus. I'll send a text when I get home, I don't want to wake you."

She nodded and faked a bright smile as he left the room to find Jonas.

Jonas was waiting in the now deserted bar watching the dying glow of the log fire. He turned as Delaney entered.

"We're heading out now. You're going out the back via the kitchens. My vehicle is parked there."

Jonas cocked his head and seemed wistful. "Feel bad ruining your Christmas, Delaney. Got to say that's one of the best meals I've had in a long while. Seems a pity to discover this place the day before it closes."

"Yeah, it's a shame. There's a lot of history here."

Jonas smiled. He pointed to one of the many photos on the wall. "Jimmy Carter standing with Governor Keane six months before he became the 39th president. My father ran the Governor's campaign. They were supposed to be campaigning, but I suspect they came for the fishing."

"According to Zuki, the population here rises by thirty thousand over the summer. So, I guess you grab votes where you can. You ready?" He placed a small log on the fire to keep it going. He was going to miss Christmas with Asha, he felt really guilty he was quitting on her.

Jonas stood up. "Yeah, I'm ready. Kinda sucks to leave huh, I could get used to this." He grabbed his little bag, then paused a moment. "You sure Asha knows how to drive stick?"

"Asha drives a little Fiat with stick shift. The bigger problem is getting your Rabbit back to you in the New Year."

"I'll figure something out."

Zuki appeared at the kitchen door. She came forward and embraced Delaney, handing him the coffee flask. "An hour till Santa arrives. Give him a wave Delaney."

Delaney smiled. "I shall keep my eyes out for him. Take care of Ash, Zukes. She's a bit upset I'm going."

Zuki smiled. "She won't have time to be upset. We will have fifty plus guests to feed breakfast, lunch, and dinner. You ever tried cooking for that many people?"

"Not since camp when I was twelve. Never want to see that many pancakes ever again. Good luck Zuki. I shall think of you."

"Will you come to see me in New York?"

"If Asha allows me to share." He smiled. "Go to bed, you look beat."

Zuki nodded. "I am beat. Go. You've got a three-hour drive. Shit, I need to find the Santa costume. Grandpa's playing Santa at breakfast tomorrow. Hotel tradition. Gifts for everyone."

"He'll love it. Sorry I won't be here."

"Me too. Go, Delaney, it's late already."

Jonas left ahead of him, and Delaney quickly followed. He wondered if the FBI would be trailing in their wake – at least they'd be able to see them, there was unlikely to be any other traffic on the coast road.

Jonas slept for the first hour. Delaney listened to WCRB classic station grateful for digital radio. The snow and rain had combined to make the road treacherous, and he was dreading the coastal route as they got closer to Berg City, memories of his plunge down the cliff were still fresh in his mind.

Jonas stirred. "What is that godawful racket?"

"Shostakovich Waltz Number 2. Sounds like jazz to me."

"You got any Chicago?"

"Chicago. The band?"

"I only listen to stuff made before 1986."

"And drive cars made before then too. You have a thing against contemporary music Jonas?"

"I have a thing against almost everything. The people in the newsroom all worship Taylor Swift but give me Chrissie Hynde any day. 'I go to sleep' – now that's a classic. The Pretenders were a real band."

"I don't think I've ever heard a Chicago album, but yeah, Chrissie Hynde had a great voice. 'Back on the chain gang', great lyrics. My late wife was a big fan." Delaney smiled remembering her dancing in the kitchen in her bare feet trying to make him join her.

"Merry Christmas Jonas, by the way. No sign of Santa in the sky as of yet."

"Jesus, Christmas already. Thank Christ I never have to shop for anyone. I'd always forget."

"You never married?" Delaney asked.

"Thought about it but y'know. I had a choice alcoholic or workaholic. She was a drinker, and I couldn't keep up. Not and keep my job." He stretched his arms and legs. "Comfortable car this."

"2021 model. You'll be missing the lack of electronics."

Jonas chuckled. "Yeah, but not the service costs. I just change the oil once a year and that's all the Rabbit needs. What are you going to do, Delaney? Once we get back?"

"I'm thinking I might go to Florida."

"You're so sure Martinet will be there?"

"He will be."

"You going to arrest him?   You don't have the power."

Delaney rubbed his face and opened the window a little for fresh air. "I'm going to ask him to hand himself in."

"Just like that."

Delaney glanced at Jonas. "Tomorrow's paper will put a noose around his neck. You'll need to get working on that the moment we get back."

Jonas raised his eyebrows. "You're so sure I'll publish it?"

Delaney smiled. "Yeah. You know you will. Story like this is Pulitzer stuff, Jonas."

"You know I won't be able to keep your name out of it."

Delaney nodded. "I know."

"What about Brin Martinet. He's your client. He's not going to be happy."

"He's still in isolation in hospital. No one can get near him. I'll give him the full picture after Florida. Let him see what his father was, then I'll let him know what really happened. It might soften the blow. It might not. Either way I'm guessing he won't be paying his bill."

Jonas chuckled. "Yeah, I can see that would be unlikely. You think Emily is a credible witness? She's tough, lot of anger there."

"She's suffered a lot of trauma in her life. Bound to leave a mark."

Jonas stretched his arms. "She confessed to me that she burned down the gallery. She regrets it now that she understands it was 'evidence'."

"Yeah, she's definitely a shoot first kind of woman. I could have happily answered her questions without being smashed over the head. Luckily, we have the digital photos as back up. You going to reveal she did it? It would mean a long time in jail for her. She's already got a record."

Jonas shook his head. "Apparently, she witnessed someone running from the gallery just before it burned."

Delaney glanced at Jonas and smiled. "I guess the cops might want to know what she was doing on the streets at two in the morning but that's better. The story of her hard life will hammer a nail into Martinet's image."

"Weird he kept all those negatives, don't you think?"

"No. He was proud of his photography. He probably couldn't bring himself to destroy them. I'm guessing he kept them to use as leverage against his paymasters if they ever wanted to terminate him."

"Going to be a hard slog peeling away at who directly benefitted from all his attacks. It's likely to be a whole bunch of middle-management who made their teeth meet."

"Which is why every darn nut and bolt costs $85 bucks for something you'd pay fifty cents for in a hardware store."

"Bastards. Then they go shoveling cash at the people and politicians who sign off on defense spending."

"This story won't be a one-time thing, Jonas. It's going to play out for months."

"A lot of people in Washington are going to squeal. How much further?" Jonas asked.

"About an hour. No stars visible. I think it might snow again soon."

"Wake me up when we get there. I suppose you'll want to be paid for all your research on this story."

"Yeah. Got to make a living, Jonas."

"That's probably what Martinet tells himself every morning."

CHAPTER THIRTY

Breakfast Blues

Delaney woke with a start. Looked for Asha, then Rufus before he remembered where he was. His phone was ringing. He squinted at the number.

"Hey, Merry Christmas M. You're up early."

"It's a farm, Delaney. Everyone gets up early. Bunty's cooking breakfast for about eighty people here."

"What people? Don't they know it's a holiday?"

He could hear Bunty chuckle in the background. "It's twenty people, don't exaggerate. Merry Christmas, Delaney, you should be here."

"I know, I feel properly guilty. Have you woken Asha?"

Maria barged back in. "She's frantic. I have no idea why. Where are you?"

"I'm at home. Asha's helping Zuki out at the hotel. The chef had an accident. Did Santa call?"

"Santa has a hangover right now," Maria whispered. "But thanks for the trainers, they fit fine. Not that I can wear them in the endless snow up here."

"Cold and wet here too. What are you going to do today?"

"Something's happening. It's a surprise I think, but I have to muck out the stables first."

"Animals keep on pooping; they don't know you want a day off."

"Promise me you're coming here for New Year's Eve."

Delaney heard something like a plea in her voice. Maybe she was missing him after all. "We'll be there. I'm trying to get Asha to bring Zuki too."

"Yay, I think. But I don't think she likes me much."

"She does, she sees a lot of herself in you. When do you get your exam results?"

"A week after we get back. Don't remind me."

"I'm sure you aced them."

"As if. Wait, Bunty wants to ask something." There was a moment's delay.

"Delaney? Is Asha alright? She sounded very tense this morning."

"She's having to cook breakfast for fifty guests. I think they may have to rope Rufus in as well."

"Oh my, no wonder she sounds so desperate. She hates cooking."

"Put it this way, maybe the guests might hate it more."

Bunty laughed. "That's so mean."

"Give my best to Mr B. Get back to your guests, Bunty. I'll do my level best to be with you New Year's Eve."

"You'd better," Maria shouted from across the kitchen.

"Be safe, Delaney. I heard about your injuries."

"Injuries?" He heard Maria squeak. He remembered they hadn't told her. Oops.

"I'll be fine. Merry Christmas, Bunty, you too M, have a great day."

He disconnected and forced himself out of bed. He looked around the bedroom. It didn't feel right. No Asha, no dog. It's true what they say, you don't know what you miss until it's gone. He sent a brief 'Merry Christmas' message to Asha. He knew she'd be up to her eyeballs in toast and coffee.

He headed to the bathroom trying to think of all the things he needed to do before he could fly to Florida.

He ate a solitary breakfast as he checked the availability of flights to Jacksonville. It didn't look promising, and he'd have to change in Newark. Nothing available till the next day. He took a priority booking to avoid getting bumped. He hoped he wouldn't be too late for Martinet. He was certain he'd try to move on pretty quickly from Florida.

Jonas messaged him. *"Everyone hates me for pulling them in for fact checking. Thanks for getting me home intact."*

Delaney took that as a positive sign. He was thinking about what to do about a Christmas lunch when Asha called.

"I may not be so keen on the coffee shop idea as I was. Happy whatever, Delaney."

He smiled. "Happy whatever. I miss you so much. This house is nothing without you."

"Naturally. Shit man, I am exhausted already and now we have to prepare lunch. Remember that talk of 'And goodwill to all men?'"

"I'm taking it breakfast didn't go so well?"

"I didn't believe Zuki, but I had no idea how she stuck it out here for so long without killing anyone. If they aren't gluten free, they're lactose intolerant, or allergic to everything. I don't think one guest wished us Merry Christmas."

Delaney wanted to reach out to her and give her a hug. "Happy to hear you're having a good time. What are you having to cook for lunch?"

"It's all pre-ordered so we know what we have to do. Twenty-five turkey dinners. Ten for a fish medley and the rest are getting nut-loaves or bean casseroles. I'm doing the vegan stuff and the vegetables and making mash for fifty. Zuki even hired Emily for the day. She's peeling veg right now."

"And the chef?"

"She broke her wrist when she fell. She wants to sue but Zuki knows she was smashed at the time and there's CCTV of her falling over with the wine bottle. A $500 dollar wine she didn't even pay for."

"Yeah, that's not going to go anywhere. How did Santa go down? Her Grandpa show up?"

"It was almost funny. He handed out the gifts and there was about ten minutes of frantic swopping and complaints about the environmental impact of all that plastic, but he sang to them and was note perfect. I had no idea a Singing Santa was a thing. Some even joined in. So, it turned out well in the end. What about you? Got time to eat?"

"Just toast so far. How's Rufus?"

"He's on reception. Anyone approaches, I told him to bark."

Delaney laughed. "Good career move. Sorry it's so tough, Ash. I feel guilty for deserting you. Maria sends her love and so does Bunty. She had twenty people over for breakfast."

"Oh yes, she does that every year for the key workers on the farm and their families."

"I booked a flight for tomorrow," Delaney told her.

Asha was silent a moment. "Is that a good idea?"

"Probably not. But I promise to be back for New Year's Eve, ok. Try and get Zuki to come with you."

"I'll try. I had a weird dream about you last night. Woke up convinced you'd been shot."

"Shot?"

"Take it as a warning, Delaney. I know you're a skeptic, but it was so real I was shaking."

Delaney rubbed his neck, still sore from driving. "We'll speak later. You're doing a good thing helping Zuki out."

"Delaney?"

"Yeah?"

"I love you; I really do."

He smiled. "I know and believe me, I love you. Go peel something, try not to stab anyone today."

"Oh yeah, Zuki took coffee and Christmas cake out to the FBI people watching Jonas's Rabbit. They look so miserable."

"How did they react?"

"I think they're contemplating a career change."

"I almost feel sorry for them." Delaney told her laughing.

"Got to get back. Maybe go to Harry's for lunch. Call, see if they'll make a space for you."

"Good idea. I will." He looked at his phone and realized she'd already gone.

He sighed. It was funny, he couldn't remember his life before she came into it. Had no idea how he used to fill his time before her. He went to pack for Florida.

CHAPTER THIRTY-ONE

Lying Low

He watched the news on as many channels as he could find. A freak blizzard in California seemed to dominate the airwaves along with a plane going down in Mexico with two hundred passengers who were never going to see Christmas again. The assassination of Calhoun barely got a mention, except on CNN and MSNBC. Funny to think he'd made all those billions, and no one seemed to care a damn about him. It was odd to see photos of him when young, Calhoun had once been a slim and handsome guy, before becoming the bloated monster he'd grown into.

He was pretty sure it would be a bigger story in the papers once Christmas was out of the way. He'd seen the same team photo from his Olympic days on screen but nothing else with him in it. He'd forgotten about the moustache and long hair. Martinet had always had trouble with controlling his weight. Kinnerson had done a good job of scrubbing the internet of any other photos of him. Said no one would ever remember what he looked like after a while. He'd been right. He'd been skeptical at first stepping into Martinet's shoes, but it had to be done. Gus Zolloff had to die, all that pressure he was under from the bastard commies to 'deliver' – his patriotic duty. They knew he had connections, that his fellow shooters were rising stars. They'd offered money but had no idea that money wasn't his motivation, or sex. But still they came, always at a distance, never in person. He would never be able to identify them, and he knew that Kinnerson would discover it one day. That's why he'd told him. Kinnerson was smart and devious. Knew how to pressure people, even better than the Russians. It was Kinnerson's idea to ditch Zolloff. Martinet was unreliable, had no scruples, was a potential liability. The unexpected opportunity came when the deer jumped in front of Martinet's vehicle. Marty dying offered him a way out. A flash decision to change places. No one ever missed the loner Zolloff.

He wasn't sure of what his next move was. Florida the first step, change identity and head south. Costa Rica, Panama, somewhere easy to disappear in. His Spanish was good enough to get by, perhaps too formal, but practice would help. He was worried about the arthritic pain in his legs. The months of inactivity in the care facility had exacerbated the problem. The cold weather didn't help any. He wondered if he could ever set foot in Berg City again. Maybe, after a few months. People were used to him being away till the end of March. He could get the apartment fixed up maybe. Slip back into his old life.

He worried about his boat. Normally he'd have someone take care of it and get it ready for his visit. One thing he knew, you couldn't leave a boat for long on the water without it developing problems. The ocean corrodes pretty much everything.

Thinking about Costa Rica made him hungry. He thought about getting dressed, heading out to find somewhere to eat. He had a sudden hankering for hot cornbread and gravy with collard greens. People ate better in the south. Yeah, a walk would do him good, then be back for 7pm when *'It's a Wonderful Life'* would be on. Never tired of that movie. Jimmy Stewart against the money grabbing bank. He'd often wondered what the world would be like without Gus Zolloff in it. A whole lot different for Kinnerson and Calhoun, that was for sure. He rubbed his legs to get the circulation moving. He drank some water and reflected on how fortunate it was he'd never believed in hell and damnation.

"Skip all that crap," his father thundered between bottles of vodka. "This is it, my son. Grab what you can and to hell with everyone else."

Funny how you never forgot the childhood lessons. Watched his father drown in one of the few times he'd ever had a bath. Vodka helped so many like him depart from this earth before their time. He'd vowed never to touch a drop and kept his word for eighty years. Too late to start now.

CHAPTER THIRTY-TWO

The Firestarter

The flights were exhausting, the changeover tedious, the car rental stank of stale cigarettes, but he was finally in St Augustine. It was dark already. He'd checked in at Journey's End Bed & Breakfast. Initially he'd hoped to find Martinet before he became aware of the morning edition of The Star back in Berg City. Little hope of that now. The story had been picked up by mainstream media hungry for a new sensation. The question was, had Martinet already run? He folded a copy of *The Star* under his arm and went for a stroll to find the fugitive. He wondered that perhaps he considered himself safe in this quaint coastal town, thinking no one would find him. He'd just be one more old snowbird amongst thousands.

Delaney felt anxious. He needed Martinet to be there, to talk. He'd be feeling what? Despair or defeat, a little remorse? Maybe he'd thought killing his former teammates would keep him safe, never anticipating anyone would even pay attention. Shooting Calhoun had to be a tactical mistake or was it revenge for something?

And there he was sitting in a chair, sipping a bottle of Sprecher's root beer on the stoop outside his frame house on Charlotte Street. Didn't look like a man with any troubles. Delaney stood in the shadows watching him studying people walk by towards the St Augustine Historical Society, which seemed to be hosting an evening event.

Delaney's phone buzzed; he'd left it on silent.

An angry voice barked at him. "Have you seen *The Star* today?"

Delaney sighed, bad timing. "Yes Brin, I have. I would have given you a heads up, but you appear to have blocked my number."

"I haven't ... I, shit my P.A. must have done it."

"I'm surprised she's still working for you."

"What's all this crap about my father being a serial arsonist and assassin? Are you kidding me? They went to print with this shit? My lawyer will kill them."

Delaney shrugged. "I don't think so, Brin. I'm sorry but it's all true. Somehow, he thought he could kill the story by getting rid of Kinnerson and Calhoun. I heard on the news a bus driver has a CCTV image of him on a bus near Bennet Kinnerson's place just after it burned. It's his M.O. Brin; too many coincidences to ignore. They're looking for CCTV of him in Baltimore where Calhoun lived. Hard to forget the fact Arnold Martinet is a crack shot with a rifle."

"You're saying he killed his teammates too? Has the world gone crazy? No one thought to call me? My father could not possibly be in any condition to do any of these things. He's only just left Summertree. All this shit about him being at the scene at every one of those fires is pure conspiracy crap, and you know it."

"One coincidence maybe he gets a pass, two unfortunate, thirty it's indisputable. He was an arsonist for hire, Brin. Just because he gave his money away doesn't whitewash his guilt. These are his own records the paper is publishing, Brin. He kept meticulous files. How they got hold of them I'm not sure, but the evidence is all there."

"Your name's on this pile of garbage. You had access to the apartment."

"So did whoever smashed the lock and trashed the place, Brin. They obviously knew he kept those records hidden in the safe. I don't know how much the paper paid for them or if it was given for free, but you'd have to ask your father why he didn't keep them some place less obvious."

"I know you had something to do with this. Don't try to bullshit me."

"They asked questions, I answered. Remember you asked me to find him. The FBI have a strong interest in this story, might have been trying to squash it, but it's too late now, a lot of people are going to be exposed. He might have been the arsonist, Brin, but they'll want whoever benefitted from his activities."

"Delaney I'm going to see that you're shut down. I'll ruin you."

"Maybe you will, maybe you won't, I've never tested my liability insurance. You're too angry to hear the truth at the moment."

"The truth? The paper trashes my father's reputation and accuses him of being a serial arsonist and I'm supposed to accept this?"

"The truth is you're a victim too, Brin. Check your DNA against your father."

"And how will I do that? No one has seen him. More's the point, why should I do that?"

"I can see him right now, Brin. He's sitting outside his house drinking a bottle of Sprecher's; probably wondering how the hell I found him."

"Let me speak to him."

"No. You're too riled up. Just accept everything you think you know about your father is untrue. He raised you, or rather the women he paid to pretend to be his sister did. He staked you, but he was never your father."

"You're insane, Delaney. None of this craziness is true. He's a good man whose reputation you have ruined forever. He's helped thousands to get a better life."

"And murdered more than thirty people that we know of. Everyone it seems has a price on their head. Got to go. Don't call back unless you want to hear the truth."

Delaney disconnected and kept his phone on silent. He took a deep breath and crossed the street to meet the Firestarter.

"It's a long way to the nearest Denny's, Gus. Orlando if I'm not mistaken."

Gus Zolloff stared at Delaney with surprising calm. It had been a very long time since someone called him by his real name. Delaney could hear a phone ringing inside the house, but Zolloff ignored it.

Delaney tossed his copy of *The Star* to him. It landed on his lap, but he didn't open it. He already knew what was in there.

"Brought you a copy of *The Star* in case you're feeling homesick."

Zolloff continued to stare at Delaney perhaps trying to formulate the right response as he let the paper fall to the deck. "What happened to your head?"

"Someone was looking for you. Thought I could help them with their enquiries with a long metal pole."

"Must have hurt, head injuries can be problematic later. You eaten?" He asked.

Delaney shook his head. "You know somewhere good? It's been a long day."

Zolloff slowly rose from his weathered Adirondack chair, wincing as pain shot through his legs.

Delaney's eyebrows raised. "I know that look. Suffered from arthritis in my arms and hands for years."

"And now?" Zolloff asked.

"A Guru cured me. Just before some Russian bastard nailed him to a wall."

Zolloff frowned a moment. "I seem to remember reading about that, about two years ago. You like Italian?"

Delaney briefly smiled. "Yeah, always reliable. Nice little house you've got here, can't see why you don't live here all year round."

"Too hot in summer. They say St Augustine will be underwater in twenty years."

"I guess most of the East Coast is vulnerable. Be like Venice. I remember eating at a table as the tide came in and everyone carried on as normal even though the water was up to their knees. It was totally surreal."

Zolloff chuckled. "I only ever got as far as Venice, California." He found a key in one of the flower tubs and locked his front door. He saw Delaney staring at the dead plants. "Hard to keep them going when you're not around to water them."

Delaney fell into step beside the old man. "Got a call from Brin. Seems a bit upset. Threatening to sue everyone."

Zolloff looked up at the sky a moment. "Hmm, I'll call him later. You know his number now?"

"I'm blocked, but I'll give you the number he called me on. Don't be offended if he doesn't answer, he's controlled by his P.A."

"That bitch still there?"

"Seems so."

"He must be angry."

"In a way it's all his fault you're on the front page, Gus. If only he hadn't commissioned a biography. That showing of all your recon photographs in a gallery didn't help much either. It was bound to trigger someone."

"I didn't burn it down, whatever you think."

"No, that was Emily Brookshire. Remember her?"

Zolloff thought about it a moment as they slowed to let a vehicle by. The name meant something, but the Emily threw him.

"You burned down her family home with her parents in it. She was away visiting a schoolfriend at the time."

"And she burned the gallery?"

"Got very upset seeing her old house up there on the wall. She might play a big part in the investigation."

Zolloff said nothing. He pointed to a small Italian restaurant across the road. "It's nothing special but the food's good. I eat there mostly."

They crossed the busy road and entered the restaurant. Delaney was happy to see it wasn't overtly touristy with stripped back brick walls, simple checkered tablecloths and traditional apron clad waiting staff who all looked busy. A small middle-aged man with a pimp's moustache and shiny shoes bore down upon them.

"Signore Martin. You're back at last. We missed you."

Zolloff smiled at the host and shook his hand. "Good evening, Stefano. I have a guest."

"Best table for you. You are late to St Augustine this season."

Zolloff pointed to the still raw scars on his head. "Operation Stefano. Takes time to heal."

Stefano made a fuss and pretended to be interested as he shepherded them to a table by a window. A huge leafy pot plant would hide them from most of the other diners.

"A bottle of Barolo for my guest, Stefano. I shall have some sparkling water."

Delaney didn't intervene but nor did he intend to drink a whole bottle by himself.

Stefano wore a gold stud earring in one ear. Delaney suspected he was quite a different person when not in the role of being 'host'. Other diners seemed happy as they negotiated huge bowls of pasta or thin crust pizzas. Most seemed old but there were a couple of honeymooners in the room wondering what they had got themselves into.

Zolloff tilted his head a little. "I can tell you don't like it."

"On the contrary, it's nice and simple. I like Italian and I'm happy to see Fusilli Primavera on the menu. Maybe a bit of garlic bread. I'm quite hungry as it turns out."

Zolloff seemed pleased with the response. "I always have the same thing. Saves time. Linguine with artichokes."

"You're vegetarian?" Delaney asked.

"Sixty-five years now. Never touched meat. It's the safest way to avoid cancer. These people," he indicated a small group of large women dining behind them and lowered his voice. "You think they ever imagined they'd get so big. All those hormones they pump into the animals. Never touch meat or dairy. Maybe I'll die in an electric chair but never because I let my body down."

The wine and sparkling water arrived, and Delaney went through the charade of the taste test and nodded the wine through. Obviously, Stefano wasn't the type to watch the news, he might be less than happy to discover he had been nurturing a serial killer all these years. They gave their orders, and they were finally left alone.

Delaney sipped some wine and wondered where this was all going as Zolloff went quiet for moment, perhaps thinking of ways to be rid of him. He opened his bottle of water and poured himself a glass. "Why are you here?" He asked finally.

Delaney was watching a woman trying to hold on to her hat in a gust of wind outside the window. The weather report had mentioned a rapid change.

"I'm here to encourage you to give yourself up."

Zolloff made a face. "You seem convinced I'll do that."

"No. Far from it. I'm pretty sure you've made plans to run. I imagine you have a boat somewhere here, or access to one. You could aim for Bermuda or Cuba. Might be hard to extract you from Cuba but then again there are risks of people handing you over for reward money there. Or perhaps Panama. I imagine you have some money stashed there. I would; if I were you."

"And why would I hand myself in, Delaney? It is Delaney, isn't it. I'm not so good with names anymore."

"It is and you would be treated better. The FBI are desperate to speak to you, but then again so are the other people."

"Other people?"

"The ones who trashed your apartment. The ones who organized the killing of the man who was writing your biography. I can't imagine they have your best interests at heart."

Delaney could see Zolloff was going to object.

"It doesn't matter you killed Kinnerson or Calhoun. They have lieutenants, others further down the food chain who wouldn't want to be exposed. I'm thinking a plea bargain, you could give them names, associates. The FBI will be your only friend. If I can find you, they can too." Delaney sipped some more wine. It was better than he'd hoped.

"I guess you weren't aware some busses are equipped with CCTV these days. There's almost nowhere to hide. There's a camera in the corner right behind you."

Zolloff didn't turn his head. He didn't care about the back of his head.

The hot garlic bread arrived, and Delaney fell on it, tearing off a chunk and offering some to Zolloff who followed suit. Zolloff's forehead was sweating a little, a small tension knot was showing between his eyes.

"I know a thousand places to hide in Panama or Costa Rica. Cuba was never an option, who the hell could you trust there? Nice garlic bread, don't you think?"

Delaney nodded. "I haven't eaten since breakfast. So, you think running is the way to go?"

"I'm not afraid of jail. I live a solitary life. No luxuries, other than my little house here."

"It looks very nice, what I've seen of it so far. I always wanted to visit St Augustine. Nearest I got was a school trip to Cape Canaveral. Got to watch one of the Shuttle launches. April '85. God I must have been about seven or eight. We were a long ways away from the launch site but the whole air shook. Made a big impression. Back then I had a plan to see all America's lighthouses. Saw the one at New Smyrna. Weird what kids fixate on huh?"

Zolloff nodded. "It's very fine lighthouse. There's one here, near Anastasia State Park. You should add it to your collection."

Delaney laughed. "I don't think I'm collecting lighthouses anymore. Come to think of it, one of your photos in the gallery had a lighthouse in it."

Zolloff smiled, remembering. "Alaska. Sitka. I was there on business. I did a calendar series on American Lighthouses about twenty years ago. Sold out twice. Rare for black and white photography."

Delaney wrinkled his nose. "Ah yes, business."

"It was only ever business and photography, of course. I took that very seriously."

"Some fine work too."

"Thank you. I'm only sorry I never got to see the exhibition. Was it successful?"

"Very well received. Believe it or not there's a positive review in The Star Magazine this weekend. It's with the paper on your stoop."

Zolloff pondered that for a moment. Delaney could tell it mattered to him.

Their food arrived and the conversation died with it. 'A true Italian never speaks when he eats,' he remembered his wife saying, but doubted this was true as she talked all through her meals and she was half-Italian.

Stefano topped up Delaney's wine and enquired if the food was good and went away reassured all was fine. Delaney mopped up the plate with the last bit of garlic bread.

"I'm curious, Gus. Why kill Kinnerson and Calhoun? Why would they be a threat to you? They've never been a threat before, have they?"

Zolloff shrugged. "We had a deal. Seems they decided to break it. I went to my apartment after I saw you. You were right, it was trashed. My records were gone. They'd cleaned out the safe. I thought no one knew I kept records. It was always going to be my defense if they ever threatened to expose me."

"You can't be sure who broke in. I mean, I saw the Maytag man, but you don't know if he was working for Kinnerson or Calhoun."

Zolloff wiped the sweat from his forehead and swallowed some water. "I know it wasn't the FBI. I watched him. He was asleep at the wheel."

"But if it was one of your people, how did the files end up at The Star?" Delaney asked, aware that he was being provocative here. Zolloff had no idea it was Asha who took them. "I can't see Kinnerson or Calhoun wanting that outcome."

Zolloff shook his head in sadness. "I don't know. I don't even care anymore. It doesn't name names. It was my personal notebook and a digital backup for my photographs. Part of my training. It only incriminates me. No one else."

"But you still went ahead and eliminated your team-mates."

"I had to act quickly. I had no doubt that Kinnerson was behind it. He never wanted me to retire. I always knew I was on borrowed time. One day they'd want to tidy up."

"Perhaps you hoped they'd forget you."

Zolloff shrugged. "Perhaps. They were happy for me to be this great benefactor; thought I was a fool for giving away my money, but it was a good cover whilst it lasted. I had no inkling my son would want to commission a biography of his reluctant father. Fate, I suppose. What do people say? No good deed goes unpunished."

He looked away a moment. "I should have stopped after the second job. Nearly did. It was a disaster. Wrong house, wrong people, right address. Completely the fault of Kinnerson. He got the city wrong. I knew something was off. Ended up having to go in and pull them out. There were too many people in there. I couldn't have that on my conscience. If I'd hung around, they probably would have given me a medal." He smiled at the irony. "If I had stopped then history would be different for a lot of people. And maybe a few billion might have been saved for the taxpayer. There, that's a confession. I screwed up. Never made that mistake again."

Delaney understood that was as close as he was going to get to extract any remorse from him. The man's eyes were still sharp and clear but the puffiness in his face and the way he was taking shallow breaths indicated underlying health issues. If he chose to run, he wouldn't last long wherever he went.

"So, what do we do now?" Delaney asked.

"We can part ways."

"Will you explain things to Brin, especially the part where you tell him he's not your son."

"You know this for sure?" Zolloff teased.

"Yes. We figured it out. You did right by him. Can't fault you for that."

"I wasn't there for him when he needed a father though. Turns out I'm not much good at being one of those. Better than my own father, but a son needs a hug from time to time. I'm not really the hugging type. I won't tell him. Will you?"

"It might come out. The media can be relentless."

"A pity. He wouldn't understand. But then again... I know nothing of psychology."

"Why did you adopt him? You could have left him on a doorstep somewhere."

"I never killed any children. I couldn't abandon a baby. Turns out the mother had kept it secret from her own parents for reasons unknown. The boy deserved a good life. I gave him one."

Delaney didn't comment. Zolloff signaled for the bill.

"No regrets at all?" Delaney asked. "You ended a lot of lives prematurely."

Zolloff shrugged. "It was never personal."

"Emily Brookshire might disagree with you," Delaney remarked, pointing at his still purple bruising.

"She's still alive, isn't she?" Martinet signaled the waiter to hurry up with the bill.

"I had the wine. I'll pay." Delaney suggested.

"No. It's my choice. I pay. I'd invite you home for a coffee, but I have plans and no coffee."

"You know the FBI will be coming for you now."

"I'm surprised they aren't here already. You found me; they can't be far behind."

Delaney wiped his mouth. "I'm not going to wish you luck."

"No such thing as luck. Go home, I'm sure there's someone waiting for you."

The bill arrived and Zolloff paid, tipping Stefano well. He saw them out, told them he was looking forward to seeing them again. Zolloff promised him he would.

They parted ways at the next intersection. Delaney watched him saunter along towards Charlotte Street, no sense of panic in his step at all.

A short woman in a grey suit and black leather shoes approached him and fell into step beside him as he made his way to his guest house.

"They ever teach you people how to blend in?" Delaney asked her. "You see anyone else wear suits these days?"

She gave him a withering look. "Give."

Delaney handed over the tiny recording device and detached the miniscule microphone they'd fitted into shirt pocket.

"You're arresting him now?"

"Something like that. You think he's meeting anyone else?"

Delaney shook his head. "He's a professional loner. He's not going to lead you to the people who made the money. But you should be able to connect the dots."

"Dots are what we do best. Good night, Mr Delaney. I hope you're going home tomorrow."

"Yeah."

"Make sure you do."

She left him on the corner, and he shrugged. He checked his watch. 9pm. He walked over the square and knocked on the window of a waiting cab. "Take me to see the lighthouse. Round trip."

The Mexican cabbie smiled. "Get in senor, the Lighthouse will be my pleasure. Very pretty at night."

Asha called at eleven pm. She sounded exhausted. "Sorry, couldn't call till now. Kitchen duties. Thank God the last guests leave after breakfast tomorrow. Zuki's on her knees."

"I guess you can understand why Zuki was keen to escape the hospitality business."

"God, yeah. Where are you?"

"I've just returned from looking at the Lighthouse which opened in 1874."

"So, you're on holiday whilst I'm a kitchen slave?"

Delaney laughed. "Sorry babe, it was on my bucket list."

"You have a bucket list?"

"Since I was a kid. American Lighthouses. I used to collect them. Well photos anyway. Blame it on another kid at school I had a crush on."

"You had a crush on someone who liked Lighthouses? That is beyond weird Delaney."

"Didn't you have a crush on a tennis player at school? I remember something about that."

"Hmmm, ok. Crushes allowed. What about Martinet?"

"You hear about Senator Chasen? Baltimore saint and paragon of virtue."

"No. Did I mention I've been a kitchen slave yet?"

Delaney smiled. "He shot himself about an hour ago. Seems he was on the Senate Committee investigating fraud. Big pal of Regie Calhoun and Bennet Kinnerson."

"And so, it begins. I guess he got a nice payoff."

"There will be hundreds who accepted kickbacks right through the armaments industry. News of Martinet's arrest travels fast. I suspect a lot of paperwork is burning right now."

"When are you coming home?" Asha asked.

"I've got a flight booked for tomorrow."

"You're not in trouble? You sound on edge."

"I'm not in trouble. The moment I bought a ticket to fly south two FBI agents were at my elbows, they flew down with me. Put it this way, I cooperated."

"And Jonas?"

"He's safe. He's protected by the First Amendment. He's going to make a meal out of the Senator's suicide. I filled him in about Martinet. He admitted to me that he was working for Kinnerson."

"I pity Brin Martinet. He's going to be trashed in the media."

"Yeah, he called me. He sounded pretty angry."

"Believe it or not his P.A. paid his bill. I'm guessing she'll finally be fired for that."

"We aren't giving it back, that's for sure. Is that Zuki I can hear?"

"We're both shattered."

"You still want to run a coffee shop?" Delaney asked.

He heard her suck in her breath a moment. "I might have been overly hasty on that idea."

Delaney smiled. "I miss you, Ash. Any news from the farm?"

"She's had fun, but just maybe had her fill of snow and shoveling horse shit."

"Wow, she's a city girl after all."

"Will you drive straight there?"

"I'll stay one night at home and drive up first thing the next day."

"I was going to suggest that. I don't want you driving at night in the snow. Zukes wants to know what Martinet was like when you found him?"

"Totally unemotional. He's old, his legs hurt. What can they do to him? There's no death penalty in our State and he's used to being locked up at Summertree. Hard to punish a guy like that. They'll squeeze him for everything he knows. Maybe they'll seize all his assets to compensate his victims. That would be the best option."

"I hope so. Shit, I'm so beat. I'm going to sleep. Please drive safe."

"You too. I hope that the Rabbit has snow tires."

"I think so."

"Go to sleep. Love you babe."

"Even with my dishpan hands? You cannot believe how many dishes I've washed."

"I always had a thing for waitresses."

"I bet you did, Delaney. I going to have to watch you. Night."

He lay back in the bed and examined the photographs he'd taken of the Lighthouse. They seemed to have come out better than he thought. He tried to remember the girl he'd had the crush on. She spurned the pop stars all the other kids were into. Now he thought about it, she'd made a conscious effort to be different. Sara Dougal suddenly popped into his head. The ginger girl with green eyes and freckles who pretended to be indifferent to his attentions but got annoyed if he ever talked to another girl. 'I'm gonna see every lighthouse in America and Canada before I'm sixteen." Her father was a pilot, so he wasn't surprised when she completed her task half way into her fifteenth year. He'd taken her in his sailboat to Gilbert Island to celebrate and she'd thrown up both ways, mortified and humiliated by the experience. She avoided him from that day on and moved to California that winter. He wondered what had happened to her. He was certain she would have achieved whatever goal she'd set herself.

He frowned as he turned the light off. He wasn't certain of his own future anymore. Maybe Asha was right. Running a coffee shop would be a lot safer. But then again, his pragmatic side considered the other option. Flipping the boathouse. That insurance guy wasn't wrong, now restored, it had to be worth at least triple what he'd paid for it. It had business development rights, parking. Great location in summer when people crowded the harbor.

His phone rang. He didn't recognize the number.

"Delaney."

"It's Sheena, Mr Delaney, Brin's P.A. Brin has disappeared. I went to the hospital at nine tonight. They say he checked out, but he's not well enough to go anywhere. He's still on antibiotics and can barely walk, his lungs are damaged. He's had death threats all day and I'm worried about the state of his mind."

"Did you check his home? He must be in shock about his father. Sheena, I may not be the right person to look for him. I spoke with him earlier tonight; he isn't happy with me. He didn't mention anything about death threats or leaving the hospital."

"He's in shock. I'm afraid he might kill himself. *Please* Mr Delaney. I love him. Please find him."

Delaney sighed; his P.A. loved him? He wondered if that was reciprocated. "I'm in Florida right now. I should be back by midday tomorrow. You sure he hasn't been home?"

"I'm there now. He hasn't been here. There are TV crews outside the gates."

"Do not engage with the media. Call me at one-thirty pm tomorrow if he hasn't returned. He might just be hiding from the press. I don't blame him. They will be brutal now his father has been arrested."

"I will call you Mr Delaney. Brin has done nothing wrong. He's a good man."

Delaney winced. He'd heard that before somewhere.

"One-thirty pm tomorrow, Sheena. Don't forget."

Delaney sighed. He didn't think Brin was in shock. Full of anger, for sure. He'd definitely want to stay out of the media's eye. He didn't think it was anything to worry about. He was being sensible. Hide and hope it all blows over. Except, of course, it wouldn't blow over, not for years. Just one more life Gus Zolloff had wrecked.

< FIN>

The Sam Hawksmoor Novels -
(All available on Amazon and Kindle)

We Feel Your Pain - so you don't have to
ISBN-13: 979-8-69908-7693
Hammer & Tong 2020
The first Delaney and Asha investigation: They run the Office of Berg City Oversight. Their role is to keep the city safe from unscrupulous people. When something looks too good to be true – it's a scam, right? But what if the scam works? What kind of scam is that?

Mission Longshot
ISBN-13: 979-8- 73565-1390
Hammer & Tong 2021
As the climate changes 3000 kids are sent into space on a 70-year voyage to save humanity – only one girl, Celeste survives. How far would you go to save one life?

Girl with Cat (Blue) – Hammer & Tong
ISBN-13: 978-1-5451-56629
War, secret tunnels, pre-historic monsters, and airships. Two London's separated by tunnels filled with monsters. Two identical teenage girls who should never meet...
Shortlisted for the International Rubery Book Award &
Honorable Mention in the Writer's Digest 26th Book Awards

Another Place to Die: Endtime Chronicles - Hammer & Tong
ISBN-13: 978-1-5028-35437
Think you can survive the next lethal pandemic? Kira and her dog Red try to escape the virus and the Firestarter's who follow. (A Sam Hawksmoor & Sam North novel)

J&K 4Ever - Hammer & Tong
ISBN-13: 978-1-5306-24225
60 years after the apocalypse. Jeyna and Kruge are two young orphans determined to stay with each other despite the odds. They must escape into the unknown, but behind them will come the cruel Enforcers ready to hunt them down.

The Repercussions of Tomas D – Hammer & Tong
ISBN-13: 978-1- 4910-32015
Tomas accidentally goes back in time to London in the Blitz.
The day after Tomas disappears, his girlfriend Gabriella wakes
up to realize she's the only one who remembers that Germany
was supposed to have lost the war...

Marikka – Hammer & Tong
ISBN-13: 978-1- 5119 94224
The Girl who ran from the fire - The Boy who crashed the car
& Anya, the girl who can read objects – An intense story about
a father's search for his missing daughter

The Repossession of Genie Magee - (Book One)
ASIN : B093LM4LG1 (Published by as TOZ in Turkey)
2nd Edition now back in print - Hammer & Tong 2021
Genie Magee is imprisoned in her own home and Rian, her
boyfriend, has to bust her out on the eve of a great storm.
They run straight into a trap where scientists are running
lethal experiments on runaways who may not be as dead as
they think.
Winner of The Wirral 'Paperback of the Year'

The Hunting of Genie Magee - (Book Two)
ASIN : B093LJLB2X (Published by as Golge in Turkey)
2nd Edition now back in print - Hammer & Tong 2021
$10,000-dollar reward for the capture of Genie and each of her
friends. Who now owns their DNA? What is the secret buried
in Radspan?

The Heaviness of Genie Magee - (Book Three)
Hammer & Tong (Published as Rüya in Turkey)
ISBN: 978-1-49750-8033
Rian is snatched along with many other genius kids to work on
Cary's anti-gravity theories. Genie has just 48 hours to save
them from ruthless kidnappers.

This is the eleventh Sam Hawksmoor novel. A former Senior
Lecturer in Creative Writing, Sam lives in Lincolnshire where
the stars are only visible on nights of a Blue Moon.

Printed in Great Britain
by Amazon

16343038R00183